THE PILGRIM

SETH I FRIEDMAN

2014 Humble Libertine Second Paperback Edition

Published in the United States by
Humble Libertine, New York City

Friedman, Seth I
The Pilgrim / Seth I Friedman

ISBN 978-0-9851057-4-7

www.thepilgrimbook.com

Cover and book design by Seth I Friedman

CONTENTS

THE PILGRIM

Part 1

The Orphan and the Druid

Elton, England

September, 1170

It was going to be another sleepless night. Claire couldn't resign herself anymore to just lying there in the darkness, terrified, listening to the wind rattle through the night. She had finally decided to break one of William's few rules. She had held off doing it as long as she could. She hadn't been ready to admit that it didn't matter anymore what William wanted. Six months is too long, and she was just crazy now to believe that there was any chance he would be coming back. So she got up, crossed her heart, struck the flint, and lit a candle. The slight glow was just bright enough for her to imagine that William was there and she was warm, and she finally slept through the night.

Normally, the ten by twenty-foot block of air that Claire and William called home was constricting at best, but they had always made the best of it, and these fond memories gave her comfort. Then she would look down at her growing belly and curse the man whom she loved so intensely. After six months with no word, she hated him a little more each day for doing this to her—and missed him twice as much.

Other times she just hated herself. She had never failed to mention her dreams of a larger house, and William, predictably confident and eager to please, jumped at the chance to secure a buyer for the Manor's sheep wool. It required traveling farther than either of them had ever gone from home, but Claire was boundlessly proud of her ambitious husband and their chance at a better life.

It was entirely possible that William was in the arms of a new woman. At least in that scenario, he was still alive and might change his mind and return. After six months without a sign of him, her hope broke, and she began to accept that she would bear a child who would never know its father.

When the time came, after roaming as far as she could to seek help, unsuccessfully, she returned home to do what had to be done, alone.

For a long time she scratched at the floor and pushed out, and tried to catch a breath that was not there. All she yearned for was his face, and maybe his hand on her shoulder. She struggled not to think of him, not to focus on the anguish, and not to give up. She imagined William watching over her from a Heaven that she was never sure that she believed in, and in this she found peace, and then strength.

She clenched her teeth, opened her eyes wide to let the tears drain away, and knew with certainty, for the first time, that she would do anything to bring William's child into the world safely. She forced the final push and heard new life cry and gasp for its first breath. Their son was born. She named him Uther.

†††

It was three months later, just as the post-harvest sun ducked under the horizon, that she heard the sound of an approaching gallop. The dismounting, the steps, the knocking—there was no mistake. She could feel the charged warmth of excitement as strongly as the cold zip of fear that had risen from her stomach in times before when outsiders had approached. She opened the door, and William smiled.

"Come and meet your son," was the best that she could muster through her tears.

†††

William spoke softly as Claire dressed his wounds.

"They attacked me on the road, and I woke up on a ship to Flanders where I was bought as a laborer. I was able to escape, but not without a price."

William held up his right hand. His two middle fingers and thumb were gone. He flashed a wide, inappropriate smile that Claire recognized as his way of looking foolishly happy when a situation seemed darkest.

William walked over to his infant son. He picked up Uther, taking extra care to be gentle to compensate for the newly acquired shakiness in his hands. Looking at his boy, William saw his wife's eyes, steely light brown—almost grey, staring back at him, and he also recognized Claire's slightly large, but still cute, ears that William sensed were listening closely. And then he saw himself—a strong chin, a heavy brow, enlarged cheeks, and the shoulders on the boy! Even at such a young age, they seemed built for a larger body—just like William's. Uther's mouth was his too, though William noticed that it rarely smiled.

Placing Uther back down in his blanket, William walked over to his wife. She was just as he remembered her, the perfect blend of innocent beauty with sharp eyes that radiated a will that could pull an ox-plow through snow. He had done his best not to let on to Claire how deeply his ordeal had affected him. She had been through enough already, and there would be time later for her to understand. She would have to because he knew he couldn't hide it forever.

When William finally slept, Claire watched him, noticing how his rest was different now. It was as if his mind was on a choppy sea, with his eyes tighter behind their lids. It didn't matter how much his trials had changed him though; he was home—and she thanked God a thousand times that day.

William allowed Claire to keep a candle lit that night so that, if she awoke in the dark, she could see him sleeping next to her and remember more quickly that he was home and it wasn't just a dream.

†††

"Reeve! ... Reeve!"

William slowly pried his eyelids open. The sound was drawing closer, coming right up to their house, followed by an urgent rapping. William rose carefully, so as not to disturb Claire, and opened the door to find the reeve of the manor, Graint Heresack, the absolute last face he wanted to see.

"I'm gathering all able-bodied men. There aren't many of you around this morning, so you'll need to move quickly. You'll be required to fulfill your duty in protection of your lord's lands."

"What?"

"Go to the church; I'll explain more there. Bring whatever tools you have, preferably a pitchfork or an axe. We'll have extra weapons there, I hope."

William detected a streak of nervous fear in Graint's voice, and then that was it. The reeve rode off while William dressed, grabbed a mattock axe, and despite his better judgment, left soon after.

When he arrived at the church, there was already a small gathering. Though William carried a small dagger at all times, he had little skill with fighting and had avoided armed conflict for most of his life. This was a deft feat in a world that required regular defense of property and kin. The thirty mysterious knights on horseback surrounding the church were the latest evidence of this.

Wearing brown crosses assembled from strips of monks' torn tunics—the mark of Crusaders—the horsemen were calm, still, and mostly quiet. William noticed that their clothing underneath was ragged and pale, which could be the result of battle fatigue or a sign of poor thieves in disguise—or worse, a little of both.

That William and six other men should defend the manor against a group of hostile Crusader knights was laughable at best. William walked up to the reeve, who stood in front of the church door.

"Mr. Heresack, please remind me why I'm here? I'm familiar with my obligations to Lord Monroe, but in thirteen years I've never been asked to raise arms for him."

"Today you are here ... because you may have to be ready to defend all property, not just our lord's manor."

"What goes on in the church?"

"Negotiations between the inner circle of these men and Father Parist."

"Negotiations for what?"

"They are claiming Papal immunity to collect supplies from the village before their fulfillment of Crusade. So the answer to your question, William Andage, is *whatever they want*. Pray it does not extend to your winter storages. Or your wife."

†††

Inside, Father Parist struggled to keep his hands steady as he emptied the church collection into the grip of a smaller knight who counted the coins. Behind this man stood what Father Parist could only assume was the dumb-muscle of the group, a far larger, bearded man who stared at the priest without a blink. As the smaller knight finished counting, the larger man stepped forward and spoke.

"It's not enough. We ride for the Holy Land and need all the supplies that the village can provide. As the man of order here, we humbly request that you assist us in keeping the peace while we fulfill our needs."

Father Parist saw that, up-close, the man's beard was wet and scattered with white chunks, and his face was streaked with the crusted, earthen spray that was once, surely, hot blood. But what truly shook Father Parist was how this shadow from out of the woods spoke with the eloquence and poise of a genteel nobleman.

"Good Sir, this tithe money is all that my lord can consent to. I must insist, as God's own voice amongst this flock, that you make your way, with blessings many, and know that you will find a hundred times greater treasures in Jerusalem."

The bearded man shifted his shoulders, gave a sideways glance to his helm-wearing consort, and then unleashed a great bark of a laugh.

"You? No. *We* are God's voice; we who crusade; and who will be forgiven of all sins for it, we who are protected under the Pope's own decree to do what we wish as we take up the sword in his name. We, not you, are God's voice."

"There is little I can do to stop the men of this manor from protecting what is theirs."

"This village rabble will not prevent us from gathering what we need."

"You are in God's house, and I am His voice on Earth. I command you to desist, leave these lands, and obey God's word in His church!"

This was Father Parist's last, best chance. As a priest in a church, this *Word*, which both the weak and the strong across the land had come to fear as the only truth, was the only power he had left that might move men.

Not these men.

"This is not God's house; this is your house, and you have no authority upon us. Do not mistake us for common thieves—we have done our work. You were put in this church by your Lord Monroe of this manor, not by the Pope or the Bishop, not by God, but by a mere man, and you will not tie our hands today. If you won't help us keep the peace, then there will be no peace for anyone."

The bearded man was familiar now with the effect that a burning church had on simple village folk, and accompanied by the sight of a priest with his chest torn open, blood spurting and entrails leaking, it was the best salvo for instilling terror in the hearts of the common people and lining them up for easy dispatch.

The bearded man was fascinated, to the point of obsession, with efficiency.

†††

William was long gone from the church when the chaos erupted. If the reeve had noticed him slip away, he would settle with him later, when, of course, there would be a tax for desertion. It was an easy trade-off; taxes, as they were, would come and go, but William would have no need for money saved or spent if he were dead. Thus, he made his choice and found his way back to the home path.

He soon discovered that it didn't matter; they had either circled around him, or, possibly, there were more horsemen stationed throughout the village. He slipped by a few on his way, but when he reached home, door in sight, he was charged by a small knight who held his sword awkwardly to the side, and bellowed, "Hold!"

William was close enough to the door that he could hear Claire trying to calm his crying son. He should have just gone inside, but instead, he froze while his mind began to spin.

"Sir, do not threaten my wife or my young son, and you may take all you wish from my meager supplies."

These were to be William's last words as, without a sound, the horseman rode up on him and a sharp steel blade cleaved through William's skull, across his right eye, and down his face. He felt his lip split in two and his throat burn—and then his shock melted into the great, quiet darkness.

✝✝✝

Godfrey Sheval pulled back his horse's reins and came around to see that he had achieved the perfect killing blow to the serf, without so much as a nick to himself.

If one called him Sir Godfrey, one was assuming a lot, because he was neither noble-born, nor properly knighted. He was nevertheless a man with a horse and armor headed to the East. No matter what the other men did, as soon as he had acquired enough supplies, he would cross the channel at Portsmouth, use the old Gallic trails through France to Rome, and then by boat, arrive at the port of Acre in the Holy Land. He would go, and he would make his name there, following the slickest path to Heaven.

Before he arrived in Jerusalem, however, Godfrey needed to learn how to kill. He had to be able to kill with ease, not just the enemy but common people of all colors, tongues, and class as well—anyone who might be the enemy in waiting. He was determined, but there was this part of him that knew that no matter how much he practiced at killing, he was not born for it. This war was not for over-thinkers; this was a business for the reckless, the coarse, and the mindlessly bold, and so he had to numb himself. He had to kill, so he killed this man, some wily serf, protecting what little he had. It had been quick and clean, and he could do it again. Soon it would be many running at him, and then others on horse. He would kill them all, and God would forgive him, as was said by the bearded man, the Bishops, and the Pope, repeating God's own crisp, immaculate word.

Godfrey needed a new helm as the used one for which he had traded was a problem. The straps were worn, and it drooped over his left eye; though it was better to deal with reduced visibility than to risk an axe to the brain. It wouldn't hurt to replace his chain-mail shirt either, stolen from his uncle's storage. Soaked to rot with the blood and sweat of battles past, it was still wearable but brittle, rusted, and rotted like everything else he wore. When he had seen his reflection in a lake, he was shocked at how green he looked. The irony of how this color was often used to describe those who lacked experience was not lost on him.

The serf he had just killed had made it close enough to his house that his wife had heard the man screaming for her to open the door, and she did so, just in time to see Godfrey cleave down on her husband's face. Luckily for Godfrey, the shock of this had prevented her from slamming and bolting that same door.

Godfrey's eyes went wide at the bounty inside, including oat wheels, dried mutton, bacon, beer, iron horseshoes, wool cloth, some leftover stew, wine, and five pennies. It would be more than enough to barter for a new helm. What Godfrey thought would just be a practice kill, now turned out to be a stroke of luck and perhaps a sign that God truly approved of Godfrey's quest.

He lost himself, greedily assessing the fresh-widow's every possession, when behind him burst-in two hungry banshees. These men from Godfrey's "Crusader" band were red-bearded, fire-eyed, and ready to rip and tear. They were not interested in the kind of spoils for which Godfrey was there. Maybe they would pillage later, but for now, a quick, sharp punch to the woman's nose would suffice. Claire felt a blaring pain spread across her face which signaled that her cheekbone had just cracked in half. Maybe Godfrey would not have noticed if she had remained unconscious, but when he heard her weak sobs, with his arms full of her belongings, he could not help but turn. He froze at what he saw; one of the attackers was using his knife. Blood covered his hands as the other invader hit her face repeatedly, scattering her teeth in view of her child and dead husband. Her sobbing stopped and was replaced by a noise much worse than anything Godfrey had heard before. *How much can one person take,* he thought to himself.

Sir Godfrey unsheathed his sword and, with shakily decisive action, surprised the two men, easily killing the first with such a hard, precise swing that it cleanly decapitated him. This being the first time that Sir Godfrey had ever cut off a man's head, he gagged, barely holding down his morning ale.

The second man pulled his hand out of the woman's mouth, grabbed his sword, and rose to stance far quicker than Godfrey had expected. He lunged at Godfrey, who lost his balance, and pulled the man to the earthen floor with him. They both rolled around, swinging wildly, until Godfrey ascended, swung his weight over onto the man, and with all his focused strength, drove his sword down through the man's throat.

Breathless but triumphant, Sir Godfrey looked around and assessed four lives that had ended at the edge of his sword: the husband, the two attackers, and the mother, who had taken a stray stab to the neck during the scuffle. Sir Godfrey looked at the freshly orphaned child, and their eyes locked. A boulder dropped on Sir Godfrey's soul, and he suddenly questioned whether he could ever be forgiven for what he had done, no matter how many Crusades he joined. He decided to begin redeeming his sins immediately, if only to give himself some space to breathe for the many more sins to come. As Sir Godfrey and the child rode off together, he vowed that he would leave the bearded man's Crusader band and set out alone.

†††

Sir Godfrey rode briskly. Word of the butchery would travel equally fast, and right now, he reeked of blood and trouble. The child would give him some cover, but would also come with questions, so Sir Godfrey pushed himself to go farther than he might have ridden under different circumstances. When his exertion produced thirst, he found that the ale that he had stolen was sour. By nightfall, his barren throat was pasted dry. With his sight blurry and his limbs sore, he veered toward a village. A single woman walked the road.

"Can I trouble you, my lady?"

"Seen enough trouble today."

"Maybe then you will take pity on a humble knight, bound for the Holy Land."

"I have nothing to offer you, good sir. If you are truly a knight of Christ, you will leave me to my keepings. There are many women of lesser virtue around here to endure your questionable intentions."

"My purpose is simply sustenance, lodging, and trade in the morning. Though, I must admit, I have trouble believing this description of your virtue to be true. You are much too stunning to have not been charmed by now."

A smile—success.

"I have kin who make ale in this village," she began. "They host at a tavern tonight to celebrate the tapping of a fresh batch. You may follow me there if you wish."

Sir Godfrey put his horse in the tavern's stable, taking his time to ensure that the still-sleeping child was well covered before laying him close-by in a hay pile. It was a short walk to the tavern after that, where, to Sir Godfrey's thanks of both God and the blessed angels of the choir, not only did cold ale await, but also roast game! Sir Godfrey devoured the crisp thigh of a small bird. It was stringy, but moist enough and most importantly, hot. He also inhaled some hearty, dark peasant bread, not like the bleached loaves he was used to, along with herring stewed with peas and cabbage, and a bit of hard cheese to go with the bread. After surviving for weeks on nothing but rock-stale loaves, watered down cider, and whatever he could steal, this was a feast to rival his father's best table. He must have looked like Chronos devouring his children, with not a care for time or appearance.

And then he saw her again, the woman from the road, and remembered the life that pulsed in the manger. No matter how much he only wished to curl up in the hay next to the child, rest his unsteady mind, and wait till the next day to find a good home for the orphan that he had created, at that moment he knew that his best chance for that was sitting across the tavern and giving him the ale-eyes.

Walking towards the young woman, Sir Godfrey found the ale barrels again and dipped his cup. Of course, in a world where water was foul, ale was the lifeblood, and a good cup from which to drink was a commodity. Sir Godfrey's cup, like much else of what he currently possessed, was taken from a dead man—a well-off carpenter killed by one of Sir Godfrey's former band. It was a little bit of treasure: a golden goblet that was most likely a communion cup, possibly never drunk from and received only as a bauble. It was supremely striking, simultaneously beholden of a divine beauty and a simple grace. Its thick, clay makeup imparted humility, as if designed for the table of an unassuming tradesman, but the golden bands and blood-red rubies encircling its exterior left no question that it was the product of wealth. It certainly caught attention, particularly in a world that was often caked with the dirt of poverty. Godfrey didn't mind it, which was a likely artifact of his time raised amongst wealth. A glorious cup was a beacon, giving indication of who you were and what you could offer. Everyone saw something different—hope, opportunity, plunder, but they saw it, and it was but mere seconds before he was approached.

"You intend to drink ale from that?" questioned a surly man.

"I'll drink whatever I can find with it as I simply wish to slaughter this great thirst that has taken me over lately."

"This is a cup to drink wine from, and you foul it with ale?" snickered the man and then, seeing the woman's eyes on the stranger, continued, "Which either makes you the ass of a mule or the most unrefined knight this side of Sicily. Whichever you are, you just had to choose tonight to stop here, eh mystery-man? It's the only night this month that Glorianna is free, and you just had to stop *here,* with your shining cup and your fancy face, and be the man of her interests, on the only night I get to talk to her, you green, rusted scavenger."

"Leave us be," demanded Glorianna, who then pulled Sir Godfrey toward her and whispered in his ear.

"My quarters are not far from where you found me on the road; you need rest."

As the two departed from the tavern, Sir Godfrey discovered that Glorianna was the first maidservant under the house-woman who attended to the lord's manor. Upon learning this, Godfrey felt a great sinking inside, as it meant that leaving the child with her was as good as leaving it in the river. Still, he revealed the orphan, who could also benefit from sleep inside the warm home where Glorianna led Sir Godfrey to spend the night beside her.

When Sir Godfrey woke the next day, Glorianna was still in deep slumber. The child was awake now, with bright eyes and blood-enlivened cheeks, and he stared with calm, wide, knowing eyes as Sir Godfrey dressed and prepared his horse for travel. When, three hours later, Sir Godfrey entered Portsmouth, and saw the surging, icy channel that would lead him to the Holy Land, the child was no longer amongst his gear.

†††

Beacan Pendraig's pitchfork sank smoothly into the post-harvest ground. He did not gouge as if breaking up roots, but simply gave a gentle push allowing the fork do the work. This was no haggard strip-land used for peas and barley—this was the special place. Separate from any of the lord's or church's land strips, connected only to Beacan's holdings, and situated in hearing distance of a babbling creek, it was his very own personal slice of untarnished perfection. At eight-foot square, it wasn't much, but it would do just fine.

The heirloom wheat that he had reaped the previous day and would now replant, was his own private stock, given to him by his father, who had received it from *his* father, who claimed it was passed down the family line all the way back to the druids, and this reserve patch was planted for a very specific outcome: beer. Beacan's father had been an amateur brewer, a skill he had passed to Beacan along with the seeds.

The manor's previous lord, Lord Anquitate, had recognized Beacan's talents as a farmer and was wise enough to understand that it was best to take advantage of these when they would be most critical. Thanks to this, Beacan was able to pay for the privilege of something as ludicrous as taking his indentured two-days-a-week of work and moving them all to one span of time during spring planting, thus leaving the autumn harvest cycle free to work uninterrupted with his wheat field.

Eventually, just as the weather ebbs and flows with the seasons, Lord Anquitate died and his son took over, at which time there was progress to be made and old agreements to reassess. Now, instead of spring planting, Beacan's lump of time for the new lord would have to be paid at harvest during the yearly gather. Thus after a month and a half of straight work on the lord's land, and then two more weeks of shoulder-aching work to gather his own harvest, finally free of burdens in the gleaning days of late autumn, Beacan could work his brew-field in peace.

The previous day, Beacan had risen early to harvest his wheat patch. When he arrived, the stalks were shimmering in the wind, and he broke one of the buds off and chewed it fully to paste. He swallowed and let the malt taste linger on his tongue. Breathing deeply of the honeyed air, despite having been worked to the bone already, he conjured up the strength of ten men and cracked the field in two.

The morning after the reaping, when the sun seemed not nearly as tall in the sky as the previous day, Beacan rose to begin the post-harvest work.

At breakfast, where one mug of ale to wash down the cold barley pottage was the norm, he had the robust three, and whereas three mugs was an indulgence, Beacan had one more while preparing his tools. Once at the field, he began grooming the dirt for replanting, turning the ground, as he focused deeply on the dark, clotted soil mixing underneath his fork. He marveled at its every bit, each clump a part of the greater mass that blanketed the land, constantly regenerating itself and giving everything it had to those who demanded so much of it.

Beacan's father had been put into the very same ground only a few months before, during the early harvest. The lord's steward had given Beacan one day to bury the old man and grieve. "Unfortunate time of year to lay a man to rest," the steward had said glibly, words that still rose quickly to the surface like steam, coalescing into Beacan's utter hatred at having to work for the lord for the privilege of growing crops to feed his family in dirt that truly belonged to no one. This same hatred simmered into a steady boil at the notion that the current "landowner" had gained it through no great glory besides being sired by another undeserving rich man before him.

It was only in his work with the land that Beacan found true peace, turning the dirt and working the dry, top terrain till it yielded to the moist batter of the deep soil. He tried to refocus, but the ale coursing through his blood only helped push forward more thoughts of his father's body, already decomposing, discharging nutrients for the worms to feed upon and create compost from which the crops would grow once again. Beacan knew that the body was a temporary vessel, but it was his father's soul that he wondered about. Beacan wasn't sure about anything that happened after life, or if anything happened at all. Even if he knew that the body simply became one with the ground, he had a hard time denying a yearning for something more—for a soul to somehow continue on as something, somewhere.

If Beacan's father was anywhere now, he was, with all hope, in the fabled Land of Cockaigne. There, every path was made up of spiced sweets leading to cakebread houses with walls held together by sugar frost. It was where lamb steaks and goose legs were the clouds in the sky and rained down even when the sun shined. Where pigs roamed the land, fully roasted, knives in their mouths to offer a slice of rump at a moment's notice. Where men burned their spades and sickles in great smoking piles fueled by bacon fat that reached to the sky. Where maidens poured a man his breakfast of milk and honey over their shoulders so that it rushed down their backs and collected in great chalices, and the only daily work was to lift the cup to one's lips and drink. Where the lying-eyed churchmen were beaten by their servants, and all of the landowners were given only dented crowns and britches to wear.

Beacan knew that Cockaigne was not some fabled land in the afterlife but a state of mind on Earth, if one could find it in themselves to see the world as joyfully as one would if food really did fall from the sky. If Beacan didn't believe in Heaven or hell, it was not because he hated Christians, he just saw their dogma for what it was: ideas invented by Jews that were then spread by Romans and barbarians. There was nothing essentially wrong with any of these people, but at heart, Beacan was a Briton. He had learned the old rituals from his father, along with the faith of his ancestors who had populated the island of Briton before men could remember how they had arrived there, all of which made sense to him on a level that he could feel in his bones. Though the land had been yoked by the Romans, decimated by the Angles, fleeced by the Saxons, ravaged by the Vikings, and finally, lined up and dissected by the Normans, it was still more alive and vital than any man who hoped to stand on it and call it his own. Beacan owed more allegiance to this dirt he had been born on than he ever would to any lord or landholder. That soil would always take care of him, and no matter what man set his mark upon it, it would outlive them all.

Beacan had married up. He was handsome and bright enough to land his golden bride, Alfreda, who was the butterfly daughter of a rich, old Saxon who had not had a chance to marry her off before passing. Her father had been a gambler, so there was not much for them to revel in, just enough to provide a more comfortable life for their small family than the average. If it was not for his wife's inheritance, Beacan would simply have been the village drunk. In the eyes of others, no matter whom he married, he would remain that anyway, and none of it changed the fact that he was tied, like a bridled horse, to the land he worked. Without enough coin to rise fully from his station, all Beacan could do was claw by, work his piece, and hold out desperately till such a day as luck would bless him with the opportunity to climb, if that day ever came at all. Beacan knew it and almost came close to accepting it most days.

As the sun reached its daily height, Beacan finished hand-tilling the field and was drained and weary when the Green Man emerged from the horizon.

The mysterious knight on horseback had halved the distance by the time Beacan had focused. His mind reeling, Beacon wondered, *Could it be?* He rationalized that it was probably just a result of his midday hunger tussling with the jagged finish of his morning ale. None of these really explained the Green Man though, as real as the pitchfork in Beacan's left hand.

As a boy, Beacan had heard stories of the Green Man, a god of the plants, who rode through the forests to bless and impart new life to the ravaged land following the harvest. The story captivated him, and he would sit on the autumn days, waiting and watching the forests, hoping to catch a glimpse of the Green Man.

If this form approaching Beacan was truly the vegetation god of old, then something of the midday air and Beacan's dewy constitution made it easy for him to accept the lack of horns, along with the missing vine-like appendages that should have been growing from the god's every pore, and the beard of wispy leaves that did not spring out from under the Green Man's helmet.

Beacan's heart pounded, his breath picked up pace, and he tried to find another explanation for what was plainly in his sight and moving toward him. It was especially hard for Beacan to deny the image when the knight with the green chain mail and helm rested his sword-point on Beacan's throat and demanded a name.

"Beacan Pendraig."

"Do you have lands and possessions enough to support a family, Beacan?"

"I do sir. As you might suspect, I have finished this year's harvest only recently."

"Are you a God-fearing man?" the creature barked at Beacan.

"I am sir; I praise Christ," Beacan said definitively, now lying to a god.

The Green Man turned and released a bundle from his gear and held it with one arm, never for a moment moving the sword from Beacan's chin.

"You will take care of this child. You will not harm him or otherwise abandon him to the elements, but instead, you will do your best to nurture him and see him to growth. If you refuse, I shall slash your throat."

Beacan did not say a word, feeling suddenly as if invisible vines held his mind and tongue in place. He received the child as naturally as the Green Man handed the infant to him, followed by a stunning golden cup, tossed to Beacan, that at first glance would seem to be worth the equivalent of the manor's entire harvest.

"This will help you to pay for the expense of the child's care. His mother called him Uther before she died."

And then the Green Man turned and rode off.

Beacan stood, transfixed, watching until the stranger was a twinkling green speck down the road. In Beacan's arms, two squinty jewels peered up at him, filled to the eyelids with adoration and fear.

†††

"Alfreda, please, calm down."

"Damn that, Beacan! Are you crazy? I want you to march your pickled brain down that path to the church, and don't come back till you're empty handed."

"How can you say that? You of all people?"

"Just go!"

"Alfreda, my ultimate love, you know I'm not going to do that. Why don't you just relax, let me put the baby to sleep, and then we can talk when we're both calm?"

She stopped, pushed her long blonde hair back, and with cheeks flushed and blue eyes wide, grabbed Beacan by his shirt and shook him, completely disregarding the child in his arms.

"You damned, drunken fool! You're obsessed with that old pagan nonsense again! We CANNOT take in this child! I won't …"

Alfreda's eyes begged him with sadness more than anger.

"Please don't call me a fool, Alfreda, while I'm trying to convince you to take care of an abandoned baby that was forced onto me at sword-point!"

"I cannot lose another one Beacan, even if he is not of our blood. I cannot bury another little face in the cold dirt. I cannot. I will not."

She gritted her teeth, swallowed, and looked at his frowning, wide face. Unable to help herself, she cupped his face in her hands. Tears welled up as she spoke.

"Is it so wrong for me to view it this way, to not want this burden on an already burdened life? Even after the last one died at three weeks…when you wanted a second child, when you begged me for the daughter to bring good luck to your harvests …"

"The harvests did get better after her birth!"

"For a few years Christ favored us with a bounty to feed our new young, but then it was back to the forever meager harvests and the struggling. Please, Beacan, give this child to the church; let them find a good home for him, or a life in a monastery, where he will attain the peace that his no-doubt restless soul will require."

Silence lingered in the air longer than each of them thought it would. Beacan exhaled wearily and broke it.

"I'm so sorry my love, but I cannot. It would haunt my days; I know it. If this is what it's like to hear the voice of God, like you often speak of, then now I understand."

Alfreda broke her silence with sobs, freeing her tears.

"Forgive me ... I'm sorry..."

"Alfreda, it will be all right; I promise you. This will not be a burden, but a blessing. Just listen to what I say now, as if it was the only thing that I've ever said of any worth: we will have a better life from now on. I believe it. I want you to believe it too."

Smiles emerged on both of them, as well as some relief.

"Alfreda ... You have made me a better man. Because you married me for love, instead of choosing a nobleman, you have forever lifted me up. I hope you will understand someday, that when a person helps you like that, if given the chance, you owe it to the world to do the same for another."

She cried more, and they kissed through the tears.

Beacan put the baby to sleep. He checked on his own children— five-year-old Manning and three-year-old Sally, taking extra time that night for a tighter tuck, a fix of the hair, and one more light kiss. Then he took his wife and sat with her, close to the dying embers of the hearth.

"We'll be all right, I promise. I ... I just have a feeling. I know this is the right thing to do. For all of us."

"I know darling, I know. You are a good man ... a great man. You do too much sometimes, where anyone else would do the least they could. It's why I love you."

†††

In many ways Uther's restless soul vindicated his new mother's predictions.

He developed into a stocky child, not fat, but unbalanced and misshapen. Not helping matters was a dour, often expressionless mask of a face, and though neither mute nor lame, he was withdrawn and quiet.

To add to this, Uther was possessed by an internal affliction from the earliest times that he could remember being aware of himself. It was not because he was adopted; Beacan and Alfreda had kept that from him. Uther would have been this way no matter where he was raised. It was part of the smallest fibers of his being, lodged in the foundation of who he was. The source of this feeling was often related to a particular talent that he had. Even as a very young boy, he was tremendously aware of all that transpired around him. Though there were obvious benefits, Uther only felt it as a curse, like having a bright burning torch always held right behind his head, which both illuminated the world, but also made it difficult to see through the brightness. It pained Alfreda to see this. She silently begged God to release the lonely ghost that seemed trapped in Uther's heart. Beacan often brought Uther to healers to coax his spirit with forest herbs, certain that if there were just some way for the boy to be rid of the fury in his blood, he would find peace. All of these qualities created the impression that behind Uther's still-young eyes there was a soul that had, sadly, endured much beyond his years.

†††

While the adults worked the day, Uther spent his boyhood on the manor, playing and exploring the woods, mostly by himself. His loner status eventually drew him to another child in the village named

Mar Inculpus. Mar had no father, and in addition to being from stand-out, curly-haired Roman lineage he was of such weak will that it seemed as if he might blow away in the wind. He was the only boy lower than Uther.

Alfreda encouraged Uther to befriend Mar, and the two became a sort of contrasted, yet balanced pair, both realizing, even at that naive age, that they each viewed the world from the unique perspective of the outsider. There was a mutually agreed upon contentment in their often silent journeys, mostly to fishing spots. Both would rise early and meet to hike far past the village, finding the places where they could throw a line without being cited for trespassing. Uther often caught food to put on the table. Mar mostly lost his bait. Neither was very concerned; just being far from those who sought to keep them low was good enough.

✝✝✝

Uther was fortunate to grow out of his doughy boyhood and into a broad, sturdy teen. He was strong enough to work with Beacan in the fields, while Mar's frail body was often bound indoors with sickness. But Mar would eventually heal, and on occasion, he and Uther would still meet late in the day, after chores, and fish at some of their more choice spots.

It was on the day that Mar started out early, and Uther followed later, that instead of meeting Mar at the stream, Uther found him still on the path, and not alone. Mar was on the ground, covered in dirt, and surrounded in a circle by three older boys.

"Your dad's dead," one of boys taunted.

"How long do you really think you'll survive? Another year? Probably die of the shivers next winter."

One boy held Mar down while another slapped him. Uther, observing at a safe distance, could hear the sound. As Uther watched, they all started kicking Mar at the same time.

Uther ran over and without a word drove an uppercut into the first boy's chin and head butted the nearest one after that. Stunned from the head butt, Uther was sent to the ground by a kick to the back. There, Uther bit the second boy's leg so hard that blood streamed from his teeth. The first boy scrambled to his feet and ran, bleating awkwardly through a fractured jaw.

"Help! Hue and cry! Help, assault! Hue and cry, hue and cry!"

Uther punched the bite mark on the second boy's leg, causing the boy to crumble. He vigorously pushed the boy's face into the dirt until he heard crunching sounds. Rising, Uther charged the third boy, driving his fist at the boy's brow. Through the haze, Uther watched the boy go down in an unconscious, flopping heap.

Panting heavily, Uther ignored the pain in his back as a smile emerged through his stoic gaze. For the first time that he could remember, he was at peace.

Lost in his triumphant rush, Uther was barely aware of his surroundings. When the father of one of the unconscious boys, accompanied by a farmhand, grabbed Uther by the collar, the man was repaid with Uther's knuckles smashed against his teeth, knocking him out cold. The farmhand backed away as Uther picked the unconscious man up and began repeatedly punching his face.

It was a century of red before the farmhand gathered enough reason and courage to pull Uther off. Later, it would be ascertained that two or three more of Uther's punches would have killed the man.

Beacan and Alfreda paid a good share of fines and spent the afternoon berating Uther, before determining what extra chores would serve as a worthy punishment.

"Beacan, what shall we do with him?"

"He's just a boy, Alfreda. He's trying to control it, but boys do things …"

"It takes a lot of punches to almost kill a man. Would you describe that as 'control'?"

"You're right. But I don't have any answers."

"He'll follow the dark path … and be an outlaw before there's hair on his chin."

"You're being dramatic. Yes, he hurt some people today, but he was defending the other boy. Loyalty is a rare commodity in this world."

She nodded skeptically, and they both furrowed their brows, uncertain as to what the future held for Uther. The next day, before Uther left for the fields, Alfreda stopped him.

"I want you to remember one thing, above all, about what happened yesterday. Everything we told you last night is the truth and the way it must be. You have to learn to control yourself. But there is another side of things. It is me asking you to befriend that boy, because I saw the way he was tormented by others. I believed that you could prevent that just by being near him because others stay away from you. But not just that; in my heart, I always knew it would eventually come to this, that you would stand up for him and fight. You should know that I don't regret that decision one grain's worth."

†††

As time progressed, Beacan was gone for long stretches of time for business on the road, and there were other changes. Beacan's clothing shifted from drab, loose, and rough-edged, to colorful, well-fitting, and finely tailored, with pointed shoes and jewels strung around his neck. There was also a distance in Beacan's eyes and a different way that he hugged Alfreda, as if she were more like a sister than his wife.

Beacan explained to Uther much of the details of how his

business had grown from that first extra-large harvest. With the great, new bounty had come surplus. With surplus came the need for new markets and eventually the money to buy even more strips of land. More strips and more profit allowed for the purchase of full furlongs of land to be converted to sheep-grazing ground for wool. With the guaranteed income generated by the wool came the transition of Beacan from indebted farmer to moneyed merchant, with greater holdings than even the lord of the manor.

Uther knew that much had changed, if from nothing else than the larger house in which they now lived, and the food on the table that was superior to the scraped together stews that he remembered subsisting on when he was younger. It was with the growing prosperity that the family enjoyed the degree of luxury and security that Beacan had promised his wife on the night that Uther had arrived so many years ago. None of it changed the discontent that remained in Uther's heart, however, nor the way in which his mother worried about him to the point of obsession.

"I wish you were here more, Dad. Mom's so hard on me. Since the fight, she makes me come home right after my work. She thinks I'm going to hell; I'm sure of it."

"Uther, your mother is right about many things, but not everything. Death isn't hell or paradise. It's peace. The only hell is *here*, and the only way it happens is if we allow ourselves to suffer for our mistakes. And no matter what the church tells you about the dangers of sin, there's nothing wrong with making a mistake. Now, I always knew you would be a good luck charm for us. A year after you arrived, our harvest was fuller than I'd ever seen—and it wasn't the last. It only confirmed to me that … I made the right choice … wanting to … to have you, my son."

Beacan looked Uther in the eyes, before looking down. It seemed for a moment as if he was about to say something else, but he only smiled and turned in for the night.

Part 2
Three Quests

With the day's work done, Prince Richard gave his armor and sword to his squire for polishing. After three days of fighting, the armor was barely scuffed, but the sword was streaked and dull. The rebel barons had been sent a clear message. Richard had wiped out their army, sparing only the leaders who were each blinded by a single swipe of his sword. Now Richard could relax and allow his countrymen some time to rethink their actions, as any chivalrous knight should do.

Putting these thoughts out of his mind, Richard turned to dinner: hearth-roasted fish plucked that day from the local Garonne River in Aquitaine, France where Richard, the Prince of England and son of its King Henry II and Queen Eleanor, had been raised in his mother's homeland and where he was currently ruling as Duke.

He pulled the stopper off of a bottle of local Cab Franc and poured liberally. After finishing his fifth cup, a defiant smile spread over his clean-shaven face as he tossed the empty goblet and put his legs up on the table. The invaders he had dispatched that day would not be the last; his vengeful father would see too that, but Richard did not care. He would take it and give it back twice. King Henry II was tired now and growing frail. He would never submit easily, but Richard was resolute; it was finally time to rein-in his father's destructive pride, and do it with such intense finality that maybe, at long last, there could be peace.

As his servants cleared the table, Richard tried to relax by sipping on a sixth pour of wine. He wanted to hear songs by his minstrel, Blondel, an old friend who was asleep. Instead of waking him, Richard tried to enjoy the silence.

As the night advanced and the second wine bottle was drained, Richard's constitution turned unexpectedly grim as he dwelled on his predicament. He searched the pores of God to understand his father, whom he feared, and loved, and hated, and missed. As he dug deeper, Richard eventually found his answer: his father could not respect another who was so like himself because he saw only the flaws mirrored back. It had forced Richard to ally himself with Philip, the King of France and a man whom Richard despised even more than his two-faced family. Richard's mother Eleanor was the ex-wife of Philip's father, King Louis VII. Though the marriage was dissolved before either Richard or Philip were conceived, it had forever linked them through the traditions of nobility. They were friends as children, but the years since had forged them into very different men. Richard was brash and unpredictable, but also brave, loyal, and pragmatic. Philip was brilliant and cunning, but also cowardly and untrusting. To Richard, Philip would always be the boy hiding inside of himself. Nevertheless, Richard would have to find temporary comfort in the arms of his enemy to defeat his father's armies.

As Richard fumed in his own conflicted emotions, plotting against his own flesh and blood, he truly longed only to wash it all away. After years of struggling to prove himself to his unappeasable father, he longed to find his own quest, and do something that really mattered for the world. He had already fallen to his knees in the presence of bishops and sworn to take up the cross in the Holy Land and free Jerusalem. He had the prestige, he had the power, and soon he would have the money to make a pilgrimage to join the only fight that really mattered. Though he could not yet depart from his home-bound concerns, he had begun to turn the wheel.

He had sent the word out to loyal nobles in England, that if they had faith or sins to absolve, and money to burn, then now was the time to spend it for their salvation. With their help, the Crusade would come to life.

As the night hours strained toward morning, Prince Richard finally let his skittering thoughts settle enough to discover sleep. Seconds before he drifted off, he was once again content. Soon his battles with his family would be over, and he could focus on his own glorious dreams and on making them a reality. Surrounded on all sides by enemies, forced to defend the very dirt on which he had played as a child, he was unmoved. Jerusalem was calling him, and nothing would stand in his way.

†††

The following year, Uther joined his Frankpledge tithing, a fellowship that included nine boys from local manors that were formed into an interconnected, self-policing unit. At a vulnerable, mischievous age, a Frankpledge was an age-old tradition for young men to join to help provide order and unity to the land. Chief pledge was Kay Gilhad, and each member was responsible for the other's behavior, to the penalty of treasure, labor, and if necessary, blood.

Uther had to bail out his brothers routinely, like when Bed Drydant became drunk and threw the cocky steward's sword in the river. Uther testified in Frankpledge court that the breakfast pottage was rotted and made them both dizzy. He felt a pinch for lying to the Elders, but he knew that the only true harm done was to the steward's pride. Uther began to realize that he held a certain power that grew with each similar opportunity. By making the right decisions, as fairly as he saw them, and not manipulating anything for personal gain, his reputation shined among his brothers.

†††

"Does anyone know how to make a bow?"

Uther asked the question at a late date; maybe too late.

With five dead children discovered and one still missing in the village, it had been a long, dark two months. The blanket of fear and distrust only grew with each new shocking revelation. No taverns had been opened for weeks, and the migrant workers and merchants had all left. As each day wound down, the manor grounds were quickly scoured of life, and home doors were shut early and tight.

It had all started so simply the past summer, when on a warm night, a light scratching on the door interrupted the evening's supper at one home after another. Once opened, it revealed the dirt-smeared cheeks and stick limbs of a girl not much older than five. She said that her name was Joan, that she was an orphan and starving. Each time, the pleas for help seeped out of her tiny, split lips like the quiet murmurs of river toads in the morning, and each time she was denied. The next morning, her lifeless body was found floating under the bridge that led to the church, with one arm outstretched over her head in an eternally futile attempt to hold back the abyss.

†††

"And God has revealed Himself to us, as He RIPS back the

curtains and shows us His TRUE revelation!"

The new priest spat when he talked, not just the minor conversational drop, but gobs of froth that built up around the corners of his lips. He paused to dab it away every so often with a yellowed cloth kept close at hand. As he continued speaking, his eyes boiled in his head and his voice peeled through the small church that Uther's family attended.

"And the wrath, dear lambs, is what you have sown with your sins, and now reap as evil prospers. And like so much spent chaff from the harvest, so now go your earthly lives, tossed about, to forever wither in the fires below, as He decrees it."

Uther hated this new priest. Since the last one was dragged away in shackles for hoarding vegetables, Uther thought that anything would be an improvement. This man, however, with his high hair, mutton-fat fingers, and eyebrows in permanent arch did not strike Uther as anything close to holy.

"Make no mistake, little sheep, He has punished you, and it is only the first salvo. Soon His wrath will draw up like a wave, before crashing down, and ALL OF YOU will understand what it truly means to be denied!"

Uther could not take it anymore. He knew it would reflect poorly when he rose to leave, but he didn't care. He would trade scorn for *true* salvation that day and looked directly at the priest before turning for the door. The priest's eyes expanded, and he paused mid-sentence before continuing.

"If my words are not reaching you this morning, then let me offer up some stark truth instead. You are ALL to blame for that poor girl's death. Had you sheltered her, had you given her some food as if she were the Lord Christ begging for an olive, then she would not have died just short of the bridge. Had she been able to cross, she would have found comfort, security, and alms within these four walls where we sit today, where all are ALWAYS welcome and salvation is free…"

The priest's voice rose as Uther drew closer to the door.

"Keep your sword and cup close, for the time has come that will test you greatly. You will be with the LORD, or you will be alone."

It took every ounce of Uther's willpower not to slam the door on the way out, but in his heart, Uther could not deny that a trace of the priest's dialogue rang true.

†††

The murders did not stop. A young boy who played by the river during the workday had gone missing, only to be found days later floating near that same bridge by the church, with his eyes gone. And then others—a brother and sister were lost for a week before the girl was found dead. The boy was still alive but horrifically beaten, as if something terrible had dashed him against the earth, trying to crack him open. He was unwell for two days before dying in agony. Then a young girl did not return from bringing the family's alms to church. The body was found mutilated in such a way as to render her unrecognizable to all but her parents, who identified the small scrap of pink fabric that she kept for good luck.

A month and a half after the first death, the sixth child—a teenage girl—disappeared. By that point, the priest could have been the most decrepit, corrupt bureaucrat to ever draw breath; it still would not have prevented the people from looking to him for any answer he could give to the ghastly affliction that had befallen them.

†††

The last baked wheat loaves leftover from the fall harvest were turning stale when the annual Frankpledge court came. All of the previous year's shortcomings would be assessed and paid for.

The old court table was rotted, so Uther's fellowship was tasked with making a new one. Uther sarcastically suggested a unique *round* design, and what started as a joke was quickly embraced by the group and carried out. The group was fined six pence each for a lack of a place at the head of the round table for the steward, but they all agreed it was worth it to see the rotten-fruit look on his face.

Court was done for the year, and they set out on the walk home. Uther waited till everyone had stopped talking so that he would be heard clearly.

"Does anyone know how to make a bow?"

There was an awkward silence before Uther awkwardly pretended to continue.

"...that way I can put an arrow in the steward's horse before next year's court and keep him stuck on his manor."

The group laughed it off and turned to other topics, like the village girls who would attend the upcoming holiday feasts. Later, Ambrosh Aurelius, a thin, stern-faced boy of Roman lineage found Uther alone.

"You know, Uther, I've heard you make jokes like that before and I can tell that you don't really mean it as a joke, so why don't you tell me why you really want to learn how to make a bow?"

Uther was surprised and looked around carefully before speaking.

"I want to do something … about the murders. They've all taken place near the bridge. I'm going to find out why."

"You really think you can solve that problem with a bow?"

"Is it too much to ask to have the skill of firing a bolt when trying to catch a killer?"

"What do you really think is behind all of this? What do you think you're going to find at the bridge?"

"I think it's a man. I have my guesses who. The murders

coincided with the arrival of that angry new priest. Do you think that's a coincidence?"

"You should tell the others, for help in numbers, at least..."

"They'll never all agree. If I'm going to do this, I have to do it alone, and take the consequences myself."

"You're not being realistic. If you're found with an unpermitted bow, we'll all suffer the charges."

"Well, I think that the cost of doing nothing outweighs the price of getting caught."

As Aurelius contemplated the situation, his face never changed. Eventually he spoke again in hushed tones.

"When I turned thirteen, my father told me about the aqueduct ruins, past the plains at Arcapelicus. It's a refuge left from the days of the Saxon invasions that's known to descendants of Roman Britons. No one has been there in ages, but my dad believed that there were supplies and weapons there, and that I should know...just in case."

"You'll help me then?"

"I've always been curious to see if it was real; I just had to make sure I was going there for the right reason."

Aurelius stared at Uther and fixed on his eyes for a few seconds before speaking.

"I am, right?"

†††

When they finally met for the trip, it was October 30th, the night before All-Hallow-Even—the official end of harvest and the start of winter. They left as soon as the workday ended and night came quickly. The walk was filled with the pained cries of wolves and owls crossing between the tree lines, along with thoughts of the many real threats that no doubt surrounded them. If something existed in their own village that had been doing such terrible things, then they could only imagine what other mysterious horrors existed out in the dark depths of the night woods.

Luckily it wasn't long before the aqueduct materialized on the horizon exactly as Aurelius had predicted. It was a thin bridge across the valley, thirty feet high and half a mile long, supported by the characteristic arches and made up of endless small stone blocks, cracked and jagged, yet unmoved by time.

While Aurelius rummaged for the shelter entrance, Uther stood mesmerized by this breathtaking expression of ancient dominance, like the colossus vertebrae of a long dead beast. Though a shadow's worth of its former glory, the decaying edifice would still be there long after Uther was gone. It was designed to carry water, but Uther saw it for what it really was, a message to impressionable natives:

We are here to tell you how to live.

Uther continued to stare, transfixed, when he heard the call.

"I'll need a hand here."

†††

They pushed away a boulder to reveal a locked door. The keyhole was mangled, but the lock was rusted and shattered easily to reveal a small room built into the valley wall. The morbidly stale air gave them the feeling of stepping through time to Ancient Rome itself.

"Aurelius, I don't think anyone has been down here in a *long* time."

"It's a misty memory that Roman Britons needed such precautions, but there was a time where it seemed as if the whole world had ended. When the empire fell and the barbarians took their day, the Romans living here did not cower; they collected themselves, fought back where they could, and bided their time."

Inside the room the boys found a variety of archaic supplies— glass vessels filled with pickled vegetables, animal hides for beds, a small, unused hearth, and a set of dresses and tunics piled neatly. And weapons— a gladius sword rusted to uselessness, three small helmets, and one bow that snapped in two when Aurelius drew it back.

Their further scouring of the enclosure revealed a set of shelves housing more time-forgotten objects: taut scrolls, ancient pottery, idol charms wrapped in scraps, and then, upon further inspection, a hidden area behind the shelves. As their eyes opened wide with astonishment, the boys discovered a secret stash containing pristine bows, arrows, swords, daggers, shields, and the remnants of what appeared to be a deconstructed lance. It all looked newer and more recently gathered than the other items.

"You can take a bow and the arrows, Uther, but we leave the rest here."

Uther did just that, rounding up the arrows in a makeshift quiver from one of the dresses. They left all the rest as it was and then departed. The walk back was uneventful, and they arrived home in the early-morning light.

Before parting, Aurelius reached into his left boot and handed Uther a dagger.

"Never bring a bow n' arrow to a knife fight, eh?"

†††

Uther hid the dagger, bow, and quiver and began the workday neither awake nor asleep, remembering the previous night hazily, as if it had all been a dream. When the work day was done, resisting the urge to sleep, he grabbed his mother's hooded cloak and used ash from the hearth to blacken his face. Keeping his head down, he made his way out into the village.

It was a mellow Hallow's Eve as compared to those past when Uther's ancestors called it *Sowin* and lit bonfires to the frighten spirits that had escaped the afterlife on last night before the start of winter. The tradition had evolved into a mischievously celebratory night where children wandered in simple costumes, pretending to be those same spirits, with gourd lanterns to light their way, seeking pork-ends and apples from village houses. Uther knew that it was the ideal situation to mask whatever he might have to do when he got to the bridge. When he arrived there, it was darker than he had expected. He found a spot that was hidden, but still in range of a solid shot, and practiced drawing his bow. Finding it harder than he had expected, he wished he could let a shot go, just to see what it felt like, but he was there to hunt in secret, so he waited.

†††

The noise of the arrival jostled Uther from sleep. His accidental nap was so seamless and tranquil that it was almost as if some forest sprite had enchanted him to keep him unaware of the horrible truth.

He had been right, it was a man—at least technically, but certainly not the priest. The braids and clothing style revealed Saxon heritage, but beneath those simple identifiers breathed something far from normal. It was hunched over and moved in a slow, peculiar gait, as if it was attached to puppet strings. The grizzled skin holding it together was patchy and warped from exposure, and its face was angular and distorted as if beaten into place with a blacksmith hammer. Uther imagined that it was born lame. It moaned an unnatural, anguished sound as it plunked down its quarry of half a deer as if presenting it to something out of site. When it did not receive the reaction that it apparently sought, it crouched and muffled its howling screams in its massive hands.

Uther tried to steady the bow as he drew back the string with nervous hands. The first arrow only grazed the creature, and it turned and ran toward Uther with such speed, that by the time Uther had steadied another arrow, the man-creature was on top of him.

The smell alone forced Uther to gag and drop the bow. He felt an onslaught of unfocused pummeling that imparted all the wrath of the uncivilized world. With the creature on top of him, pressed up against its soiled, leather tunic, Uther frantically grabbed a sturdy handful of beard and, summoning every ounce of his determination, hauled the beast's head into his own right knee. The creature's screaming reaction vibrated through Uther's bones, and the pain flowed through his knee as if he had split it with a sword pommel. Instantly, gigantic hands fastened around Uther's throat.

Shocked and immobilized, Uther did not grope, or even gasp for air; he simply floated. As his breath drained and the picture faded, he felt small, just one more man who had made a wrong choice that was about to cost him his life. This impending reality was almost frozen in place when Uther's limp hand brushed against his calf and he felt the blade Aurelius had given him. Grabbing it, Uther used the last of his dwindling strength to bury the dagger in the wild man's chest as deep as it would go.

It was enough. The creature projected one last, distorted shriek, as if damning God for bringing it into existence and then, with a gurgled whimper, slumped onto Uther. A line of saliva drained onto Uther's brow, as Uther felt the burden go limp.

It took Uther ten minutes to escape from under the dead being, starting and stopping many times before quitting from exhaustion. When he finally emerged, it was another ten minutes before he could stave off the dry heaves and walk.

Uther ducked under the bridge where he found a hole within which was a girl, the last person that had gone missing. Though emaciated, she was beautiful and near his age. She shivered and barely pulled her gaze away from the ground as Uther, still woozy himself, cut her binding ropes and covered her with his cloak. Apparently still in shock, she quizzically looked around, before slowly retreating back into the hole. Uther helped her out again and back to her senses.

"My name is Uther Pendraig, from Caerlon Manor. I'm a friend. Are you ok?"

He received nothing in return but silent, stricken eyes.

"If you will let me …"

He held his shaking, blood-speckled hand in the air for many minutes before the futility dawned on him, and he put it back down.

"I'll walk with you to your village; I know it's not far from here—your father posted a reward yesterday."

They walked, ending the night in silence as Uther left her at her house.

†††

Another sleepless night for Uther was followed, this time, by a harder day of work. At its end, Uther was possessed with the kind of rest-deprived energy that allows a man to keep himself useful and aware long after it should be possible. He accompanied his mother to the Feast of All Saints at the manor house to celebrate the start of winter.

Uther spoke to no one about the events of the previous night and claimed no reward. The girl's clenched silence told him that whatever had happened before he had found her was not something from which she could be so easily rescued. Despite the fact that he had saved her from unimaginably worse horrors to come, he did not feel like much of a hero. However justified, he had taken another life and the thought of that made his young head thump. He wished he could be anywhere else but at the feast.

In the waning hours of dinnertime, a seeming stranger arrived—a gray-bearded man clothed in red silk and a fur hat, with a cherub smile and the wide, jolly eyes of a soul finally returned home.

"Dad?"

Beacan knew how to make an impressive entrance. His arms overflowed with gifts of spices, gems, bright colored clothes for the adults, and dolls and puppets for the children. He was recognized by a cousin who began a back-slapping round of greetings. Although Beacan was heavier with a grown-out beard concealing the edges of a more weathered visage, what had not changed was his smile stretching almost wider than his face could contain.

"C'mere my boy; it's been far too long!"

The bear hug from his father brought a decisive change to Uther.

"Where've you been?"

"Germany, Kiev, the Land of the Rus, the Black Sea shores, and East too, to Bethlehem and the Holy Land. We've got a lot to catch up on, and there will be time to do it, but for tonight, let's find ale and sing the winter carols. Ha ha ha, my boy, my boy! Come, let me show you something outside."

Beacan giddily led Uther out, where, tied next to Beacan's horse was a pair of bizarre, hoofed animals, broad and high, resembling forest deer that had supped on bacon for a year. Out of the head of one jutted a great nettle of branch-like horns.

"I brought them back from Kiev; they're Rhine deer. I rode one for a number of clicks into Germany before I found a decent horse trader. Aren't they stunning beasts? I made sure to get one of each so we can breed them. The milk is six times fatter than a cow's, and wait till you taste the meat!"

It was increasingly evident to Uther that Beacan had not lessened in his favorite habit of keeping the cold away. The same stains that used to appear on a humble farmer's tunic now covered red silk and testified to Beacan's merry consumption of whatever fermented drink was offered to him. But that was part of what Uther loved about his father—his infectious, albeit inebriated, sense of joy; something that Uther lamented not inheriting.

They returned to the manor house and enjoyed the night's festive celebration together, and afterwards Uther finally enjoyed a night of solid sleep.

In the morning the family assembled, and Beacan spoke of his travels over breakfast.

"Alfreda, you'll be happy to hear that your other son is thriving. I met Manning on break from his studies at Bologna. That school is costing almost half of our holdings, but he laps up whatever the old Italians throw at him. I feel simple in his presence."

"I should visit him. Mom, we could all go!" Uther enthusiastically suggested.

"Oh, you won't get me trekking across France," Alfreda said with automatic revulsion, "though, it would be lovely to visit Rome. Oh, what am I saying, I've never even ridden past the northern borders."

"Actually I'm afraid it would be a bad time to stride across the continent for any of us. I have news…from the Holy Land. It's not good news…"

Beacan used his sleeve to clean the crumbs off of his beard and cleared his throat.

"Jerusalem has fallen to the Saracens. Christian hands no longer control the Holy Land, and the spot where Christ rose to Heaven now rests under the crescent flag."

A startling chill shot from Uther's toes up through his spine, as it did similarly for his mother. Beacan continued.

"Unfortunately, that's not all. The news was relayed to the Pope and that night he dropped dead. Every priest, doctor, and soothsayer from here to Constantinople is trying to read the meaning in this.

These are uncertain times that we now enter."

Alfreda let the news soak in grimly.

"If the Holy Land has indeed fallen and the Pope is dead, can all Europe be far behind? Should we not prepare for the Moors and Saracens to be streaming up through Spain to our doors?"

"All hope is not drained," Beacan said in what he hoped was a reassuring tone. "King Henry may be sick, but Prince Richard has sworn to take up Crusade; same as Barbarossa in Germany and Philip of France. The Templars are massing men in Antioch as we speak. The pilgrimage will start soon, and it will be a massive host, dwarfing the first two Crusades. We will pray that their victory ensures our safe keep here in England. Till then, we will do what we must, let the seasons pass, and try to enjoy our harvests."

Beacan put his arm up and around Uther.

"I know that I've been a stranger to the air here, but that's going to change. A few more short trips, and I'll be coming back to England for good, to retire and man the farm. Before I head out, however, I want you to take a short journey with me, just for a few days; we've got some things to discuss. Tie up your plots tomorrow, and we'll set out the next day."

When Tuesday came, Uther and Beacan traveled south for the day, stopping for the night at an unassuming lodge. Once settled, Beacan ordered two ales, along with an entire carafe of whiskey, made by the lodge owner himself, who was shocked at the ability of one guest to buy that much at a time.

Uther drank his ale, and Beacan used his to wash down the whiskey. As Beacan began to feel the effects, Uther was discovered by one of the owner's daughters, and Beacan saw the tensed curls of a smile unfold. Struck by the moment, Beacan once again felt himself pull back from the edge, not wanting to take that joy away from Uther with what he was about to reveal. When the girl finally headed off, Beacan, now well inebriated, decided that it was time to get on with it.

"Uther, sit, and let your drunken old father ramble for a bit."

Beacan smiled forcibly, but it lasted only seconds before it shrank back to the pained expression that it had been before. He swallowed hard and spoke again, this time more quickly.

"Uther … I love you like my own flesh and blood, and that will never change, but you are not my real son. A stranger gave you to me when you were a baby. I am not your real father. Alfreda is not your real mother. It is the truth."

Uther smiled awkwardly but said nothing.

"The reason we're on this journey is for me to tell you this. Tomorrow's day trip is only to help take the sting away."

"What do you mean, Dad?"

"No Uther, I'm not your father—not by blood at least. This is not a joke or banter. I wasn't kidding, and I am sorry I do not possess the talent with words to reveal this to you more delicately."

"I don't understand. Why are you telling me this now?"

"Because it's an unpredictable world, and I still have travels to take. When I leave England, I'm not sure when I will see home again, and it's past time that you knew the truth."

"What you're saying then … it's real? You? Mom too?"

"Yes, Uther, she is not your birth mother. Your brother is our only living blood offspring. We have always celebrated the day that you were given to us as your birthday, but true as the old trees, I do not know the real day that you were born."

"Dad, I … is there any more that you know? Of my real parents? Of anything?"

"I will throw myself at your feet now and tell you that there are always gray areas in life, no matter how much we want to idealize it into the dark and light. It grieves me that I even have to tell you this now, and that I have allowed you to believe the lie for so long. Please be assured that it was only because I have let myself believe, in my own heart, that however different you were from us, you were still my true son. But you aren't and your life has been part of a greater drama that I, as a flawed man, have created, and I am just so sorry. "

"I don't understand. What is it? What have you done? Say it, without guilt. You've been a good man, a good father to me, and I know that won't change ... I love you, Dad!"

"I love you too, Uther ... son. This isn't easy for me, but I have, from the day you entered my house, believed that it was my purpose to help you and give you a good life despite whatever turmoil you emerged from."

"How did you find me?"

"You were brought to me in the morning while I was working the fields. A sword was held to my throat, and I was forced to take you from the man who wielded it. I could have brought you to the church, but I knew I could provide a better life for you. And, there is another reason..."

Beacan's hands shook as he reached around to his pack and removed a bundle, wrapped in coarse cloth. He placed it on the table and unwrapped it, revealing a goblet made of rough-hewn clay, with flawless gold sections grafted onto it—a fusion of the humble and the high.

"When I was in the Holy Land, a fellow merchant guided me to the place where Christ was crucified on Golgotha Mountain, where the church of the Holy Sepulcher is built and where I bought this cup. I had the gold added in Paris. It's for you."

Uther picked up the chalice awkwardly and turned it around in his hands.

"Uther, I don't know if the man who brought you to me was your father or a kidnapper, but he insisted that I take care of you, and when I agreed, he gave me an exquisite golden cup as a means to help feed and care for you. It did that, and much more. My greatest sin and mistake of the heart was not to tell your mother about the gift, which I used to create wealth for our family. When you arrived, things were not so good for us, I knew that I had to have that new wealth; I knew I was not strong enough to give it up once it was placed in my hands. But I also knew that if I had accepted it and then given you away to the church, the money would have brought a curse on my head. So I kept you, and I kept the secret."

Uther was speechless for a long while, fidgeting with the cup, searching its exterior with his bulky fingers, not knowing what it could possibly mean to him in the wake of the unsettling revelations that were only just beginning to sink in. Out of respect, Beacan observed the vigil quietly, taking infrequent sips from his cup, and wishing that he knew the right words to say so that they could forget this minor detail of their otherwise unbent relationship. As the tavern emptied for the night, Uther regained himself.

"So where are we going tomorrow, Beacan?"

"I'm taking you to a healing place. If you were born in Briton, then it's a place important to all of our fathers, no matter who they were. You may have heard the village crones speak of it. It's called Stonehenge."

†††

The next morning they started out early, with Beacan in shockingly spry spirits despite the full carafe of whiskey that he had drunk the night before. He and Uther journeyed outward to the site by foot. Along the way, Beacan collected herbs and wild vegetables that he used to prepare a mid-day meal, and told Uther of his work as a trader, guide, and caravan leader that had taken him farther than he could ever have imagined. He had seen the origins of civilization in the deserts of Egypt and the forests of Samaria, where he had acquired the kind of knowledge incomprehensible to those on the manor.

"I was searching for something, but I didn't know what. If I had known the lonely places to which such a quest can lead a man, I would never have stepped foot off of Briton. But I do know things now, and today I will use what I have learned to help cleanse you of the pain that you feel, either from last night's revelations or otherwise."

They walked farther until they reached the edge of the dense woods. Before entering, Beacan paused and spoke.

"We will seek out the age old truths in the forest together, but we must enter separately. Find your own path in, and we'll discover each other again when the time is right."

Though dubious of Beacan's vague, high pronouncement, Uther did as told, hiking far into the woods alone, with no sign of Beacan for hours. He turned back toward the direction from which he had started and eventually, he found Beacan, who was pressed against a tree and shaking awkwardly.

As Uther came close, he realized that Beacan was using a long stick to hold something down. It was a snake.

Beacan handed Uther a small, steel blade embedded in a slick, silver stone.

"Been waiting for you. I've kept it at bay, but you have to finish it."

"I can't. I'm afraid of snakes."

"It's not a particularly fast one, and I've already stunned its head with a stone."

Beacan held down the head of the snake so that Uther only

needed to strike the killing blow. He did so with his eyes closed.

Uther watched as Beacan skinned the snake, drained its blood, and then mixed it with the venom from the fangs. He rationed it into his own cup and into Uther's.

"It is said that the oldest truth is found in the snake's venom. Only its blood will serve as a sufficient dilution to the poison's effects for you to be able to ingest it and experience the wisdom. Drink with me now."

They finished their cups and walked on, reaching the Stonehenge site when the sun was almost at its high point in the sky. As they broke through the woods, a wide field came into view, stabbed on its visage with an encirclement of tall stones. Beacan led Uther to the center where he stopped and whirled around, looking grey and ancient, with the light seeming to enhance every time-worn pore in his skin.

"Our forefathers called it Stanhence. Very great things happened here; and terrible things too. But the stones still stand, and they will watch it all come and go and then see it happen again and again. And again.

Uther started to feel an unusual sensation like being drunk, except his mind was still clear. He felt as if he was watching his body move, as if floating above it, and this was such an infinitely peaceful sensation that he imagined he would never feel angry or upset about anything again. He felt his mind flying across everything as if it were set free from his over-confining body. The thoughts came fast, with each new idea colliding into the next and all of it interconnected in one great unified truth that was impossible to look away from, yet comforting in its endless, chaotic perfection. Beacan's revelation from the night before seemed to mean absolutely nothing in the grand scheme of things. A feeling would come over him as if he wanted to get up and run, but it would quickly be overcome by another feeling of how wonderful it felt just to sit and stare. It was almost dark when the faces that had materialized in the rocks started to look craggy and bare again. Back at the tavern, it was only a short time before Uther retired to his bed and faded into a cavernous sleep.

†††

They rode home the next day without stopping, and Beacan left for the last of his travels a few weeks later. In addition to the cup, he gave Uther a sizeable gift of coin, not only allowing Uther to hire migrants to work for him, but also to borrow horses for his remaining tithing brothers to take a trip together. Uther had always wanted to see Mynid Baidan Hill, where legends said King Arthur had won his greatest battle, and he hoped that a journey away from the home that he thought of as his birthplace might help him to forget that it no longer was.

Of the nine original brothers of Uther's tithe, only four remained, with the rest either moved away or dead. They set out in early summer as Uther did his best to keep his mind off of what Beacan had told him, rationalizing it as not an unusual fate in the precarious times in which he lived. At least he did not have to be raised by the church and live a cloistered life in a monastery.

Eventually crossing into Wales undetected as far as they knew, the four companions rode hard for the site of Mynid Baidan Hill. It took them until mid-day to reach the destination, only for them to find that it really was just a hill, and barely one at that—an upward dent in the ground was a more appropriate description. There would be no triumphant stand on a soaring, elevated peak in the heat of the mid-day sun, as Uther had imagined, in the spot where King Arthur supposedly had, after twelve battles, finally defeated the Saxons along the Welsh border. They made the best of it, spending some time there, sitting, standing, talking, and joking. Uther dug his hand into the grassy dirt on the top of the hill and let it run through his fingers, only to rest again on the ground in that disappointing, holy place.

They camped close to the hill that night, in the place that for Uther held his *true* intention of the trip. As they arrived near the spot, they saw a peculiar sight confirming the legends of the sword handles projecting out from the ground.

"Sarmatians are buried here," Uther said. "Beacan told me about them; they were master horsemen collected from the Eastern border of the Roman Empire to fight the invading barbarians in England. They were flung far from their families to ensure that they would fight hard and finish the job quickly so they could return home."

"I heard that they were buried with their swords," Gwayn Lot said. "Sure enough."

Uther pulled one of the handles as hard as he could, but it was held tight in the calcified ground.

That night, Uther kept his eyes closed until he was certain that the others were asleep. Even then, he gave it some more time before using whatever he could—the edge of the bronze plate in his supply pack, the dagger, and even his own hands, to dig out one of the swords. As night transformed to dawn, the last bits of the confining ground relented and the blade came free.

Uther gripped the sword firmly and, just for a moment, held it aloft. It was a blessed prize, tarnished but still sturdy, and last held in the hands of a man who had probably died using it. He swore to polish the blade till it was reborn. As morning arrived, they began the ride home, with Uther keeping the sword close and hidden.

Part 3
Terror and Riches

A year passed, and the Sarmatian sword rested, underground near the wood pile, where Uther had buried it. During that time, his days were spent in a flurry of activity, plowing fields, clearing weeds, managing migrant workers, and gathering hay for the animals in winter. He was happy to work hard on the land that his adopted family owned; it filled him with so much pride and satisfaction that all he could wish for at any moment was a refreshing cup of ale and a good woman to refill it for him. It was on a particularly hot, mid-summer's day that while thinking of exactly that, *she* appeared, holding a cup. He nodded graciously and gulped it, while his eyes met hers. Then he heard her voice for the first time.

"I wanted to thank you; not just for saving me."

He had not seen her since that time, over a year ago. She looked well, and he had the urge to say something that sounded funny and a little smart.

"I came close to needing saving there myself, if memory serves."

"...You didn't ask for the reward. You didn't say anything. Thank you."

She paused before her next words.

"... I haven't told anyone either ... about any of it."

Uther wiped sweat from his eyes and fished for the right words.

"I don't need the money; I've got my own plots here. My ... father is a successful merchant; my family owns half of the manor... I'm Uther."

"I know. That was the first thing you ever said to me."

"Will you tell me your name?"

"Maybe, if you're good."

"Do you think, possibly, I've been good enough already?"

"Gwen, Gwen Igrane. My dad is Cornwall Igrane, but I guess you already knew that. I'll see you around Uther."

✝✝✝

Uther did know who Cornwall Igrane was. Even before the reward had been posted, Uther had remembered overhearing Beacan mention the prosperous merchant who lived on the next manor over. Igrane had disputes with the manor owner, Lord Tintagel, and although Beacan sympathized with a man who did not respect authority, Igrane took it too far. He held raucous feasts with his merchant guests at the manor house against the lord's will, and hired dangerous looking knights from outside the realm to guard his holdings. This did not sit well with anyone; there was a reason that men such as Cornwall Igrane did not become titled nobility simply because they desired it and had the money to buy it. The aristocracy was wary of people who did not have experience with authority but were anxious to claim it; it was a sure sign of someone who would abuse power.

It was rumored that Igrane had ties to Templar bankers and was conducting loans on their behalf. This was the only aspect that prevented the lord from arresting him; no one interfered with the Templars, for it was a name that inspired awe and fear. Templars were the only men that the Pope permitted to charge interest on lent money, and if one owed a Templar money, one looked over one's shoulder till every last coin was repaid.

†††

That fall, Uther was elected steward of the manor. It was a respected position and a good step toward being voted reeve when he was older. With the extra pay came extra tasks, which at that time of the year, with winter approaching, mostly meant chopping wood.

"Do you always furrow your brow like that when you chop?"

She appeared again at midday, like an apparition formed from the shadows of the swaying leaves.

"It's not easy you know…"

"You look like you've lined up demons on those trees and you're splitting their necks. What else could vex a man so much to look like you do when you chop?"

He readied another defensive remark but realized he was being played with.

"Perhaps you can show me what kind of face you make when you chop?"

He did not expect that she would smile, grab the axe, and proceed to squarely work the tree almost better than he had. She took a few more swings before giving the axe back.

"Have you gotten enough chopping done that you might take a walk with me?"

Uther did not work for the rest of the week. Instead he spent a generous sum to hire workers to finish his tasks while he spent those hours with Gwen. Hand in hand, they wandered far from their homes and talked for hours. Uther, a young man forever of few words, opened up to her about Mar, about his tithe brothers, about the trip to the aqueducts, about Beacan, Stonehenge, Mynid Baidan, and even the sword buried in his yard. She hung on every word with her silent, fascinated eyes. When he finally turned to kiss her, it was not that she was simply willing; she had, it would seem, been waiting desperately for it, as her lips met Uther's with enthusiasm.

†††

The scared, confused girl that Uther had brought out from under the bridge had not spoken to anyone during the year that had followed her ordeal. Not to her sister, not to her father, not to the other children, not the village officials—not a living soul. She did not know why, yet the longer her silence had lasted, the harder it had seemed for her to come back from it. Uther changed that.

After he had rescued her those many months before and walked her home, she had thought about him often and hoped that he was still there, nearby, maybe even thinking of her too. She wondered who this person was, this man, really a boy, who had risked everything to stop the monster that had hurt her. Discovering that he was, in fact, living on a nearby manor, had made her happier than anything she could remember. She began to watch him from a distance, until she could no longer hold back. She had to find something to say— anything—so she could meet him, look at his face with courage, and see if he would talk to her. When she finally did approach him, he had let her in as easily as she had let herself fall away. She spoke again, and the words flowed with ease.

Slowly she learned who he was and why he had been there that night to help her. Then, she saw the strength with which he had dealt with his own burden; discovering that he was an orphan and that his life had been a lie. She knew that although it troubled him daily, he carried it with quiet grace. From his strength, she was inspired to find her own way back out from her silence. She at last broke through and spoke again to her sister Igerna, first apologizing for the silence and then making up for the hushed year by gabbing about all the village happenings and, of course, about Uther. Autumn winds pushed through the trees when Gwen's father left for several weeks on business, during which time Gwen and Igerna conspired to invite Uther to stay one night.

After finishing his day's work, Uther hiked briskly the half hour's distance until he arrived at Gwen's home; a stunning residence made of polished, fitted stones that was double the size of Uther's own impressive home, reaching off the plot and onto unused farmland. It was common law that all excess farmland must be used to plant surplus for the lord, but Igrane had offered to pay twice what it was worth, and Lord Tintagel was not a fool. Igrane had also assumed the mantle of village blacksmith by paying twice the price for the title, though Igrane himself did not assume the role and continue service, instead hiring migrants to work it specifically for his own purposes. If the villagers needed anything, they were charged double what they had paid in the past. Gwen explained this all to Uther before they ate the lavish meal that she and her sister had prepared of mutton, quail and apple tarts, so that Uther knew that what they were about to enjoy came with a price.

Nevertheless, they ate and talked and drank ale till they would laugh at almost anything. Later, Uther and Gwen slept in the same bed for the first time. They both hit the pillow, nodding off instantly and slept with a kind of peace that neither had ever known.

†††

The next morning, Uther helped Gwen with her early day chores.

She packed a meal of sausage, mustard, and pickles, and they ate out in the pasture at mid-day. On the way there, they passed a man who Uther could swear had given them a cross look. Gwen knew the man, Abner Albern, a veteran from the second crusade.

Abner had fought in the battle at the base of the Hattin Mountains, called "The Horns" for the double sharp hills in view and because it was a massacre. The Crusaders had marched into unrelenting desert heat. The water source had dried up, so when the arrows started flying, they were exhausted, thirsty, and easily decimated. Losing this crucial battle had set off a chain of events for the Christians that culminated in the surrender of Jerusalem to the Muslims.

When a man has as many hours contemplating his own death as Abner did on crusade, what more could he wish for than to be with his wife (now dead from sickness) and his new child (also dead) and to resume his inherited trade to feed them and hold up the roof? After returning from the Holy Land and visiting his wife's and child's graves, Abner planned to head straight for his old forge and pound out horseshoes, hinges, and swords to the tune of his pain on the anvil that had been given to him by his father, who had taught him the trade, learned from his father before and on up their family line. For Abner, that forge was more of a home than the house in which he had grown up.

When he did finally arrive, the sadness outweighed the shock, as he found out that he would no longer be needed. The forge was now owned by another, as paid to the lord by the merchant Cornwall Igrane. Though Abner had not technically owned the forge before, it had always been the Lord's customary preference to have it passed down through a family of blacksmiths. So, hobbled by circumstance, Abner was a beggar at Cornwall Igrane's door.

"Please my lord, as a proud soldier who has fought for God,

please give me my job back; it's all I know. I won't even look for payment."

Igrane's face seemed sympathetic, stirring hope in Abner that Igrane was a man who was at least capable of pity. It was all Abner had left.

"My friend, I had no intention of specifically wronging you, but please understand that the old traditions are fading. Time progresses and change is inevitable. I need a forge I can depend on. If I were to throw a poorly crafted shoe on a horse that was meant to deliver goods to market, it would affect my reputation. Eliminating risk is my intent; that's why I hire men who are young, strong, and straight in sight—which is to take nothing away from your valuable service in defense of this realm ..."

"In the Holy Land, King Guy de Lusignon dubbed me a knight after I survived 'The Horns.' I killed and killed and never took a cut, no matter the heat! That should tell you all you need to know about my ability to do *good*, proper work..."

Abner peeked over Igrane's shoulder at Gwen and Igerna eating breakfast.

"You have daughters. I know that they would want to grow up in a place where chivalry to a good knight of the Crusade is upheld, so that they can be proud of their father."

"Good Sir Knight, let me speak directly. Please understand that, in no way do I wish to prevent you from practicing your trade. I will be primarily using this forge for my own purposes. No one is preventing you from building another forge and catering to the village's other minor blacksmith needs. In fact, I encourage it!"

Abner realized that it was futile, and the façade that he had been holding up disintegrated.

"You would speak to me like this? I should cut your guts out.

You know very well that I can't assemble my own forge. We didn't exactly haul back overflowing riches from the last Crusade if you hadn't heard."

"I heard very well, as we all did, good Sir Knight, that you *lost* the Holy Land to the Muslims! Are you honestly looking for a reward for such abject failure?" questioned Cornwall sarcastically.

After that, tables were thrown, girls screamed, bowls of fruit were broken and fruit was smashed underfoot to a runny pulp. Abner was a broken man after years at war, and Cornwall took advantage of this, repeatedly punching Abner's limp-leg. As Abner fled, Cornwall lost his composure, cursing the man out with Templar-driven death threats.

The blacksmith knight wasn't fully beaten just yet. A cluster of extra supplies were stored in his house, and the final small quantity of his saved veteran's payment helped him to buy a few more essentials. He transformed his home into a small forge and started the fires up, working tirelessly from sunrise to sunset, and collapsing in a corner at day's end to sleep. With hot irons cooling too close to straw walls, however, eventually it all went up in a blaze.

It was pure luck that as Uther and Gwen were sharing their midday meal, they caught a glimpse of smoke rising in the distance. It was soon followed by a visible flare-up. Uther exhaled slowly and spoke with a tone of responsible disappointment.

"I'll go check it out."

"I'm coming too," Gwen replied.

When Uther burst through the wall of Abner's burning home, the old soldier, his senses hazy from the smoke in his lungs, saw only a muffled shape of a broad figure, before feeling his useless body scooped up and carried into the blinding light.

Uther caught his breath, rubbed his stinging eyes, and turned to face the waterless reality of trying to put out the fire. Luckily, the walls collapsed in on themselves, and snuffed out the blaze almost instantly.

"Bless you a thousand times, kind son. I owe you everything."

With his lip quivering and the sweat still hazing his vision, Abner spotted Gwen.

"But you, girl, can rot in hell! Your father is Satan's spawn, and I swear that I will pray every day for you to suffer! You may think that you're innocent and safe, but you will taste it the same as your father will!"

Uther left quickly, to avoid association with the whole mess. It was futile though, as Cornwall returned from his trip and immediately heard about what had happened from neighbors. He was thus, very curious to know about the man whom his daughter was spending her time with in his absence. Gwen, possessed of a mix of shock and childlike guilt, told him everything; how Uther saved her, how he had not claimed the reward, how she had found him, and how he had saved Abner from the fire.

"Naturally, I'd want to meet this young hero. Will you bring him by for dinner Gwenofire, my lamb? Tonight, perhaps?"

"Yes, Father, I will ask him to join us."

Uther, too, had an encounter with a parent that day. On his way home, he found Alfreda tending her garden and was startled by her question.

"Do you love her?"

"How do you even know about her?"

"I was at market today. The women of the villages know everything."

"I do love her, but I know that her father won't allow it when he finds out."

"He will do what all rich men do when their daughters love a poorer man; he will find reasons not to accept you until he realizes that his daughter's happiness is worth more to him than a dowry from some baron's son. I have a little experience with this, you know."

"Are you ok with it?"

"I'm not a crone just yet. Your happiness is what's important to me. Only God chooses whom we are to love and who loves us in return. I won't lie to you—I had hoped you would find another way … maybe a nice girl of moderate means … so as not to have the worries of trying to please a rich man's daughter. It seems you really are Beacan's son."

†††

Gwen thought about the awkwardness of trying to introduce Uther to her father. Uther—all lumpy and thuggish eyes at first appearance; simple, glorious Uther. Her savior, so humbly unaware that with every step he put lightning down where his foot touched. In even his dimmest look, he shined like a sunrise over the water to her. Her father would never understand her love for him, how it was instant and permanent. Cornwall would test and prod Uther until he found some defect or failing on which to focus and use to his advantage. It would not end pleasantly, and she had no desire to expose herself or Uther to that, especially after Uther had come to her and explicitly requested to see her that night for some mysterious purpose. Gwen made the decision to skip dinner, knowing that the pain of having to explain it to her father in the morning would be an acceptable trade for being able to run off into the night with Uther.

†††

"No, I don't want to marry you!"

"But, Gwen … I thought …"

"What? You thought what?"

"That you loved me … that this is what you wanted?"

She strode over to him and kissed him softly on the cheek, then harder on the lips.

"Someday, yes, I do want that, but let's stroll a little first before we run. Besides, there's my father to deal with. He knows about us; he found out from the fire. He wanted to meet you tonight, but I wanted to be alone with you, so I left without word. He'll be angry, but I'll smooth it over in the morning. And I *do* love you."

"Who cares about him? Let's run away together, and we'll never have to worry about what he thinks again. I … I have a priest waiting in the clearing for us at midnight. I thought you would accept."

"Uther, I can't do it. I'm not ready for this. Please, slow down. It's ok."

She kissed him again and lingered with it.

"Look …" she asserted, grabbing his face, "I am not getting married today."

She took his hand, and they walked until she whispered in his ear, "I say we meet that priest tonight, tell him he can go home, and then we find a quiet, hidden place by ourselves."

After telling the priest of their change in plans, they found a spot in the deep forest and eventually slept. As deeper night gave way to the release of morning, they went their separate ways. Gwen, blissful and content, floated through her village to her house, while Uther, feeling hopeful and at ease, strolled the path back to his own village with a new rhythm in his step.

†††

He had to see her again and imagined that she must feel the same way. Grabbing only bread for supper, Uther ate as he walked toward her manor. The night was warm, and he thought of another spot that he knew of to bring her to. When he stopped to spy from the trees, to see if Gwen's father was home before approaching, what he discovered was an altogether unexpected scene. He was unable to speak to Gwen, so he had to trust in the story told to him by the reeve.

The previous night, as Uther and Gwen had slept together in the forest, two men broke into the house while Cornwall and Igerna were asleep. Igerna claimed that the men were knights, or at least dressed as such, and while forcing Cornwall to watch, they raped her. After that, they slit Cornwall's throat and left, well before Gwen returned to find her father dead and her sister ravaged.

The reeve would not allow Uther inside the house, so, frustrated, he left the scene just as stares and suspicious thoughts began to gather.

†††

When Uther arrived home, he headed directly to where he had buried the sword, marked by the equal space between the old oak tree and a large, half-buried stone.

Nothing.

He knew exactly where it should have been, and even dug around and deeper to be certain, but it was gone. *Dug up by someone else. Had to be*, he thought.

Uther did not hear from Gwen for a few days, so he stirred up his courage and crept back to Tintagel Manor after dark. Entering her home, he found her still wearing the same dress from when they had last been together.

"Is it true, Gwen? Like the reeve told me?"

"How should I know what the reeve told you?"

"Is it true?"

"He's dead. My father is dead. It's his own fault."

"Who did it?"

"Anyone who was decent and crossed his path, for all I know!"

"Has anyone figured out who did it?" Uther asked softly.

"It doesn't matter," she sobbed. "It's done!"

"They can't get away with it. It must have something to do with the blacksmith."

"Didn't you hear me? I don't care. It's over. Whoever it was got their surely-deserved revenge against my father!"

"Let me speak to Igerna ..."

"You can't ... she's dying."

Uther grabbed Gwen's arms and looked into her eyes, and she saw something inside of him that she had not seen before. It scared her a little, and this time, when he insisted on seeing Igerna, she let him in without protest.

In Igerna's room, Uther found a blanched, quivering ghost in place of the bright, beautiful girl he had met just a few days before. He took Igerna's fingers in his much larger hand and clasped them tightly. There was nothing there. Regardless, he squeezed tighter, as if helping to hold in the life that was leaking out by the second.

"Igerna, it's Uther."

She locked eyes with him briefly before her gaze scattered again, and then surprisingly she whispered, "Will you rescue me now and take me away?"

"Yes, of course, I will take you far, and everything will be just fine."

She smiled and looked at Uther, not at his face, but far off behind him.

"Igerna, can you tell me who did this to you?"

"Men in the night came, to steal, stole from us, taken ... "

"Do you remember anything about them? What they looked like? What they said to your father? Anything?"

"Nothing said ... they spoke in tongues. Foreign. All tongues and fingers."

Water rose to the surface of her eyes and rivers streaked down her cheeks.

"Dad? Where are you? Are you back now ... is it over?"

Uther responded in the same voice.

"Igerna, it's your father; I'm here now. You are safe. Do you remember anything about the men who did this to you? Were they Crusaders?"

"They took off their helmets and chain mail before they got onto me. It was honorable of them, chivalrous ... "

She trailed off. Uther felt her hand tense in his and then go slack. Gwen screamed and ran from the house into the woods, faster than Uther could follow.

†††

Uther found the church where Abner was staying. The old soldier was sleeping when Uther smacked him awake, grabbed his neck, and put him against the wall.

"This is how you repay me for saving your life?"

Before Abner could answer, Uther hit him again.

"Who attacked the girl and her father? Tell me names! Tell me where they are!"

"I don't know anything ... It wasn't me; I swear it."

"What wasn't you? Tell me what you know!"

Uther picked Abner up and threw him out the door. Dragging him by the leg, Uther pulled Abner to where the trough of holy water sat, and then held Abner's head under for a five-second count. He pulled Abner's head out and moved in close.

"I know this is a house of sanctuary, and I will respect that enough not to kill you. But I will make you wish you were dead!"

"Enough! Let me speak!"

Tears welled up and then flowed from Abner's eyes, along with the truth.

"You have to believe me … I didn't do it; I didn't do anything ... I just wanted to be a blacksmith again … I never wanted to hurt anyone … ever again."

"Do you think me lame? After I saved you from the fire, you said that you would take revenge. The next night a tragedy befalls the family that you cursed …"

"You have to believe me … this wasn't my doing … it was never my intention to go through with that … just words … just angry words …"

"You know nothing of the attackers? There is no one you told? Because it is said that there were knights involved, and you're a knight."

"I went to a tavern after the fire. I took in enough ale to either kill the pain, or myself. By the time I was kicked out to the lane, I was ranting to the Gates of St. Peter about the man who took away my forge. That's all I did. You have to believe me. If not, then kill me now. Do it, and do me a favor."

Between sobs, Uther could see unmistakable guilt in Abner's eyes, so he released the old soldier, but not before learning the location of the tavern.

The next night, Uther borrowed his mother's hooded cloak again. Using his steward's key, he entered the manor house and spent the next hour collecting whatever he could from the tool shed to substitute for the missing sword. An old hammer was the best he could find. No armor, no chain mail, no sword or lance.

The next morning, Uther made his way to Tintagel where he found Gwen still wearing the same dress and Igerna's body still in the bed. After burying Igerna, he helped Gwen change out of her clothes. She crawled into bed and finally spoke.

"You don't understand. It's my fault. If I hadn't left with you that night ..."

" ... You would be in the ground next to Igerna and your father. You only wanted to get away for one night, you didn't mean any harm."

"No ... my father asked me to have you join us for dinner. Had I not been such a coward, you would have been here, in the house. You could have stopped it."

"There's nothing we could have done to change it ... If I was here, I probably would have been killed too."

"I can't believe they're gone. I'm all alone."

"You're not alone, Gwen; you don't have to go through this by yourself. First though, I'm going to go to that tavern and see what I can find."

"No. Don't go. It's done. I don't want any more hurt to come out of this. My father was a man who could not be content with his lot in life. It wasn't a coincidence that this happened to him, not on that night, or any night. He made his plans, others be damned, and it came back to him. I accept it. It was the risk he took."

"The hell with that! Igerna didn't deserve this ... I'm going there ... I have to see what's at that tavern; I have to do *something*!"

Gwen grabbed Uther's hand and held it tightly.

"If anything happened to you, it would destroy me. You're all I have left. Don't leave me ..."

"That night I intended to marry you and for us run away together. It was all I wanted—to have you to myself. Your father was the only thing standing in the way. I knew I would never measure up to his expectations, and so I daydreamed of him being killed; and then this happened. I've got to go there, and at least try to find the men who did this and bring them to justice. It's just something that I have to do."

✝✝✝

The two French knights, Duloc and Salofard, had been sitting in the tavern for two hours. Only recently returned from fighting in the Holy Land, and now on a mission in hated England, Sirs Salofard and Duloc were exhausted. They needed refreshment and what better place to learn of local, vulnerable women than in tavern? There was luck on the first night when a stammering drunk pointed the way to a hated local merchant with money, two young daughters, and no guards. The rest had been easy, but they had left the girl alive, and Salofard knew it was a mistake and now his paranoia was setting in deep.

The only other man at the tavern had ordered an oxen steak, which was not a small luxury. Salofard watched out of the corner of his eye as the man ate methodically, savoring each bite. *Was he listening to them?* Salofard was certain that the man had looked up and stared straight at Salofard for a few seconds, as though the man had recognized him. Salofard was not crazy; he knew that something was not right.

"Maybe we should go," Salofard suggested to Duloc. "Someone might be looking for the source of last night's fun."

Duloc took a large swig of wine and grimaced dramatically at Salofard.

"That's what *guilty* people do. The last thing anyone expects is for us to stay close. And must you always ruin the fun? You're as predictable as the damned rain here. We've survived Hattin, Montgisard, even the Siege of Jerusalem, and now you're yellow-livered over this? We're envoys of the French Crown; no one can touch us here, which is why we did it in the first place. So please just let me drink in peace."

"If you insist," Salofard said as he smiled through chipped teeth.

"But after that next bottle, I may have to take another rich man's daughter, and maybe his wife too."

By now, the wine had touched Salofard's brain, and he had lost care for the volume of his speech. It was not long before the other man had come to sit with them.

"Did I happen to overhear that you brave knights are seeking some fine English women tonight? I think I can help. My name's Uther."

†††

That night Uther discovered that he had a decent skill for acting. Making friends with the knights, he promised that, in exchange for payment, he would lead them to a local manor house where three unguarded female servants resided.

They trudged out into the moonlit night, with Uther doing his best to appear as drunk as the two knights who stumbled alongside him with abandon. Uther led them on until it seemed as if they were far from any villages, and then as swiftly as possible, he slipped the hammer out of his belt, spun around, and sunk it into Duloc's collarbone.

After tossing Duloc's sword far into the woods, Uther swung around, striking Salofard just above the eye and kicking his dropped sword into the brush as well. This was the fight Uther wanted—no weapons, no more death, just the guilty brought to justice with fists. Uther tossed his hammer, balled his hands solid, and drove a punch so hard to Duloc's sternum that Duloc felt it through the chain mail. He collapsed to the ground, and while Salofard was still looking for his sword, Uther dove wildly at him, sending them both sprawling into the woods. Instantly Uther scrambled on top, pinned Salofard, and let the skin on his fists tear as each punch crashed against Salofard's chain mail. Moments later, Uther sensed Duloc rising up behind him, and in one fluid motion, Uther cocked back his arm, turned, and with all of his young strength, aimed an upper-cut square at Duloc's jaw. He miscalculated though, and instead of cracking a jaw, Uther drove a raw, bony fist straight into Duloc's throat. Upon contact, Uther heard the crunch and felt the anatomy crumple under his bent knuckles. Duloc clutched desperately at his neck, spitting blood into the air in clipped sprays. He fell over, and his agonized gasps drew to silence.

Salofard saw Duloc's body go limp with Uther standing over it. With his sword gone and his partner dead, all Salofard could think to do was beg.

"Please, no, no, please … we work for the French Crown…we can pay you … Please!"

Uther rediscovered his humanity only to decide that he would ignore the request. A rock was hastily located that was substantial enough, when combined with Uther's strength, to crush the side of Salofard's face, until it all stopped.

Wiping his bloody hands in the dirt and collapsing to the ground, Uther sat for a long time with his head pulsing and heart beating violently fast in his chest, until the feeling finally faded enough for him to take hold of his surroundings: silence, bloodied faces, and two pairs of dead eyes.

It was harder for Uther to remove the chain mail tunics from the bodies than he had imagined it would be. Exhausted and drenched in sweat, he tried to drag them both, as they were, to the river, but there was no chance.

He started to dig, but that too, was futile. In his weakened condition, even the shallowest grave would have taken him till the following midday, so he scraped both knights' faces against some sharp rocks so that the features were no longer recognizable. That was the last of Uther's strength, and although he felt like he would pass out on the spot, he forced himself up, piled the bodies as deep in the brush as he could, and started for home. As he stumbled on the path, one question haunted him with black terror, echoing inside of his head.

What have I done?

†††

Alfreda had the look on her face that Uther could only rarely remember seeing from the stern, impassioned woman who had raised him: helplessness.

"They were here looking for you."

"I made some mistakes. I never meant to kill anyone but it didn't go how I'd planned. They were important men ... knights working for the French king."

"Where will you go?"

"I don't know; away from here, for now. I've heard stories of a church by the eastern shore where sanctuary is given to those who would leave the country by boat."

"You're leaving England?"

"Do I have any other choice?"

"Won't they be looking for you, even in France?"

"Then I won't go there."

Alfreda hugged Uther.

"I always knew this day would come. I prayed with every ounce of my soul that you would find another way ... but it was not meant to be."

She hugged him again and pulled him close and down, kissing the top of his head.

"I will pray every day. Remember that your father and I will always love you."

"I know, Mom; I love you too."

He packed lightly: three days dried pottage, a small cask of ale, some medicinal herbs, and the cup that Beacan had given to him. As he collected his few possessions, Alfreda reached behind the mantle and handed him a long, loosely wrapped bundle.

The sword.

"I found this awhile ago. I hid it from you because I didn't want you thinking about what you might do with it."

"May I take your hooded cloak? I can use it for bedding."

She wrapped the cloak around his shoulders.

"I will come back one day, when I can, Mom."

"Goodbye, Uther, my son."

Then he streaked away, headed eastward with no idea what he would truly find there, and no better ideas than that.

†††

Move at night. Sleep in hidden spots by day. Stay aware. Keep moving. Although this pattern continued for what seemed like weeks, it shouldn't have. The eastern shores would have been a four-day trip, at most. Eventually Uther was truly lost, with no idea whether he was walking in the direction he intended, or back the way he came. He passed villages, but avoided contact. Eventually the flatland changed into the beach and the sea. For two days he walked, thinking he would find the church. Deep down, he knew it was only a rumor, but he had not accepted yet that he would need another option. Only slowly did it begin to sink in that there were no boats coming to take him anywhere, and that there was also no going back. Even if he could find his way home, he would be forever cursed as a criminal who murdered two envoys of the king of France.

And what about Gwen? He had not even had a chance to say goodbye. He could visualize her face so clearly, and it dawned on him that in his memory was the only place where he would probably ever see her again.

Soon a fever overtook him. He writhed in his boiling skin by day, and shivered at night. Having no food or water, nobody to care for him, and nothing for which to live, he started to believe that this was how his life would end. Eventually he collapsed and slept long enough that if anyone had been watching the body, they would have assumed that he was dead.

✝✝✝

When he awoke, it was to a morning sun that felt, to his eyes, brighter than any that he could remember. His blurry first sight was of feet, encased in ripped, cloth-tied shoes. A voice boomed down from above them.

"Thank God. I almost thought you weren't going to make it. But then I decided that you were a lot tougher than that. Actually, all you needed was a little honeyed-milk. Perked you right up."

"Who are you?"

"Who am I? Who are you?"

"Uther. I'm ... a pilgrim."

"Headed east then? Not many boats docked on beaches like this one."

"I was looking for something, a church by the water."

"Many people are."

Uther tried to stand up, but was still too weak.

"Don't try to get up. You've still got a bit of a journey to get to the light. Not ready to leave just yet it seems. Have a drink."

A gaunt, sturdy finger pointed toward Uther's cup, sitting nearby, filled with what looked like wine.

"Drink! It's the blood of the land to help fatten you back up."

Uther took a few sips. The cool, earthy aroma sliced through what was left of his clouded head. He took a larger gulp and wiped his mouth.

"I hope you don't mind that I inspected your belongings, Uther. I assure you, I only wished to see if you had anything left that I might help nurse you with. I'm not much more than a beggar these days, and I tend to travel light."

Uther opened his eyes wide to see the person in front of him. The man was not much older than Uther, maybe in his thirties, outfitted in the robes of a churchman, but worn, frayed, and muted, with time having had its way. The man's hair was cropped short, and his face housed an unruly beard, along with the dirt that confirmed his station in life.

"I wonder, Uther, what are you running from exactly?"

"How do you know that I'm running, and why are you helping me at all? Are you some kind of priest?"

"Was. A monk, to be more exact. Actually, I've lived the spectrum, my father being a rich lord, and I being sent to a lauded monastery. But the closed-off life wasn't for me. Bit of the wandering ghost that sits on my bones does that to a man. I am as you see me now—all and nothing."

The man pulled a fist-sized loaf of bread from within his robes and handed it to Uther, who ate ravenously. It was magnificent—soft and ethereal so that it practically melted in his mouth.

"Take it easy, son. There's enough time to eat it all."

"Why do you give so much without asking for anything?"

"Isn't that what a Christian is supposed to do? Are you not a God-fearing man? Or don't you believe in God?"

"I must confess; I'm not an easy follower of the church."

"Ah, then we do have something in common."

"I know that there is more to all of this than what one finds on Earth."

"See; a God-knowing man after all. Good. Who needs to fear God anyways? After all, as you can see, there is clearly nothing to fear. If God can bring you here to the water's edge, where you mean to find your salvation, and then help you back to health, why worry of anything ever again? You gave Him your plan, and He gave you your wish."

"It seems in this life, it's not always that simple."

"It isn't eh? I will let you believe that if you wish, but God will keep showing you a different story; I promise. It may not always be pretty, but it is, most certainly, simple."

"Who are you?"

"Not simply the answerer of your questions. I prefer not to keep with my old name, but know that I have seen a better way than all that has come before and will spread that message as long as the wind and the spirit push me on. And then when I have seen its day come, I will spread whatever message comes after that one."

Uther suddenly found himself feeling overtaken by his lack of full health, and with his belly full, he lay back down, drifting off with the man still speaking to him.

†††

When Uther awoke the next day, he felt surprisingly more alive than he could remember feeling in a long time, even before all of the troubles that had led him to the road. With renewed vigor, he realized that the cuts on his knuckles from punching the knight's chainmail were almost healed. The monk was gone without a sign—not even a footprint in the sand.

Without a plan or even a direction, Uther walked the shore. When he eventually saw a ship on the horizon, he waded so far into the water that it almost topped his shoulders. Holding his cup high, Uther let it catch the sunlight and reflect a sharp glare, signaling the ship.

With a granted stroke of luck, the ship came in close and anchored. Uther watched as a small skiff emerged and quickly made its way toward him. Seeing four, dark-faced men dressed in rags, Uther suddenly felt a surge of fear course through his body. Before Uther could retreat to the shore, the men hauled him onboard, overwhelmed him, and pulled a sack over his head. Once again, Uther was returned to unconsciousness, not from illness this time, but from the broad side of an oar introduced to his skull.

†††

Each new scorch of pain from where the whiplash edge struck Uther's skin quickly became part of a broad throbbing that switched in a continuous network from one wound to the next. When the throb gave way to white-hot shock, his captors took mercy on him and lashed him to the ship's stern for the night.

As the rains increased, it seemed to Uther that the ship might splay itself on the enraged waters at any second. With nothing but the dark sack in front of his eyes, Uther imagined and hoped that his captors had abandoned ship. This fantasy was blasted away when someone cut the ropes that had held him to the mast. With no sight and his hands still bound, he tried to stand and find balance on the shifting, rain-slicked deck. He knew that they were watching him; he could hear their laughter, and as he found the edge of the ship, two pairs of hands rushed in and tossed him over the side and into the slosh.

Salt water rushed straight through the wounds and into his veins, practically paralyzing him with pain. With hands bound tight and sackcloth crushing his gasp for air, he thought to himself, *This is how I die.*

Instead, he was grabbed and thrown back onto the deck. They must have valued the profit to be made from selling him more than the enjoyment of watching him die, but it occurred to Uther that it was only because he had gone overboard and almost drowned that it was even possible for what occurred next. They removed the hood so that he could breathe. It was their last mistake.

Uther used the disadvantage of his still-bound hands to his favor, wielding them like a mace. He willingly lost control and released an animal from within that was no longer afraid of pain, or weapons, or his chances. They came at him from all sides, yet he just hit harder, with less focus, and little care for what damage he did to them or himself. One by one, he pummeled the members of the crew into submission or death, until there was just the sound of the rain on the deck, Uther's shallow breathing, and the pained moans of anyone else still alive. It did not matter that these men had been sick, or desperate, or had not seen food in three weeks, or had living mothers, somewhere, who cried for them at night. They had chosen the wrong day to push a sad, broken man with nothing to lose, too far.

†††

Though Uther did not know how to write, for many nights, to help him fall asleep, he rehearsed a letter in his head that he would have transcribed if the chance ever arose:

To My Dear Gwen,

I have no hope that this letter will reach you, but I have had it written so that, were I to be killed and somehow discovered honorably, it might find its way back to England and give you some closure about my fate.

You must know that thoughts of you give me comfort on dark nights. I hope that it is the same for you and that you have not forgotten me, and that you forgive me for what I have done. My meeting with the knights at the tavern did not turn out well, as I'm sure you know by now. As a result, I fled and sought escape aboard a vessel that I would soon find out was a devil's carriage of thieves who intended me no good options. After enduring capture and scourging, I was given an opportunity to reverse the odds, and now I run the ship with the survivors as my crew.

I plead your forgiveness for my actions that followed. We robbed any ships that we encountered. To say that I did it because I was starving is a weak excuse for not going to port and finding a better solution. To say even, that my goal was simply to find food is untrue. I sought only to lose myself in the downward spiral of my brutal victories.

The only positive effect of my exile at sea has been healing. As I now have drunk fully from the cup of the criminal, I can no longer hold a grudge to those who don't make the effort to do any better. My actions at sea have thus relieved me of the burden of judging others, since I have placed myself in no better of a spot. But what has brought me true peace has been this time that I have given over my fate to the whims of the sea. All I must do is take a few moments to stare into the great, flowing abyss to remember that I am at the whim of forces much greater than me, forces that do not judge me a quarter as harshly as I judge myself.

As such, what the other men here do not know, is that my true intention for this ship and its newly acquired riches, is to sail as far in the direction of the Holy Land as I can, and contribute our stolen treasure, along with my own skin, to the Crusade. If by some chance I survive, then like others, I will seek the greatest possible forgiveness, as is the known reward to those who have taken up the sword in the name of Christ. Despite my fears and lack of fighting prowess, I know it is the only way to be truly relieved of the burden of the crimes I have committed. I hope that someday I will find you again and hand you this letter, and that after you have read it and listened to my pleas, you will forgive me. Until then, I will hope that you are safe and that this letter is not given to you separate from me. I will do my best to be a true and good man again, to fight with a steady hand, and to return to you when I am done.

    All of my love,

    Uther

Part 4
Sicily

Damascus, Syria

September, 1190

Salah ad-Din returned to his sister's palace, directly from the front lines at Acre where his army was whittling down the Christian siege forces. As he settled into his quarters, he shook the sand out of his beard and hair, or at least as much as he could remove without close inspection. He could never get it all out.

As he finished his prayers, he reflected on his predicament. He had encouraged Jihad to inspire his downcast people, but in truth, he was long weary of the wretched, never-ending struggle with the Christians. Even after he had forced them out of Jerusalem and burned their army alive, more still arrived daily with a seemingly infinite desire for stubborn conflict. He tried to find avenues of diplomacy as often as he could, but it was perpetually futile. He yearned for a leader to emerge from their side who was reasonable and strong, someone that he could work with.

Soon Ba'ha, his personal biographer and close friend, arrived. They chatted and even laughed a little, but Ba'ha could see that his friend was weary.

"You're taking the right approach; we must show them our strength and bring a final terror into their souls that will drive them back to sanity, and to their own lands. You know these things; you have always understood God's way better than other men. I think he chooses this moment for our greatest triumph."

"No Ba'ha, he does not. The spies bring news of the kings of Europe massing new armies for another crusade. For the first time, I find myself questioning my mercy when we recaptured Jerusalem. Maybe I should have been harsher."

"Men respect and tremble at the name Salah ad-Din in the far edges of the known lands. Let them bring a thousand kings. You will take them, and one at a time, introduce them to their maker."

"I fear that my time in this world is waning. I hear God calling me a little more with every prayer. I hear him whisper and tell me that I've done all that I can."

"He is only testing you; testing your *faith*. In him, and in yourself. A test, that is all, and you have passed so many of them before."

"Not this time, and maybe never again. I am unable to ride and inspire like I used to. My sons are not like me. When I'm gone, they will fight amongst themselves and lose all that we have built. The Christians will outlast us Ba'ha; I have seen it in my dreams."

"I will never believe that. They see themselves as believers of the One, but they are pagans who look to trinkets to shore up their faith. They are children in the eyes of God."

Salah ad-Din took a deep breath, followed by a light exhale.

"You're right. I'm sorry, I know that I get lost in my thoughts sometimes, but that doesn't change the fact that it is our duty to cleanse our lands of these unholy men as long as we draw breath. I will wash them away with a bloody sword and God's holy grace."

†††

For the newly crowned King Richard, it had begun to sink in that his father was truly gone. When Richard was a young boy, he had dreamed of the day that his father would happily pass him the kingdom. Instead Richard had had to pry it from his dead hands.

As Richard prepared for Crusade, England yielded up its gold willingly for the Royal war chest. They were proud of their new king who was the spirited image of his brick-tough father combined with his charming mother. Though naturally disdainful of England since being raised in France, Richard remembered riding through the English countryside as a child with his father who truly loved the place. As he left the English shores to join his fleet in Marseilles, he almost missed it, and he was happy, and hopeful.

A few weeks later, just after his thirty-third birthday, Richard beamed with pride as he surveyed the great fleet at the departure point in Marseilles; the grandest fighting force that the world had ever seen. Eight thousand men would blanket the Earth, and respond to every nuance of his will. No matter what boulder fell onto his path, Richard would go around it, over it, or if necessary, pound it to dust, as he drove this great sword of the Western world straight through Saladin's heart, and walked over his corpse through the gates of Jerusalem.

†††

"Where's my sword?"

It was the first thing that Uther had demanded from the graying captain after Uther had crippled most of the man's crew. They had been starving and near mutiny when they had spotted the desperate looking man onshore, alone and built for slave trade, and holding aloft a brilliant gold chalice. It had sent the whole ship into a lurch, but the captain knew better; this man, holding an expensive cup high without concern, was trouble. Now with a third of his crew dead and the kidnapped man's hands around his throat, the captain would probably have to give up his ship. Uther tightened his grasp and spoke in a weary whisper.

"I'm going to beat you, every day, like you would have done to me, until you submit. But I don't want it to be that way. I want you to stay on as captain, lead these men as you would have otherwise done, and leave me alone. I will depart peacefully when I have reached my destination."

"Whatever you say, my lord. You are the captain now."

With that, the captain and his remaining crew sailed eastward as Uther demanded, and otherwise, they left each other alone. Uther spent most hours simply drinking whatever they could steal and facing out at the waters with a vanished look. The crew continued to raid though Uther did not join them at first. Whenever a particularly useful acquisition came along, he would assist, until eventually he simply led them in the attacks. Then one day, he ran out of drink, sobered up, and reflected on how far he had fallen. It was at this point that he made the decision to join the Crusade.

In desperate need of food, and wanting to avoid the docks as much as possible, it occurred to Uther that perhaps he could put his old fishing skills to use. Of course, the sea was a much different sport's ground than a creek, but as soon as he put a rod together, the muscle memory came back. Uther taught the crew to fish as well. It was astonishing how quickly these men, so distant from the behaviors of civilization, adapted to becoming hardworking fishermen, fleecing all manner of meals from the sea. *If these men could change*, Uther thought, *then it is proof enough that I can find peace, one way or another.*

Unable to sleep one night, Uther crept onto the deck and settled down by the port side. He looked out at the calm, flat waters and saw a startling sight, a larger ship with the unmistakable coat-of-arms on its sail.

He hastily roused his shipmates from sleep as their only chance would be in numbers. The captain cursed in seven languages and stroked his beard with nervous repetition. Uther just stared at the colossal red cross on the white sail—the mark of greatness and secrecy, known by many names: monks, wizards, number-counters, killers.

Templars.

The other ship slowed and came close enough that Uther could make out figures on the deck. One of the men stepped forward.

"Who speaks for this crew?"

Uther and the captain looked at each other before Uther walked to the port edge. His only comfort was in knowing that if they really wanted to kill him, he would be dead already.

"My lord, will you allow a ship of humble pilgrims to find peaceful crossing?"

The Templar lowered his hood to reveal dark, searching eyes.

"Are you titled?" he asked Uther.

"No man on this ship hails from noble birth."

A line of four Templar knights in full armor advanced from behind the speaker and nimbly crossed the bow onto Uther's ship. Fanning out, they surrounded Uther and his haggard crew. The Templar speaker continued.

"What is the task of your journey?"

"Forgiveness and atonement. In the Holy Land."

"We are not naïve. This is a raider ship. King Richard and King Philip sail these waters on Crusade. We will make sure that they have safe passage."

Uther was ready for a fight, even if it was to be his last, but as soon as the speaker finished, one of the Templars rushed him with inhuman speed, striking him in the neck and causing everything to go to black. When he awakened, it was to the feeling of a foot holding his head to the ground and a blade pressed to his throat. Someone spoke.

"Joseph, do not kill that man."

Uther felt the foot move and the blade pull away, as its owner responded.

"Commander, what do you wish?"

There was a pause, and the Commander spoke one word.

"Assassin."

At this, Uther was picked up by two Templars and taken to their ship. No words were exchanged as they led him to the hold where the same Templar that had put Uther under his boot earlier, sat nearby, unarmed. The man could not have been much older than thirty, yet his appearance seemed dusty and worn.

"You have no reason to fear your confinement. If your death was desired, I would have killed you myself. I was more than ready to do so, but apparently it's not your time yet. In fact, you're being given an extraordinary opportunity. Have faith in the events that have occurred to bring you here, and know that soon all will become clear. Please, tell me your name, your birth land, who your father is, and his status."

"I'm Uther Pendraig, from England. My last name is that of Beacan Pendraig, a merchant of no title; however, he is not my birth-father. I was abandoned to him by another and know nothing of my true origin."

The Templar frowned.

"You know who I am now, good Sir," Uther said. "Will you give me the same knowledge?"

"My name is Joseph Gaston, son of the Outremer, born in Ramlah of Sir Armeth Gaston, a knight of the second crusade."

"Well, thank you, Joseph for sparing my life, even if you hadn't planned to. If it's any comfort, I would have killed you too."

"Yes indeed, Uther; that's why you're here. My Commander believed you would have killed us all if you had the chance before you would have surrendered. We are in desperate need of men like that."

†††

Uther knew little accurate truth about the Templars. Since they had formed, a short hundred years before, their story had quickly become diluted with myth and speculation, possibly because they wished it so.

During the first Crusade, after the Christian army broke through the walls of Jerusalem in the middle of sweltering July, 1099, they slaughtered everyone and took control of the city. At that point few men possessed the will and ambition to defend the prize. Most were weary, sick, and anxious to return home. Those who stayed included wealthy lords who were tired of feasting and sought greater meaning to their privileged lives, and also poorer types who wished only to escape the constant yoke around their neck of those above them. The desert air had cleared all of their heads, and the best of them made a pact, choosing to believe in something greater than each of their individual lives.

They took over the Al Aqsa Mosque, an Islamic shrine

constructed on top of the holiest temple of the Jews, built by King David's son Solomon on the place where ancient Abraham had been willing to sacrifice his son to God. They dug deep into the dirt below, sifting through antiquated layers, until they found something that gave them great pause.

Some say that they unearthed a fabled relic so powerful that all who opposed them were defeated. Others say that they found knowledge that allowed them to control the outcome of events. However, it was most widely believed that they found evidence of the true life of Jesus that was so controversial that the threat of releasing it was enough for the Templars to demand anything they wanted from those who wished to keep it secret.

Soon the Templars became the first church-sanctioned moneylenders in the Christian world. With this, came fees charged, and the acquired sum eventually dwarfed the treasuries of the wealthiest kings in all the land. The *Poor Knights of the Temple*, were now the richest men in all of Europe. They were feared and respected, not because of the money, but because of the power it gave them to get things done. That was all Uther cared about. Now, thanks to his ironic luck, they might just be his ticket home.

†††

Uther was left alone again for long enough to contemplate whether they still intended to kill him or not. Eventually Joseph returned.

"It's time, Uther. They're waiting for you."

Uther left the hold. As he emerged into the light of the ship's deck, he was immediately tackled by a group of fully armored knights. They pinned him down with arms outstretched, and the Commander brandished a dagger.

Inserted under Uther's armpit, the dagger cut—first the right sleeve, then the left, and then the rest of the shirt.

"Uther Pendraig, do you vow to uphold the principles of The Poor Knights of the Temple and swear loyalty to none but the brotherhood and to God?"

"Yes."

"Fellow knights of the poor brotherhood of Solomon's Temple, do you accept this new initiate?"

In tandem, all of the knights recited a booming, definitive, "YES!"

Uther was brought to his knees, and the commander thundered in his left ear.

"Your life, given to your brother, before yourself!"

The commander smacked Uther on the left shoulder with the flat of the sword, and then bellowed into his right ear.

"Humility and piety above all!"

He hit Uther on the right shoulder and then stood in front of him.

"Bring the surcoat."

A fresh, white tunic was brought, and the sleeves of Uther's old shirt were fashioned into a cross that was pinned to the front. Uther put it on.

"I dub you a Knight of the Holy Temple. When you rise, you will no longer be a man; you are now the living embodiment of an idea. Never forget that."

The commander swung the flat of the sword at Uther's head, snapping it hard against his cheek.

"Rise, brother."

†††

Later, as Uther finished sewing the cross made from his old sleeves onto the new surcoat, Joseph visited him again.

"I'm glad you're here, Uther. I believe that you will do your job well."

"I look forward to fighting with you, Joseph."

"Don't. We will soon part; I to England and you to Sicily to begin your mission. My commander believes that you are the type of person who should be assigned a very special task in the war against the infidels."

"What kind of important mission is staffed with an unknown fisherman?"

"Everyone here knows you are a wanted man, Uther; no person as bright as you turns to sea-trade unless forced. Understand that, in our view, all that you were before today is forfeit. You are reborn and thus scrubbed as clean as Adam before the fall. Either that, or you are a criminal who cannot change. The version that will prevail is your choice."

Joseph gave Uther over to a leather-skinned Templar known only as the Armenian, who instructed Uther in Eastern combat techniques. He explained that in order to be able to best defeat the enemy, the Western fighters must adapt, and learn the enemy's tactics. One such method was the creation of a league stocked with men from outside of the noble system to accomplish difficult tasks, modeled after a similar Muslim group known as "Hashishans." Uther would be one of the first.

†††

Joseph found Uther on deck, staring at the sea, much as was when they first met.

"The Armenian said you were a fast learner."

"It was a quick lesson. I don't really know if I'll remember it all."

"These tactics you were taught have been adapted from our enemies, as they will inevitably adapt ours; it's simply the way of things. What is important for you to understand is that the Muslims are drugged to get their approval for the dangerous missions that they are tasked with. That is where we differ from them. For us, it must be voluntary; that's the only way it works. It doesn't take Templar knowledge to know that if you don't believe in what you are doing, then it will fail as surely as the sun sets."

Joseph put a reassuring hand on Uther's shoulder and made as if to walk away before Uther spoke, stopping him.

"Joseph, there's one last thing. I came on board with—a cup, a gold chalice. It was special to me. A gift. May I have it back before I go?"

"I'm sorry; it must be given up as part of your vows. It will become charity brought to England. I'll get you another cup."

They arrived at one of the quieter inlets on the southern shores of Sicily. Joseph was the only one to see Uther off, offering him a humble clay cup and the last few words about his mission.

"Integrate with the forces awaiting the arrival of the Kings of England and France. When you locate the commander of the local Templar forces, tell him the phrase *deus fortuna*, and he will instruct you further. Obey your superiors above all else; this is the most important part of our code. You are bound by your vows, and should you run from them, it will be to your detriment, not ours. That's not a threat, just the truth of what you are now a part of."

Uther was left onshore in Sicily. Besides his new clothes and cup, he was given a real sword to replace the Sarmatian artifact, leaving him with nothing in his possession to connect him to everything that he had been through, except his thoughts of Gwen.

He walked on till the shores faded, the open plains beckoned, and the land felt right under his feet again. Eventually he arrived at a town, where he wandered the twisting alleys for half a day, searching for food. He stumbled onto a marketplace where his senses were battered by the brilliant colors and smells of pears, figs, olives, fennel, and rows of lettuce shimmering in the wind. The possibility of consuming something only recently dug from the ground was reason enough to have taken the Templar oath and come ashore. Unfortunately he had been left without a coin to his name.

He dipped his cup deep into the communal well and bloated himself with water to push off the desire to jump into the vegetable stalls and roll around like a dog. After that, with no idea of where to go or with whom to speak, he sought out an older woman with kind eyes and pointed to the sign on his chest.

"Humphrey."

She spoke the name, spat on the floor, and pointed toward a villa over the hill. Uther made his way there, where its owner greeted him at the gates.

Humphrey of Toron was hunched-over and tan, with scars on his forehead and neck, and a mop of black hair that hung in splotches over his sagging eyes. His walk was delicate, and the tone of his speech was supremely calm, almost passive. *Not passive,* Uther thought, *defeated.*

Humphrey found Sir Uther, the Templar knight, to be a bore and a fraud, having seen this story too many times to tally—another jaded second-son, eager to quench his thirsty, violent thoughts with sacked caravans and Eastern women. Taking the oath of a Templar used to mean sacrifice: no money, no women, no drink or game. Now the only requirement for membership was enough coin to buy oneself a shirt with a cross.

"Sir Uther, that's sort of a shoddy tunic isn't it? Did they run out of Templars who can stitch properly?"

"It's the one they gave me when they knighted me a few days

ago."

At these words Humphrey took an earnest look at Uther before slowly shaking his head.

"I was told by the other Templars that I have a mission to fulfill, something that I'd find out when I got here. Do you know what my mission is?"

Humphrey scoffed, "You're joking man. I just met you. What would I know?"

Humphrey could see that this so-called Templar had not been to war. He was tough, maybe had even killed someone, but he did not have the murky disposition and sour eyes that were the marks of a soldier who had fought in the desert.

Humphrey shook Uther on the shoulder. "When we get to Messina, see about getting yourself some decent armor. Don't worry about the Templar shirt; your armor is what will keep you alive. Keep it clean, and keep it on."

Thanks for the advice, jackass, Uther thought to himself, as if they were giving away armor for free.

"Armor or not, I assure you, I'm glad to see a Templar, even one so clearly green as you. I don't wish to walk around as a known man without extra muscle. The locals have been growing severely agitated about the approaching English fleet. They are apt to start organizing into flag-waving mobs at any moment, and I have things to do."

Uther stayed at Humphrey's villa that night. Even though it was assumed that Templars gave their service without pay, Humphrey offered to buy Uther a suit of chainmail if he would accompany him on a series of tasks over the next three days.

†††

In the morning, Uther escorted Humphrey to the first task of securing feed for the waterlogged crusader horses that would soon arrive. Next Humphrey and Uther headed north to look into an order placed for six hundred crossbows. The blacksmith was behind on production, and when Humphrey picked up one of the finished crossbows, it fell apart. Nevertheless, he told the man not to worry and just to have as many finished as possible by the time the king arrived. With the last of the three chores to be completed the next day, they headed back to Humphrey's villa.

"I'm curious, Sir Uther, how did you find your way to Crusade?

"My ship was captured by Templars. They told me that they needed help from men like me, so they made me a knight. My choices were that or death. Before they left me here, they told me to find the other Templars and the king, and that eventually my mission would be revealed."

"And then what? What if it's something that you don't want to do?"

"I don't think that it really matters anymore what I want to do, if it ever did at all."

"But it could be anything, and knowing the Templars, it won't be anything pleasant. The suspense must be gnawing away at you?"

Uther shrugged, "If it's true that the king is coming here, maybe there will be some answers when he arrives. I hope."

"Well, stay by me, and you can tell him whatever you want. The man himself dispatched me directly to my missions, and the last of our chores will be done tomorrow. After that, he'll be here; we're the welcoming squad."

✝✝✝

The next day Humphrey and Uther set out early to pick up the caravan in Caltanissetta that would meet the king in Messina. It was a good twenty mile journey, and Humphrey spent the majority of this time wearing out Uther's ear with constant babble.

"There's a theory that at any time seven people are withstanding the highest of the world's cruelty, and it's only as a result of them enduring it, that the order of things is maintained. Do you ever wonder if maybe you are one of the seven?"

"If I had to guess, I'd say that even with my troubles, there's others that have had it much harder. I can't imagine that a well-lived man like yourself has suffered much."

"You do yourself wrong to assume. Riches and power do little to solve one's problems, and in many cases only increase them ... They took the only person that I loved and forced her to be with another man. She is of royal blood, and he wished to rise in rank. There was nothing I could do about it."

"You didn't ... fight for her?"

"I received notice only after it had occurred, during the time while I was imprisoned. That's where I got these."

He motioned to the scars on his face.

"Best a man of my size can do in the Saracen jails. It was only because of my wife fighting for my release that I'm standing here, instead of rinsing my teeth with piss."

"Is your wife in Toron?"

"No, and she's not my wife anymore. She's in Tyre, married to a man called Conrad of Montferrat, a satan-kissing son of a whore."

They finally arrived at the caravan that included fifteen camels carrying whetstones, canteens, and arrows—all sourced by Humphrey at the king's request. The next day they entered Messina and spent the day building. When they broke for the night, preparations were complete to, when the king arrived and upon his word, quickly erect a gallows.

†††

The Crusader fleet landed in Sicily after the first streaks of the new rising sun. Uther and Humphrey wandered out to the docks at noon, where enthusiastic crowds filled the space. For once, the men that Humphrey had paid to keep the protesters away seemed to have done their jobs, instead of taking counter-bribes.

The king's flagship arrived later, where, onboard, Richard poured himself one last goblet of the Amaro that he had obtained in Naples. He sipped gently from the cup and savored a few more quiet moments before he had to be on the stage.

Sicily was the last place Richard wanted to linger. It had a reputation for muddying the boots of those who used it as a stepping-stone to go eastward. Having spent the whole summer looking for a friendly port, however, he knew he had been out to sea for too long and, he needed a change.

Finally ready for his audience, Richard put down his cup and walked out onto the bow of his ship to address the gathered crowds.

"Good people of Messina, rich and poor alike, I bring greetings and gratitude for the time that I shall rest here. I ask merely for your prayers, as this army that I bring will soon journey to liberate the home of our Lord and Savior in Jerusalem. God wills it!"

The crowd's wild response signaled that they were, in fact, still runny cheese in his hands. Putting his feet to land, the first person Richard recognized was Humphrey.

"My good King, welcome to Sicily."

"Humphrey. How are the bastards treating you?"

"As till eternity, Sire, I float above it all."

"Floating as always. Glad some things don't change. Are the provisions secured?"

"Ready and accessible to your whim. Do I ever let you down?"

"There's always next time. Who's this man disguised as a Templar?"

The king turned an eye to Uther, regarding him for the barest second.

"This man, Sire, is a Templar true. He served as my guard for the gathering of your supplies here."

"Oh, well then, a mistake. You do a good job impersonating a commoner, Sir Uther ... You are of origin where?"

The time it took Uther to answer felt to him like hours. In his life he had been an orphan, loner, outlaw, and raider; now he was chatting with the King of England. He considered smashing his head into the bow of a nearby ship as a simple reality check.

"Uh ... well, England, Sire. Caerlon Manor in the South."

"HA, I knew it! Could spot a Brit a mile away. Those damned teeth!"

The king brushed past them both, pausing briefly to let Humphrey know his wishes.

"Assemble the gallows."

†††

"You have to know him, Uther ... He is not a simple man to understand."

Uther followed Humphrey, who stopped suddenly at the sight of another Templar exiting one of the ships. Uther heard Humphrey mutter a curse under his breath as a muscled stump of a man covered in prickly, gray-red hair adjusted his eyes to the light and sniffed the air. He practically knocked Humphrey over as he approached to give him the obligatory intimate greeting of nobles.

"Uther, I'd like you to meet Sir Reynard. I'm sure that you're well aware that he's the new Templar Grand Master. Uther is a good man, Reynard; he assisted me in gathering supplies for the king."

"All right then, whoever you are ... fall in line."

Reynard motioned his head to the ship's gangplank from which he had just descended and gave Uther an impatient look. Uther hastily boarded the ship and found waiting there ten Templars, men who looked more like local thugs than revered men of a monastic order. Reynard followed soon after, addressing the group.

"We've picked up a stray; treat him *well*, he may be a spy. "

Grinning slightly, Reynard turned toward Uther who used the pause to speak a phrase.

"Deus Fortuna."

It took a few extra seconds to register with Reynard.

"Say that again ..."

"Deus Fortuna."

Reynard exhaled a slow, pained breath and then addressed the other Templars.

"Take position behind the king, five paces. Report back in an hour."

Uther stepped forward to follow the others, but instead he met Reynard's hand, connecting with his jaw. Dazed, the next thing that Uther felt was Reynard grabbing onto Uther's collarbone and lifting him by it.

"Did you torture a Templar to get that word? I don't know where you came from, but you better tell me fast why I should trust a man who appears right before the king arrives, claiming to be a Templar, and not even wearing chain mail!"

"Humphrey was going to help me buy some when we got here. Then he went with the king, and I went with you."

"I want to know who you are and exactly where you got that word, or I'm gonna gouge your eyes out and burn the sockets."

"I was with a ship at sea ... We were boarded by the Templars. They were going to kill me, but instead they ... forced me to join."

Reynard slapped Uther rock-solid across the cheek.

"Who the hell are you?"

"I'm just a farmer … here to serve and gain my forgiveness."

"For what?"

"I … I killed men … to protect … my wife."

Reynard pivoted his head, glared at Uther, and then let go.

"Take enough gold from the ship to buy a proper suit of chain mail. Find a blacksmith, and take care of it. After that, wait on the ship for me. I'll see what information I can assemble about … *your mission*."

✝✝✝

At first light the next morning, Richard had Humphrey negotiate for all local prisoners to be turned over to the king, and then Richard had eighteen men hung in a simultaneous binge of quick-snapping death. He left the scene mounted on his royal horse, with scepter in hand, to the sound of cheers. After that he rode around the perimeter of the city with an entourage of knights, handing out jewels and food, before heading back to his quarters and summoning Humphrey.

When Humphrey arrived, he found Richard bent over a piece of parchment, sketching feverishly. It was a map of the city, with detailed topography of the surrounding area. The king's eyes looked tired.

"Were they with me today, Humphrey? I was too drunk to tell."

"It was raw meat for the ones who were, and a shiver for the ones who weren't."

"As long as Tancred hears it."

"I suppose a little reinforcement couldn't hurt anyone. That is, except for those long-necked bastards you hung. Did you really need to kill the thieves? It's a tad vulgar."

"Never underestimate the blood-parched throat of the commoner. Their whole lives are misery; all they want is to see someone else suffer for a moment. They will talk of today's spectacle for days. Maybe it will be just the amount of time we need."

"My king, I would counsel you to, just … try to stay calm while we're here. I know how you get after traveling for a while."

"It's not that. The Holy Land awaits, and I have little patience for tyrants in the way."

"Let me rephrase then. Richard, I know that you have not made peace with your father's death. I know that you wish to fight something, anything, to help you feel whole again, but I beg you not to let these emotions guide your sword in this place. I know that you are pragmatic at the core, and I want to encourage you to find that place when you speak to Tancred."

"My father would have already chopped off that man's head and fed upon it."

"Yes, and you are not your father, nor do you have to please his view anymore. Truth be told, you never had to."

"And that's probably why I never did."

"Tancred is a slippery eel. The gangs are in his pocket, and they control most of the trade here. This may not be as easy of a conquest as you wish it to be."

Richard smiled wide and nodded.

"They won't give up their coin easily, Humphrey, but the time is ripe for change. Speaking of which, you've looked like the wandering dead since I found you here. What weighs on you, old man?"

"Why ask when you know?"

"I can only assume that you still pine for her?"

"Yes, I think of her, trapped there with him, enduring God-knows-what, without end in sight. I can't let it go; I have to do something."

"It would certainly be the romantic choice," Richard said, smirking dismissively. "There will be a time, but for now, we need to focus on other things."

"I won't let it go like that. I won't give up on her."

"Maybe you should consider that she has accepted her fate, and that she may not even mind the change. Maybe it isn't as bad as you think?"

"No, Richard. I know her heart. I can feel her connection. I know she hurts ..."

At these words, the king's eyes dimmed a little.

"You speak madness now, Humphrey. You can't possibly know such things. The only thing hurt is your conscience."

"...I should have forgotten everything else and gone after her. I was so wrong."

"You have achieved great things for our cause, and greater to come ..."

"I would trade it all, every triumph, every pleasure, every good breath; I'd go back into the jails ..."

"Come now man, you despair to the point of absurdity."

"Is there nothing you will do?" questioned Humphrey.

"There is certainly nothing I *can* do right now. It's an indulgence to even allow you to propose this to me. You know how delicate these times are for our cause."

"Damn the cause! I know you have more than war-brains in your head, Richard. You must do something ..."

Richard methodically put on his chain mail glove, stepped in front of Humphrey, and slapped him, before grabbing a fistful of Humphrey's hair and pulling it taught.

"I do not discount your pain; I know you care deeply for her ... deeply. I know. You are a good friend, Humphrey, but you know that I have much larger concerns right now, so *snap out of it*. I will remind you ... for the last time."

Richard released Humphrey, who answered with pious indignation.

"I will remain as I have always been, faithful to only you, Sire."

Humphrey shook his head to himself, and Richard grabbed his shoulder.

"I promise you, with my honor at stake, that we will fix this when the moment is right. We will reverse the hourglass, you will have your wife back, and we will gain great political advantage from it in many, *many* ways. But brother, please, I need you here, now, focused in the present moment on our task-at-hand. Please, for me, try."

"Well you asked, anyway."

"I did. And aren't I a fool for it," replied Richard. "I've got more than a slice of my own concerns when it comes to women. My mother will be here in a few days—with my fiancé."

"So it's true then? *You* settling down? Don't kid me. You'll be chasing after her assistants within three months."

"I owe the queen some grandchildren. The girl is charming. She'll make a fine wife and mother. The next queen, hand-picked by the current one."

Richard trailed off these words, almost as if mocking them, before continuing again.

"I have another chore with which you can assist. I need a bodyguard."

"Pardon?"

"I worry, Humphrey, that I will let my bad habits get the best of me. I can only do so much to control the dragon. I need you to find someone to shadow me. Should be about my size, not taller, maybe a Templar, someone other than Reynard. What about that knight that you arrived with, the Brit?"

"Yes, Uther, he was English. Not a bad gesture, though I should warn you, that man is … incredibly green. I'm not sure he will fulfill your expectations of a Templar. I'm not even sure he's been in battle before."

"It doesn't matter; I don't need him to protect me, just to protect me from myself. I'm sure he'll do fine."

"I'll arrange it as soon as I can find him."

†††

Shortly after dawn broke the next day, Humphrey and the king traveled to a local pastry stand where they were lavished with free desserts that Richard brought as a gesture of goodwill to Tancred of Leece, the current ruler of Sicily.

"Tancredulus … how are you old man?"

"Hello, Richard. Welcome to my island."

Richard sat down across from Tancred and put his feet up on the table. He bit into a pastry and chewed big, open mouthfuls, with crumbs tumbling to the floor as he spoke.

"How is your wife, Tancred? I do miss my dear sister's company. I was wondering if perchance I could visit with her?"

"She is consumed with her duties as Queen, but I'll relay your regards to her."

"That's funny because I'd heard that you were keeping her trapped against her will, along with her inheritance from the former king, the man she was *actually* married to before he died, and from whom you stole everything, including this island."

Richard finished chewing and then swallowed before speaking again in slow, deliberate syllables.

"Do you think I'm stupid?"

"No, I think you're a king who stole the crown from his father's corpse and couldn't locate half the cities in England even with a map written in French. Either way, you're in Sicily now and far from either of those places, so I suggest that you come to my table with a little more respect, no matter how many pastries you bring."

As Richard tensed his jaw and balled his fists, it was not difficult for Tancred to deduce that Richard's predictable temper was rising. Tancred smiled, jutting out his yellowing, sixty-year-old teeth. His wiry eyes seemed to swirl in his face, darting at Richard and then away. Richard took out another pastry, bit off half of it, speedily chewed it up, and then spat it out at Tancred.

"You are about as much of an Italian, as I'm a Brit, Tancred, and you know it, and I know it, and in fact, let's not forget that your subjects know it. Don't pretend that they're truly loyal to you. The only thing you have in common with them is that you all hate me. Well, I'm here to tell you that you don't know what hating me is. Believe me, I will give you reason to hate me. I'll give you the kind of searing, dismembered reason that will unavoidably remind you of your hatred of me for the few bright days that you've got left. So, let's say … by morning … my sister is released, along with all of the dowry that my father paid to her dead husband, as well as all of her inheritance from him as well."

Richard rose, twisted the remains of the pastry into the table top, signaled his guards, and left Tancred with his last words.

"The money, Tancred. *All of it.*"

✝✝✝

Later that night, Reynard found Richard in his study still working on some documents before bed.

"Have you thought about what I said, Richard?"

"I've thought about many things, Reynard, too many, frankly, to consider one more tonight."

"You haven't been out there much, have you? It's not going to be as easy as you think. Half the population actually likes you."

"Well, if enough of them do, and Tancred gives in, maybe we can leave this place without stabbing a single heart."

"I know that's not what you really want. Let me start in, make an example or two."

"You know the plan; you know my intentions. What's the problem?"

"This whole island stinks of garlic and fish. Reminds me of the south of France."

"Have another cup of wine, Reynard. Find a Sicilian girl for the night, and just ... *relax*. Keep your blade sharp, and let me handle this. There will be a time for the blood to flow, and when it comes, you can bathe in it if you wish."

"We should be using our blades to scalp Saracens in the Holy Land, but I'm ready to kill dirty Sicilians just as well."

"Follow the plan ... trust me. And remember what happened the last time the Templars rushed into a fight. I don't think I need to remind you of your dead countrymen whose bones litter Hattin."

"I resent that. I'm the Grand Master. I've earned my position, and my plans are as good as anyone's, certainly anyone at least my own age. You need my Templars to fight your Crusade. You don't have warriors; all your "knights" are just well equipped nobles. I command the sturdiest defense of our interests here, and I'm under no authority but the Pope's. You would do well to recall that there are other kings that I can speak with."

Reynard stormed out, and Richard looked up from his work for the first time since Reynard had arrived.

The next morning, Reynard exited his place of lodging to discover Humphrey, seemingly waiting for him. Humphrey knew that Reynard had chosen his bed in a lodge recognized for its exceptional

Persian whores.

"Humphrey, what is it? I'm off to see to my knights."

"Yes, that's why I'm here. The king has requested a Templar guide ..."

"I'll be right with him after I clean up."

"Not you; the Brit, Uther, who accompanied me into town; requested specifically. The king requires someone unknown, someone who won't ... draw attention."

"You're telling me that that six-foot-tall, rot-toothed hayseed won't draw attention?"

Reynard hacked a ball of chunky phlegm onto the ground and contemplated further words with Humphrey before turning and marching off in silence.

†††

With his sight pried open by the morning light, Uther discovered, to his shock, that it was all in fact a dream. Her hair. Her skin. Every word. Every kiss. All a dream.

"She was right there!" he exclaimed.

He spent the morning in a daze, surrounded by his silent fellow Templars. Only one was apt to talk—a pale wisp of a man with blue eyes that glowed with radiant awareness. He introduced himself as Gabrielle.

"What does the Templar code say about dreams?" Uther asked.

"I don't know what the code says, but I know what I believe. We try to forget the things that haunt us, and that's why God reminds us, because He hasn't forgotten. If He wanted us to forget, we would be like the chickens, nipping at the dirt, free of all thoughts, bad or good."

"There are times I wish for that. Maybe that would make it easier to let go."

"Why let go? Why are you still here at all? Why push forward to certain death against the Saracens when you could be with her?"

"I seek the forgiveness that the Pope promises to all men who take up Crusade. Maybe then I will be able to find her again."

"Forgiveness is yours anytime you want it."

"Not where the English common law is concerned."

Gabrielle jutted his eyes skyward towards the ceiling of the ship's hold.

"His is the only forgiveness to seek. You need only ask for it and see it granted."

Uther had followed Reynard's orders and bought a full set of armor that would have cost him a year of labor back at the manor. Draped over his frame, it felt heavy, but not burdensome, like a solid, second skin. The links sparkled in the light, and he felt free like a child, as if nothing could touch him. Then Reynard returned.

"Aint you a pretty one? And so proud of this protection that my gold has bought for you. Your bones will decorate the frontline nicely, no matter what type of armor covers them. Follow me now; talk of your mission will have to wait."

He took Uther to the ship's hold and unlocked the door. An unpleasant surge filled Uther's nostrils, as the origin of the smell came into view: six dark-skinned men hanging from shackles attached to the walls, with their own waste running down their legs. The flies buzzing barely covered the low wheezing as Reynard surveyed each one carefully.

"Now, which of my darlings will it be?"

Reynard chose one, unlocked the man's shackles, and kicked him to his feet. When he could not walk by himself, Reynard had Uther support him as the man staggered off the ship. Holding a hinged box with a hole in one end, Reynard joined them minutes later.

Uther followed Reynard through town, dragging the prisoner. For every nod of approval, three sets of eyes squinted in scorn. Reynard led them to a nearby cliff that overlooked the rocky shores and was visible to the market. When they reached the top, Reynard unhinged the box, placed it over the prisoner's head, and then locked it.

"Now toss him."

"Why protect his head if we're going to execute him?"

"One of my inventions. He can't hit his head, black out and avoid the pain if his head is protected. He doesn't have to die quickly, so we wouldn't want him to miss out on any of the unfortunate sensations that accompany broken bones."

"What did this man do?"

"He was born. He prayed towards Mecca. That's enough for you. Toss him!"

Reynard remained calm, staring straight at Uther and waiting. Taking a breath, Uther looked away, and pushed, and then walked from the edge quickly to avoid hearing any sounds.

"Good job, son—another soul for Satan. By the time this war is over, we'll have made his buckets in hell as fat as autumn gourds. Now, you've been requested by important people, so try not to embarrass The Order in front of the king."

✝✝✝

Richard pummeled the table leg with his boot heel till it cracked. As Humphrey cautiously entered, Richard stopped and broke into sweaty laughter.

"Yes Humphrey, what do you want from me?"

"I can only assume that you've received the news?"

"I was aware of the possibility that Tancred would release my sister, but damnit, it would have been so easy if he had just refused. Why can't it be easy just once? He's not going to give me the money, so I'll be obligated to back up my threats or look like a weak fool and curse the whole damn venture; but since he has released my sister, if I attack, I'll look like a tyrant and curse the whole damn venture."

"I forget; do we seek the people's approval or God's?"

"As always, you prove your worth in my presence with your sense of humor, if nothing else. Please leave me alone now so I can find some liberation at the bottom of my wine goblet."

"I only seek to remind you, Sire, that you are, as I have always stated, much too slavishly devoted to the commoners' views of your actions."

"And once again you remind me of your lack of true talent in strategy, no matter how conniving you are. The perception of our actions by others, be they high or low, will shape our destinies no matter how boldly we fight against it. Your money and the life it has bound you to has fogged your vision as my negotiator."

"Well, maybe if you would let me do some honest negotiating now and then, we might find ourselves with options that don't cause you to destroy the furniture. In the meantime, I've rounded up the knight that you requested for your guard."

"Send him to pick up my sister."

✝✝✝

For his first job in service to the King of England, Uther was there to meet Richard's sister, Joanna, Queen of Sicily, when Tancred released her. The dark circles under her eyes blotted an otherwise youthful face, which drew to Uther with surprise.

"Who are you?"

"Sir Uther Pendraig, my lady, sent by King Richard to escort you."

With these words, Joanna rushed to Uther and threw her arms around him in a taut, constricting hug, as if she were falling. She dug her head into his neck and released a cascade of sobs before bashfully collecting herself.

"I'm so sorry, how unlike me. I'm … I was … the Queen … Where's my brother?"

"We are to take your dowry and meet him at the port."

"There's no dowry. All the bastard gave me was the furniture from that room that I was locked in for the last year. As if I wanted to see any of it ever again."

When Uther and Joanna arrived at the king's ship, she repeated the same episode of hugs and sobs with Richard, and then collected herself just as quickly.

Richard weighed his options and decided that a small showing of force would keep Tancred on his toes without tipping the scales too far, so along with a cachet of his knights, Richard claimed two local monasteries and set one up as Joanna's quarters. Once Richard had her settled in, he took Uther and journeyed to visit King Philip for the first time in Sicily.

"Sir Uther, was your new job explained clearly?"

"No, Sire. Reynard simply sent me at Humphrey's request."

"I need a man who can help me with appearances. I want you to make sure that I don't do anything too rash when my Celtic blood gets going, and there's no doubt that it will."

"Whatever you wish, Sire."

Richard rubbed his hands together, and Uther noticed they were heavily calloused. He wondered if it had something to do with the rumors that the king had brought some of England's oldest druids to teach him arcane battle techniques, which he practiced during the late hours.

They arrived at Philip's makeshift dwelling just at sunset. Richard sneered as they made their way through the well-decorated halls, walking with purpose, as if he was rushing toward something that he was anxious to be close-to and done-with at the same time. As they entered the royal chamber, King Philip sat back in his chair uncomfortably.

"Well Richard, have you made enough monks homeless today? Would it have been so hard for you just to ask Tancred for some place to stay, as I did?"

"You are mistaken, Philip, the residence is for my sister, recently released from imprisonment by the same man. You two were always close when we were all young; I'm certain that she would grab joy in the handfuls from seeing your shining face. You can come by her new residence anytime…"

Richard pulled a chair up awkwardly close to Philip.

" … Now, as far as Tancred goes, well, I'll pretend that you didn't just suggest that I beg for a piece of cold stone from the bastard who has kept my sister in prison for the last year and probably spent her entire royal inheritance on fish heads. I'll just pretend that that was one of your average exercises in getting your tongue stuck in your shoes. Meanwhile, news abounds of some of your troops killing Sicilian prostitutes. So, you enter a city where half the population hates us, and you proceed to have vulnerable women murdered. Bravo, I say, that's the spirit, old man!"

"Of course, fool, I did not approve of that. Let me ask you, while we're delayed here, have you inquired about what actually occurs currently in the Holy Land? Reynard was here earlier, and he thinks we should leave for Acre immediately. He was very persuasive."

"Do you remember what happened, Philip, the last time everyone listened to Templar foolishness? Eleven thousand Christian soldiers marched into the desert in the middle of the day with no water and were cut down like rabbits by Saladin, who then took Jerusalem.

You would be wise not to give any more attention to those who have nothing to lose, for that is the only thing they will do."

"Well, to whom should I listen then? While you're messing around with Tancred, my troops grow soft, and apparently restless. You know better than anyone, my brother, the mischief that happens when you get too many knights sitting in one place, Richard."

"There's business to accomplish here before we move on. That was always the plan. Unlike you, I do not change my tactics on the whim of good news or bad, and on top of that, you even *suggest* that I would give ground to the piece of trash that held my sister captive? *Family*—you never forget family, Philip, *my brother*."

"How ironic then that you came to me to help win a war against your own blood."

"I may have had disagreements with my father, but I never wished to see him suffer. Tancred is a villain and it is known, so you can take your petulance and your condescension and shove them both down your throat, sideways!"

Philip began to rise, but Richard grabbed his arm and pulled him back into the seat, releasing a roar of laughter.

"Can't you take a joke? If you can't relax now, then you'll be a damned instrumentalist's harp by the time we reach Acre."

Philip weakly pulled free of Richard's grip and stood up again.

"I would leave you now. I am going to take a bath. We will discuss the rest of our business another time."

As Philip left, Richard turned to Uther and chuckled the sound of accomplishment.

"C'mon, let's let him take his bath and get the hell out of this rat hole."

✝✝✝

As the king and Uther ventured back from Philip's dwellings,

Richard turned to Uther with a severe look.

"I went too far. You should have stopped me. It's what I told you to do."

"I ... Sire, I had no idea I was in the right to do such a thing. I am humbled beyond words to be in the presence of my king ..."

"Do you think I chose you for this position because I thought you were a delicate flower to speak when spoken to? I brought you on because you're *a killer*. I can tell. You're not going to make anyone happy by leaning on the tapestries. You've got to put yourself out there; I'm not going to send you an invitation. I need you to help me prevent my mouth from causing more trouble than I wish it to. I have a reputation to uphold, and I won't back down from my enemies; but if you were to remind me ever-so-gently, then it will appear that I am listening to reason and that I am wise and prudent. So next time, do your best, do something, do anything, and make me not regret selecting you. There are many others who are looking for proper, high-level work."

"I apologize, Sire. I will do better next time."

†††

It had all seemed so simple in the beginning, yet now, Uther only wished to be a dumb grunt, in fact the lowest grunt; the first one tossed into the grinder would be ideal. Why weren't they out of Sicily already? Maybe Reynard had pushed Uther off of that ledge behind the prisoner, and he was dead, and this was Purgatory.

Uther remembered being in the fields with Gwen. He longed for her simple embrace and to listen to her breathing as she slept next to him. He wondered if she called out for him in the night, or if she had just forgotten about him. Maybe she had the same exact thoughts about him, or maybe she just assumed he was dead. Either way, there was not much he could do about it, and it was only in that revelation that he could let go a little more.

Uther found a merchant with a jug of wine to sell, used the leftover Templar gold, and drank it in an hour. Instead of going back to the ship, he dropped down in an alley and curled into the wall. The armor would keep him safe, he thought, unless someone killed him for it.

When Uther dragged his frame back to the Templar ship the next morning, a familiar sight greeted him: a mass of night-dark hair barely covering beady eyes—Humphrey.

"Where did you sleep last night?"

"I … was ambushed by thieves … left in an alley."

"They must have been some pretty tough thieves. Must have been a couple of warlords with maces to take you down …"

"I had, uh … some wine before …"

"Yes, haven't we all. Well, you would do best to freshen yourself, whatever that consists of, and stand to attention with haste. The king summons you, and it seems he's not in a patient mood."

Uther adjusted his armor straight on his body and wiped the crust from his eyes. His new Templar tunic was now stained from whatever he had slept in, but there was nothing that he could do about it as he rushed to rejoin Humphrey.

"So, I heard you met King Philip?"

"Yes. He and King Richard have an interesting relationship. It's hard to tell if they're preparing to fight Saladin or each other," Uther replied.

"Yes, interesting relationship, sort of like saying bulls and the cows they mount have an interesting relationship, though often I find it hard to figure out who is the cow and who the bull."

"Philip seems like a delicate man."

"He is," Humphrey responded. "Do not, however, underestimate him, a mistake that Richard often makes."

"Can they not put aside their rivalry for the greater good?"

"These men have been friends and enemies forever. They are partners now for a purpose, but in each other's presence, they simply become blinded by the past, sometimes to the point of insanity. And this, *this* is what's going to be leading us into what could be one of the most terrible conflicts since Hastings."

"So we are doomed then?"

"Yes, indeed we likely are."

When Humphrey brought Uther to the king's quarters, Richard was working on a new hand-drawn map.

"You may leave us now, Humphrey."

Richard handed Uther the map showing a small route traced around the town and stated, "This is where you'll be going tonight. Take the rest of the Templars with you."

"What about Reynard?"

"I can't find him, that's why I'm sending you."

Richard pointed to a square drawn at the end of the path on the map.

"At this location you will find a large structure made of pinkish stone. It is owned by a rich Muslim who trades in Christian slaves. I want you to lead the Templars, along with a squad of knights, and shut down this enterprise in the name of the Crusade and my royal house. Retrieve the women, and burn the building when you're done."

Uther felt the tension pull at the arches of his feet.

"One more thing," continued Richard. "We simply cannot have Christian knights defiling themselves and this Crusade by raping Christian slaves owned by a Muslim. Kill any of our men who try such a thing. Kill anyone who does not follow these instructions. Kill me even, if you see me there and I do not comply. Do you understand?"

"Yes, Sire, I'll depart immediately."

Uther did not pause with his answer, but in his head he was reeling. What was this that the king was asking him to do? Liberate a brothel? Kill a bunch of their own Christian people? Something did not seem right about it all, and he wished he could just back out.

"Sire … a question, if you will allow. Why me? I mean why are you choosing a young, frankly inexperienced knight like myself to lead this when I'm sure that you have many other seasoned knights with much more familiarity …"

"Because you're expendable," Richard stated, cutting him off.

†††

The formation that Uther led had sinister business in their eyes. King Richard instructed Uther that the ten Templars should be divided between the front and back of the line; the symbol on their tunics would make anyone who spotted them think twice about reporting it. Between the Templars strode thirty knights who left their horses behind to downplay their presence, though the winding line of men shrouded in mail and armed to the teeth still made for a less-than-subtle display. Making swift steps along the path that the king had laid out for them, they eventually reached the back of the stone structure that matched the description.

Uther kicked in the door, and a hallway packed with guards and their waiting swords greeted him. From behind him, the Templars charged in. Their harsh, well-trained blades quickly stabbed the first floor silent. Within minutes, a perimeter was secured, and fifteen women were released.

Following swiftly behind, the other knights practically overran Uther in a stampede to the second floor. They tore into the rooms, having their way with both whores and clients. The frenzy spread like a hay fire, and Uther found himself watching feebly, contemplating the king's orders. He reflexively gripped his sword tighter and found Gabrielle.

"Gather the Templars, and follow me to the third floor."

Instead of trying to stop a flood with a leaf and engage the knights who were running wild, Uther decided that he would do better to save as many women as he could before there were none left to save. He had half of the Templars clear the rooms while the rest guided the women to safety. Uther himself cleared several rooms, finally coming to the last room on the right and opening the door. The sight of the familiar red-hair-covered frame standing in front of him left Uther struck dumb with shock as Reynard spoke.

"I was wondering what all the commotion was about out there."

"I was sent by the king to shut this place down."

Reynard scrunched back his face in genuine surprise.

"Horsecrap. Those may be the king's orders, but you answer to me, your Grand Master, so turn the hell around and go back to wherever he sent you from."

Uther's nerves were hardened and fixed, but finding Reynard was not at all what Uther had expected. Indecision scorched him; he knew he could not just turn and leave, and yet the last thing he ever wanted to do was challenge Reynard. He gathered what he could of himself and took the leap.

"I'm going to burn this place down. I'd rather you not be in it when I do."

Reynard turned near purple as his eyes bulged with rage.

"How about, instead, you take yourself out of my sight before I'm forced to take you out of it forever. That's a standing order!"

Some of the other Templars had discovered the situation and now stood behind Uther. He turned back to Reynard and pointed his sword toward him, as Reynard waved in the other Templars.

"Take this pig, and peel off his skin."

The Templars followed their orders and swarmed Uther. Two pairs of hands grabbed him from behind and held him. He heard what sounded like smashing glass, before Reynard barked, "Don't kill him. Hold him for me."

Uther's arms were pinned back as Reynard approached with the pristine razor edges of a shredded bottle. He held the glass a fingernail's width from Uther's left eye. It was then that, with shock, Uther felt the hands of the Templar who was holding him go slack, accompanied by death-rattle moans. Reynard threw the bottle to the side and dove for his sword. Uther did the same and spun around to see Gabrielle holding a sword stained with the blood of the other Templars. Uther turned to face Reynard, who stood, armed and revived.

Reynard swung his sword with frightening speed, and as Uther blocked, he could feel the weight of the hits. It was a relentless attack, and all Uther could do was fall back into the hall and shelter himself behind his own sword. By miracle or alcohol, Reynard lost his wind and stumbled, opening a defensive hole. Uther anxiously stabbed, cutting a long gash along Reynard's side that sent him reeling back.

Reynard's stunned anger seared through the drunken fog, and he charged back at Uther, who dropped down to his knees and swung as hard as he could, cutting off Reynard's right leg cleanly. With blood everywhere and Reynard gasping on his back in shock, Uther drove his sword down into Reynard's chest to bring a conclusive silence to the room.

As Uther turned to leave, he discovered Gabrielle on the ground, dead, along with the rest of the Templars. Stepping over them, Uther made his path out of the building, warning any knights that he passed, before lighting a fire at each corner of the building.

✝✝✝

After King Richard had initially given him the assignment, Uther had spent the next few hours sharpening his sword. He knew that he was not qualified to lead the mission. A sharp weapon was the one that would succeed when needed, so he tried not to panic and kept sharpening. A dull sword might have lodged itself in Reynard's femur bone and allowed Reynard to drive his own blade through Uther's neck. Instead, Reynard was ash in the wind, and Uther was still alive.

✝✝✝

In King Richard's mind, who but the lowest filth could object to liberating a brothel staffed by slaves? Regardless, the next day Richard was certain that there would be outrage. Wives and mothers, who had begrudgingly accepted their now-dead husbands' bad habits, would protest, along with relatives of the slain guards. The locals in general, disgusted as they were with all interlopers, would not take well to foreign knights running amok, whether for virtue or vice. Regardless, if events progressed the way that Richard wished, it would make dealing with the messy aftermath worthwhile. It would also be a crucial step towards making his coming plans in the Holy Land a more guaranteed success. In hope of this, he did something he had not done since setting sail from France: he prayed.

That night, at sunset, the king assembled a spirited party to help improve his mood while he awaited the results of Uther's mission. The celebration spilled out into a wide moat of lively, drunken locals all with the dull perfume of the king's free ale. Richard meanwhile, slouched a bit lower in his chair and sipped some wine. His crown felt infinitely heavier that night. It was late, and without word of success, he had begun to accept the failure of his hoped-for plans and the realization that he had sent Uther to his painful death at Reynard's merciless hand.

When Uther arrived back with his group that now included the rescued women, there was an audible reaction from the party. Uther noticed the king first, with thick eyelids threatening to overwhelm his wine-stoned pupils. Those same eyes ignited wide at the sight of the returning group.

"Uther, by God's will, could it be? I don't believe it!"

The drunken lord of all England and half of France stumbled forward, healed of his apparent malady, and grabbed Uther in a bear hug.

"…I had not put my bet on you boy, and I'm ashamed to admit it, but I'll gladly look a fool today to have guessed so wrong."

"I did what you asked, Sire. The fires burn as we speak. And Reynard is dead."

The king nodded and, lost in his joyous moment, otherwise ignored the news. He liberally refilled his wine goblet and motioned for a pour for Uther, who did a quick, reflexive scan of the room. And stopped.

He saw a ghost. Must be. A familiar face in the corner, talking to others: Gabrielle.

Impossible. Uther saw him on the ground, stabbed, bloody—dead.

"Listen to me …"

The king grabbed Uther by the neck, looked him straight in the eye, and spoke in a deep, direct growl.

"You have done a great act today, for our cause and for the greater good. You've served your country with honor and strength, and despite anything I may have said earlier, I am so very glad to see you returned. This day will not be soon forgotten."

"Sire, when I first arrived, you appeared sullen. Is everything all right?"

"Ah, bless you, old man, you worry too much. Everything is magnificent. Walk with me."

Richard put his arm around Uther, and they strolled as the king spoke close and low.

"I dispatched a messenger to Rome a week ago to tell the Templar authorities of the news. They will arrive back soon with word of a new Grand Master, and also of your mission. Till then, we'll do our best to collect ourselves and do what we need to do to leave this place and make for Acre, and then soon, Jerusalem!"

The king laughed large and motioned to the minstrel band to play louder. Uther chugged one more cup of wine to ensure sound sleep and, before ending the night earlier than most of the revelers, made one last stop.

"Gabrielle … I saw you dead."

"Maybe you don't know what you saw."

"I saw a dead man."

"Clearly you were mistaken. I live again."

"I didn't get to thank you."

"No thanks are necessary; I've long ago discarded need for such embellishments."

"Will you at least tell me why you disobeyed orders and helped me?"

"I thought for myself in the moment and disregarded rigid thinking the same way that you did. We both survived as a result, and that should be the only answer you need."

It was time for Uther to end the night, and neither Gabrielle's riddles nor the whole party could keep him from a rest to rival death.

✝✝✝

The next morning Uther was awake earlier than he had hoped,

finding himself alone on the Templar ship as the rapping sound continued. He unlocked the door to find a helmeted stranger with a familiar pair of eyes peering out. The stranger removed his helmet to confirm Uther's guess: King Richard.

"How are you this morning, old man? You missed a good, late revelry last night."

"I'm sorry, Sire. It was a long day."

"Aye. Well then, I hope your rest paid off. I want to get a solid hunt in today."

"What will you have me do?"

"Join me. But let's be on with it. I'd really like to abandon this disguise as soon as possible; it's hotter than ox piss in this helmet."

They disembarked to a swath of land ten miles south of Messina on a villa owned by English wool merchants where they spent the day hunting.

"Uther, will you express some thoughts if I ask to know them?"

"Do I have a choice?"

"There's always a choice. Consider this an unenforced request."

"Ask then, either way."

"Why are you really here? You're not a professional soldier or a zealot like most Templars. What is it that afflicts you to stay here? Maybe I can help."

"Maybe you can. I run from crimes. I know that if I join the Crusade I'll be granted forgiveness and can return home in peace, to the girl that I left there."

"What crimes? What did you do?"

"I ... murdered men: French knights on errand for King Philip. I killed them for revenge, after they'd raped the younger sister of the same girl I wish to return to. The sister was innocent, and she died the next day. So I killed them."

The king was still and quiet as he contemplated this.

"You're an impulsive man, Uther; decisive in your morals and willing to do what needs to be done for justice and for people. As your king, I absolve you of all of your crimes committed on the lands that I rule, by royal decree, as of this moment. Completely forgiven. You may return to England at any time that you wish with a royal pardon that will protect you from all laws of the land."

Was it possible? Just like that, the entire ordeal finally over? The absolute joy Uther should have felt was overwhelmed by his realization of the absurdity of the path that had led him to it, and the reminder that he had committed himself to the Templars who had authority seemingly superseding anyone. Still, now that Reynard was gone, who would even know it if he left? Uther could bask momentarily in the childlike sense of accomplishment, that, with those words spoken by the king, he was free. Unfortunately, as was often the case, it was short-lived.

"Now that you are forgiven and free to go," Richard continued, "I will ask you to do what is most noble, to stay and fight. I need all the honest knights I can find. It is a currency in the shortest supply these days, but I know that it describes you. So I request: stay, help defend your king, and provide the greatest service that you can do."

"I … do not wish to."

"That's exactly why it must be someone like you; a man who does not thirst for it. That's what I need here. Before you make your final decision, there's something that I'd like you to see."

The king led Uther to a clearing in the woods. As they drew close, Uther heard the sound: a low hum that grew as they approached. It was moaning. The source revealed itself as a large group of men. A few sat, but most were on the ground. Some slept, some drifted between worlds, some had long passed into the night from which there was no waking, and ever present was the smell of festering wounds.

The king toured the camp to the jubilant reaction of men with split bones and missing eyes. During that time, Uther saw a change in Richard whose attitude made it clear that he thought no better of himself than the others. Arrangements were made for payment to be sent to the men's widows if they died. Richard turned to Uther with a tempered tone.

"These men are the evidence that Acre is taking its toll on us. It's the first place we must go, to help recapture that once great city that is now in Saladin's hands. We are desperately needed there, as each day that passes leaves us with more armless men who won't be able to help us defend the Holy Land when we recapture it. Acre … it won't be easy."

"Sire, forgive me, but do you not feel any doubt in your actions? Are you so sure that what we seek to do in the Holy Land is the best course?"

Uther expected anger in response, but instead Richard answered him with disarming frankness.

"It's not my desire to rule over men but to lead them by example. I try my best. Someone must do it, and as long as I can remember, I couldn't look to the next man and wait for him to act first—certainly not with this damned crown born onto my head."

"Sire, you have asked me to follow you to war voluntarily. I know that I cannot disobey my king, but if you are truly giving me a choice …"

"I am. Make no mistake; I am."

"I will give you my answer, after one more question. It's said that the barons of Aquitaine, where you grew up, made war on you, not for land, or money, or even disagreement, but because … you were known for picking their most cherished fruit."

"Be plainspoken with your meaning."

"Rape, Sire. Rumors of rape."

The king, even in his mastery of disguising his reactions, could not hide a certain shock and sorrow that washed over him at these words.

"Sire, I burned that brothel to the ground to liberate women being kept against their will. How is that any different from rape? My answer to your request of me … is that I cannot truly follow a man guilty of the same crimes that I killed men for."

"It isn't a rumor, just one greatly exaggerated story. I thought she was willing. I swear that I didn't force her, but I ended up going too far. I thought she wanted it that way, but something happened that wasn't right. I know this. I pray for the forgiveness that I will never know. Not God's—hers."

"And what if she never gives it to you? What if your crime was too heinous to find salvation, even if you repent?"

"Don't doubt that I am already cursed. My soul is blackened. I … can't look women in the eyes for long. I feel like they can tell all, and it makes me feel a criminal in their presence, lower even. It affects me at times when I am intimate with them. That is why my mother, Queen Eleanor, is personally escorting a girl here for me to … decide if I can marry. She won't be the first. I will try my best."

The king reached under his chainmail and removed a necklace made from a seashell.

"This was given to me by a monk from the Cathedral of Santiago de Compostela, in Spain, after my first trip. I prayed and fasted for three days in silence at the shrine of St. James. I've made fifteen pilgrimages to Holy sites to cleanse my spirit and seek penance for my mistakes and shortcomings. I'm not telling you this to impress you; I'm saying it because I think you're a man who can appreciate going on the road to redeem oneself."

Uther wanted so much to go home, but standing there, having been an orphan farmer only a short time ago, and now speaking closely with the king, he felt completely overwhelmed, and it made it impossible for him to say no.

"I will. I'll do it. You have my word. You were right earlier though; I'm not a zealot, and I'm not trying to get to heaven. I just want to go home."

"Then we will see the shores of England again together."

The king brought Uther to a small room in his temporary castle that was furnished with a feather bed.

"You'll stay here now, Uther. If you are to serve as a true royal guard, you must be close-at-hand at all times. Just don't get too comfortable; we're leaving very soon."

Uther rose the next day, put on his chainmail, and tried to look prepared. He wandered the halls hoping someone would either stop him or tell him what to do until he found the king discussing plans with Humphrey and others. The group broke off shortly, and the king motioned for Uther.

"The horse that you rode yesterday is now yours. Treat it not as a tool, or a friend, or even a sibling, but as you would your own mother. If you do that, you will be a lump of steel on the battlefield, and it will be the wings to carry you."

"What do we do next, Sire?"

"We take a walk. It's an absolutely beautiful day, the day we get out of Sicily. But first, a stroll through the market."

Before they left, the king gave Uther a new assignment, to protect the young chronicler, Samuel, who had joined the Crusade to transcribe the exploits for history.

"Guard this boy well, Uther. I have a feeling that there will be sights worth remembering today."

King Richard decided to bring an entourage of one hundred knights to the market area to spend royal gold. Two days after the brothel fire, however, the locals' hatred of the outsiders was dense in the air. Uther had arrived early with the chronicler, to blend in and observe. Making his entrance, the king declared to the market, in fluid Sicilian, that his gold was their gold. Then he drank and ate with abandon, while his boisterous laugh conveyed a genuine expression of joy and goodwill. All of it was futile.

While Samuel wrote, Uther settled into a slice of rabbit pie. Both of them heard it all, as nearby, a young, good-willed Crusader knight looked to satisfy his hunger.

"What is the price of this bread, Sir?"

"Eight."

"Eight for just a loaf?"

The merchant pulled his bread back from the young knight.

"Ten now! Either that or starve for all I care."

The knight placed twenty coins gently on the counter and picked up a small loaf.

"Here are twenty. Keep them."

"Oh no you don't …"

The merchant knocked the coins away, sending them flying out amongst the crowd.

"I don't want a single dirty coin of yours, you long-tailed bastard. Don't you dare take that bread!"

"The money is yours now; the bread is mine. The transaction is finished."

"You're finished. You think I won't take back what's mine?"

The knight saw it in slow motion—the merchant's dagger, the

diving attempt to grab the knight's ear, and the blade missing and going up to its handle into the knight's own neck—then blood, the ground, and darkness.

Richard tried to calm down the commotion quickly, taking to the highest platform and pleading with the crowd, offering more gold and apologies, but by now, the locals were mobbed together in large numbers, without the slightest concern of facing off against a group of knights. They stormed the platform, forcing Richard to retreat, while his guards tried to hold them back. Eventually, however, the knights were overrun and trampled. Uther had thought it a good idea to lead a path out on foot for the horse and Samuel, but he too was bloodied and ended up staggering to the gates of the city where the mob had now run-out most of the Crusaders.

A great charge of joy arose from the triumphant crowd; finally they had risen up against the latest band of usurpers. A rousing cheer erupted as the people proclaimed, "Sicily for Sicilians!"

†††

The king strapped his armor on with quick precision, barely able to hide his zeal. Every one of Richard's men were told to gather and to be prepared to die.

When they arrived, each archer had their bow and quiver exchanged for one of the many hastily produced crossbows that Humphrey had acquired for the king. It was proclaimed by royal order that, on pain of execution, no man should fire, even if fired upon first, without the king's word. The dragon-emblazoned battle flag was unfurled, and Richard appeared in front of the army, mounted on his decorated horse with eyes piercing out through his oblong war helmet. He removed the helm, held up his hand, and received the quiet that he required.

"I know that you wish to save your strength for the Saracens, but today, I ask you to help me show these bastards that it will take far more than a locked gate to keep out the army that's going to bring down the walls of Jerusalem. If we leave Sicily with this outrage unanswered, every gutless coward in the land will think that now is the time to have his way with us. So we will leave this island either alive and avenged, or dead and proud."

An unrestrained roar erupted and with these last words, the army was set loose.

†††

The locally produced crossbows had been rickety and practically unusable yet had done their jobs perfectly. The archers never had to fire a single bolt as the furious Sicilian rabble was quickly dispersed by the sight of an approaching battle line brandishing weapons so brutal that the Pope had outlawed them.

With the crowds scattered, there was just Tancred's men to face. The Sicilian soldiers were fewer than the Crusader army, but they were fierce and sturdy and had knives hidden in every boot and sleeve. They were not ready to turn over the largest port in the land without a dirty fight.

The Sicilian's charged fast at the swelled Crusader ranks, weaving their way through and carving off whatever they could. Uther and Samuel saw it all, and for a time, it seemed almost a fair fight. There was a problem, though; the Sicilians were not simply fighting another would-be invader army, and as Richard led the disciplined, Crusader lines repeatedly in their charges, Tancred's men began to thin out.

Uther tried to stay out of the melee, but the Sicilians swarmed his horse and pulled him down. As he fought for his life, he drifted farther away from Samuel and his horse, till he could no longer see them. The sweat poured down through his helmet, fogging his eyes and making his hold on his sword slip. At first, he thought he was dead, when suddenly from behind a surprising pair of hands grabbed him by the chain mail and pulled all two-hundred-plus pounds of him up onto the horse, next to Samuel, and the king.

"I told you to watch this boy. Consider it luck that I chose to monitor from a distance because I didn't trust your skill. Now hold the reins, and keep this boy alive."

Richard jumped off the horse directly into a group of Sicilians. He was relentless as he fluidly sliced, stabbed, and executed men as effortlessly as breathing. At one point, he took off his own helmet and used it to beat one man into submission. Down to the last man he faced, who was without chain mail, instead of granting mercy, Richard dementedly sliced open the man's stomach with two blades, almost splitting him in half. Uther watched with mouth agape until the king's shouted words reached him.

"Pour me some wine from the sack on my horse."

Uther thought that the king was joking, until Richard turned again and looked straight at him with blood-splattered eyes that would have startled a bear.

"Pour me a damned cup of wine, fool!"

Uther did as told, bringing the cup to Richard, who poured something in and drank it all in one, breathless gulp. The king followed Uther back to his horse where he pulled Samuel off, tossing the boy with abandon, and drew out his massive, ceremonial royal sword, an almost ten-foot long behemoth blade wielded with two hands.

"Stay flat on the ground, and do not move till I'm done."

What Uther saw then was something that he could only describe as sorcery. Richard swung the sword in a circle, faster than Uther thought possible for a man's hands to move, killing anyone around him who could not duck quickly enough. Whatever was left of the

Sicilian army either fled or jumped off the docks to escape. After driving his sword into the dirt, the king motioned to Uther to bring the royal banner, and the king planted the flag next to the sword. That was the end of it.

The broken crossbows made good kindling, as Richard had the knights burn the market square. The rest fueled the fire for the next night's celebration, but not before Tancred sent Richard all the money that the king had asked for.

✝✝✝

With his wealth depleted, Tancred stewed in his castle, unsure if Richard's next target would be Tancred himself. It was only a small comfort that the battle had finally confirmed what Tancred had suspected all along: Richard intended to take not just him, not just the port of Messina, not just the treasury, but all of Sicily. The realization hit hard: Richard had only been toying with Tancred and the people to make certain that the Sicilians threw the first blade. The next day, Richard began construction of a temporary wooden castle, presumably for the winter stay, and christened it with the name Mategriffon, roughly translated as "Death to the Sicilians." It was now obvious to Uther that they were not yet leaving Sicily the country, only the state of mind. No longer would Richard allow his grand Crusader army to be treated as outsiders in their journey east. They would be viewed properly, as exactly what the locals suspected them to be: conquerors.

The king's mother, Queen Eleanor of Aquitaine, soon arrived with regal pomp and a curse of the blackest bad luck. The last time she had attended a crusade, it had turned into a glorious failure. It certainly did not help that her arrival was accompanied by the distraction of her attempt to pair the king to some Spanish noble girl he had met once. Berengaria was a slight, shy, impeccably poised girl of twenty-six years. Once she was securely wedged into the care of Richard's sister, Joanna, Eleanor departed. Berengaria adjusted well to the festive, hopeful Crusaders, and preparations began for a wedding to occur on the evening of the greatest fight of her soon-to-be husband's life.

As winter receded, King Philip packed up his troops and boarded his ship bound for resupply in Tyre, before joining the fight at Acre. Richard and his knights followed close behind. By mid-spring, when the vegetables had just burst up through the topsoil, there was not a Crusader boot left on Sicily's soil. The march to Acre had begun.

✝✝✝

Salah ad-Din's head was awash in the growing drip of anxiety that had begun since he had left the siege at Acre two days before. He knew it was misplaced; the situation wouldn't change while he was gone and the siege would remain a festering stalemate going on two years. The recent arrival of the King of France meant little; the real threat that stalked Salah ad-Din's blind spot was a man that he believed was coming to give him the test that he had yet to face. Salah ad-Din was anxious to hear from his top spy who brought news from Sicily.

"The spiced lamb is excellent as always, but I assure you that King Richard was having every bite checked by his tasters. The locals were predictably unwelcoming and tensions rose quickly. The king did not find this treatment …acceptable."

Salah ad-Din was visibly relieved to hear this.

"He is a fool then and a great weight off of my shoulders. Any man stupid enough to be trapped in a ground war in Sicily is no true threat. By the time he arrives here, he'll be cut and weary. His army will limp behind him in tatters."

The spy's smirk relaxed itself, and he weighed his next words carefully.

"I'm sorry to say, Sultan, that they will likely arrive intact. They left port a day before I did … with possession of the royal Sicilian treasury and … Sicily itself."

Salah ad-Din heard this and swallowed his next words. After a few moments, his dimmed eyes must have given him away. There was no weight to be relieved, only the tenderness in his gut that warned him that he was one-hundred-percent correct in his previous prediction; the final great battle of his life had begun. The thought drove a great pang of fright through his old body, and it made him feel more alive than he thought he would ever feel again. One gratifying sentence slid back and forth in his mind.

"Finally, a worthy opponent."

Part 5
Toward the Farthest Castle

Uther left the king's cabin and looked out over the bow of the royal ship. As far as he could see, ships dotted the horizon, as part of the triangle of one hundred thirty that constituted King Richard's fleet. It was a sight to behold. The fleet sailed eastward at a leisurely pace, and there was celebration amongst the Crusaders. Details were still pending on Uther's mission, so Richard encouraged him to blend in amongst the other knights and enjoy the trip. In truth, Uther would do whatever he could to keep the dark thoughts at bay. He was not ready to fight in a war; Sicily had shown him that. It had sunk in by now that the chances of returning alive were slim, yet it didn't matter; he had pledged himself to the Templars in hopes of arriving in the Holy Land, and the frightening reality dawned on him that he had gotten exactly what he wanted.

On the fifth night straight of celebration, he found a secluded place and drank alone while staring at the endless seas. Eventually he was interrupted.

"Looks like you could use some company, even though you clearly left to be without it. Even so, I brought something to share."

The slurred speech preceded a French knight who tilted his cup messily toward Uther's, dividing the ale between them. Flecks of spit hit Uther's nose as the man spoke.

"We've never been introduced. Coup Laroux, from Burgandy."

"Uther Pendraig, England"

"Sir Uther, what malady has drawn you from celebration to this desolate place?

"I just like watching the water sometimes."

"Ah, yes; Satan doesn't control the seas yet, though we'll doubt that if we catch the storms. Nevertheless, the Lionheart will see us through."

"The Lionheart. What's that?"

"*Who*, not what. Richard. He is called Coeur de Lion in France. Heart of a lion. If God gives favor, He gives it to your king. Before this Crusade is over and we die in strange lands, I suspect that we will see true greatness."

"What could possibly give a knight such rock solid faith?"

"Perhaps because I'm not a knight. But I do have a sword and armor, and a horse."

"Well I am dubbed a knight and know for certain that I am less of one than you," responded Uther.

"There is a saying that I once heard; 'If I have a horse, then I am a noble; if I have armor, then I am a soldier; if I have a beating heart, then I am a knight.'"

†††

Uther followed Coup back just long enough to fill his cup before the man-at-arms to the king's sister found Uther and escorted him to meet with her by request. As soon as the door closed behind Uther, she found a spot close enough to him that he could smell her perfume rising just above the ale on her breath as she spoke.

"Large brow, slight double chin, oafish ... but also intelligent, and perceptive I think. Sensitive even, and just a rub of handsome. Still, my brother may think your blood would mix well with blue, but I'm not so sure."

She came around in front of him, much closer than Uther was comfortable with. The smell of her hair pushed him to question whether he would be able to remember whom he was in the presence of.

"I'm informed, Sir Uther, that you displayed great honor and chivalry when you destroyed the brothel in Sicily."

"I followed the king's orders, my lady."

"Indeed. Yet, I'm told that you did not act like the others. One of the ladies that you rescued was a noblewoman who was kidnapped by the slavers. She claimed that you were gentle and considerate, more than a simple man is expected to be."

"The chaos of the scene no doubt aids her imagination."

"Even now, with your high, honorable modesty ... you can't hide who you truly are. I'm told that you fight for romantic love, to return to a woman you long for?"

"I ... wish only to go home and have my old life back after I've done my part. The girl you speak of no doubt thinks me dead. I only hope that I can someday provide her with a pleasant surprise."

"I'm glad that Richard has taken to you and that you help protect him, but I'm compelled to reveal the truth of what you've gotten yourself into. Richard is my brother and my king, and I would follow no other man while he lives; but he is reckless, and he is dangerous.

I'm telling you this because he likes you, and he needs people like you around him who can help him; but don't forget that for all his victories, he's just another flawed soul looking for the next battle to give him purpose. In the interest of your lost love, who surely awaits your return, be careful about Richard. I fear that his negative qualities will overwhelm the good ones, and it will be his downfall, and thus ours as well."

Uther was stunned. Joanna poured herself another drink.

"What can *I* do?"

"Anything you can."

She began to disrobe, and Uther stood speechless and frozen. As much as he knew it was a treacherous descent, he wished only for her to undress fully and lock the door, but a stern look over her shoulder as she paused told him he had overstayed his welcome.

✝✝✝

As the fleet cruised to the midway mark, the skies darkened, and a gloomy breeze pushed through the sails. Soon the horizon disappeared, and water was everywhere. Relentless sheets descended from the heavens, and the winds were strong enough to take men over the side. When the skies were clear again, the fleet formation was a memory.

The few ships drifting nearby looked to the king for direction. He ordered them to cluster and rest, and in the morning they would work with revived souls to find their people. There was grumbling about searching sooner, but only because Richard had not suggested it himself. If he had, he knew they would have grumbled to wait till morning. Either way, the ten ships in view did not bode well for the other one hundred twenty.

Richard had the fleet dock near Crete, with Mount Ida visible in the distance. This supposed birthplace of Zeus, king of the Greek gods, loomed large in Richard's vision, reminding him that his current problems, bad as they were, were only a preview of the real fight to come.

In the morning Richard organized search sweeps, with attention to finding the large ship that carried his fiancé and sister, but the quest was fruitless and the storms returned. When the rains were at their heaviest yet, Richard was the only one to venture on deck to see the storm up close. Up there, battered by the elements, he felt at peace. It seemed as if the whole Crusade would simply be swallowed by the sea, and he was not sure that he minded. He had never led anything this immense, and he suspected that he might have bitten off more than he could chew. Maybe it was easier just to let the water wash it all away he thought, and find out if the afterlife for Christians really was a paradise. Despite what the Pope said though, Richard was not sure that he would escape hell for his misdeeds, just for leading the Crusade, and so he was not ready to potentially face eternal suffering just yet.

The battered remnants of the fleet stopped again near the port city of Rhodes. It was a natural docking point for any ships that might be waiting for the king to catch up, but when Richard arrived he found only disappointment. He sent for Uther.

"You've told me of your experience at sea, old man. Limasol is the nearest port ahead, in Cyprus. Take a skiff and a skeleton crew to see if you can find any survivors."

Uther nodded, and as he turned, Richard grabbed his shoulder.

"...The ruler of Cyprus is a tyrant installed by the Byzantines to keep order so they can reap profit from its ports. He won't be as easy to dispatch as Tancred, so we must take care to avoid a confrontation."

✝✝✝

Of the two crusader ships that wrecked near the Cypriot shores, all of the passengers were captured, except the chancellor who fell overboard and washed onshore with the royal seal still around his broken neck. The Cypriots put his rotting corpse in the cell with the rest of the men and added the seal to the confiscated store of weapons and gold.

A third ship that carried the queen-to-be and the king's sister remained trapped amongst an outcropping of red-stained rocks. It was a spot where it was said that the goddess Venus was born and to which young lovers swam to sit and exchange kisses. In contrast, at the present moment, it was a place of parched isolation for the stranded ladies and their starving, petrified crew.

Uther saw it and weighed the prospects of a rescue mission that he had no experience planning and which would involve the extraction of multiple passengers from a compromised ship amidst violent surf and talon-sharp rocks, all in view of the locals that he was trying to avoid. He decided to report back to the king.

After three days, the crew of the women's ship repaired the damage enough to escape from the rocks and drift toward port. Starving, thirsty, and desperate for relief, the queens and their crew were nevertheless locked out from the port where crucial supplies could be obtained. When two emissary knights weakly rowed in to make contact, the Emperor of Cyprus himself, Isaac Dukas Comnenus, personally greeted them.

Isaac adjusted his posture before the meeting, working hard not to slump forward. He kept his delusion of being taller and handsomer at the front of his mind, even as the sweat pooled in his pockmarked cheeks. Though he tried to look regal and dashing, the reflective puddles reminded him, as they always did, of the inescapable truth. He was a stark contrast to the two tall, imperious knights standing in front of him. By their light skin, he assumed that they were far out of their element, probably from Western Europe, which meant that there was money to be made.

"Great Emperor Comnenus, Queen Joanna of Sicily and Berengaria, fiancé of King Richard of England, appeal to your holy Christian spirit to allow them to dock and purchase food and water. In exchange for this royal favor, you will be generously rewarded and held in their highest regard."

The emperor whispered something to one of his guards, and then the Crusaders watched in horror as the same guard slit another guard's throat. Afterward, the emperor motioned for the Crusader knights to come close and spoke in stuttered, broken French.

"You have invaded my waters without invitation, and now you have the boldness to expect supplies? If this is what I will do to one of my own soldiers, then what do you think I will do to you?"

"The Queen Joanna will gladly pay. We are in dire need of water ..." began the knight. Isaac shook his head and waved them silent. Interrupting, the younger of the two Crusader knights stated, "We were not wandering around your waters; we accompany King Richard of England on Crusade to win back the Holy Land. For all Christians, be they English, French ... or Greek, like you."

The insult of calling a Byzantine a Greek was enough to have both knights stripped of clothing and possessions. And now the emperor knew that he had the future Queen of England and, better still, perhaps soon the King of England as his ransom chips. He felt a shiver of anticipation at his sudden good luck.

The younger knight was thrown in with the other Crusader prisoners while the older one was sent back to the queens' ship with a message.

"Tell your queens to meet me at Dieudamour Castle, with no guards. If they are truly of royal house, then they should have no problem meeting with a fellow ruler to discuss terms and compensation for these insults."

When the older knight returned to the queens' ship, Berengaria had not had the strength to leave bed for a second day straight, while scurvy had caused four of Joanna's nails to fall off. Joanna found herself absurdly longing for the room in Sicily where she was kept as Tancred's prisoner. At least there was food there.

"My lady, I strongly advise that you not go ashore to meet with him," urged the knight.

"I can't just stiff him; that will put us in an even worse position."

Joanna picked off a fifth nail, which had been hanging by one mangled cuticle. As it came free, she flinched and exhaled, attempting to remain composed in front of the knights, who looked to her for leadership. Only one thought ran through her head: *I wish Richard were here.*

✝✝✝

When Uther reported the situation to the king, Richard literally chuckled at the absurdity of the news, before exhaling a resigned sigh.

"It seems we will attain some additional practice whether we wanted it or not."

The king cracked a barrel of the most common ale, pulled a royal chalice off of the wall, dug it deep, and chugged down a cup. A genuine smile returned to his face for the first time since they'd left Sicily.

"By my reckoning, this emperor is either the dumbest man ever to have held a title, or the most courageous ruler to walk the dirt since Alexander. Either way, we're going to create an example for all to see what this particular Crusader army is capable of when faced with such unjust circumstances."

✝✝✝

To the sudden surprise of everyone on Joanna and Berengaria's ship, the port was opened to them. They docked, and all remained onboard except for a few knights who ventured out to buy food and drink. The emperor must have discovered that Richard was close; it was the only explanation for why he would change his mind so quickly and skittishly open the port.

Richard sent Uther out again. Slipping ashore, Uther made contact and brought the ladies back to the king's ship. Seeing the depleted health of the women in his family, Richard deteriorated into a seething frenzy of anger so intense that he hacked at the ship's wall until the blade got stuck. After calming down, he sent Uther and Humphrey to make first contact.

✝✝✝

"What kind of king can't meet another ruler face to face?" the emperor proclaimed as Richard's men stood before him.

Humphrey pushed the hair out of his eyes and calmly responded, "King Richard is focused on preparations to win back the Holy Land. He only wishes, for love of God and pilgrimage, to attain peace with you. He is more than willing to forgive these slights with the release of the remaining hostages along with their gold and weapons returned."

"I'll give no money! The insult was made to me. His soldiers are mine till he can meet me in person to discuss terms."

After drinking at a local tavern in order to collect information, Humphrey and Uther headed back to the king's ship. Humphrey repeated for Richard every one of the emperor's words.

"What else did you find out?"

"The man is despised by his subjects, especially his army, whom he's fond of punishing in … creative ways. He also apparently has an excellent division of ballistas, which should be visible to us very soon on the beaches."

Richard unclipped his royal cape and stretched out his arms.

"Gather our arsenal. We're going ashore."

†††

The Crusader skiffs glided over the near-Cyprus tides. The knights had aching backs from sleeping on the boat's rowing benches, but they still rowed hard, seemingly indifferent to saving their energy for the fighting that awaited onshore, if they made it.

As the beach came into focus, Uther tensed at the sight. It seemed the rumors were true; a long line of hurling engines hugged the shore, pointed directly at the incoming Crusaders. The Cypriot soldiers, outfitted in expensive, garish uniforms, stood clustered in impressive numbers compared to the king's ragtag bunch.

The ballista assault began. The bolts fired from the oversized crossbows were not merely large arrows, but whole logs, sharpened for speed and outfitted with iron tips. In an instant, they were everywhere in the sky, and there was nowhere to hide.

Richard dodged fast left of one bolt that would have speared his head. A nearby knight was impaled by a bolt that shattered the man's skiff and sent his fellow knights scrambling for the shore in forty pounds of armor.

When his own skiff was near enough, Richard waded in, holding his sword and crossbow above his head. Uther followed close to Richard who strided onto the shore and walked into the fatal melee with the poised tranquility of a monk.

The king pushed straight for the center, slashing and stabbing his way across the beach and looking happy to be there. In the midst of his relentless killing, he stared off, transfixed for a few seconds, before slowly and serenely balancing his crossbow on his arm. He squinted his right eye, focused his left, and let fly a bolt that only barely missed its target, a short distance away, where the emperor sat mounted on his royal yellow horse. Richard turned to Uther.

"Did you see him?..."

Suddenly a flying arrow lodged into the king's chain mail. He stared at Uther, unmoved.

"... The emperor, did you see him? He was riding a yellow horse. Yellow!?"

Richard stood smiling with childish glee, as another arrow landed in his breastplate.

"I'm going to get that damn horse!"

The king charged in a direct line toward the emperor, but a man on horse will beat a man on foot every time. Nevertheless, the Crusaders had turned the tide and were routing the Cypriot army. Though out of breath, Richard's face was plastered with utter joy, as if the whole Crusade, the Holy Land, the army he led, the throne, God, none of it mattered. He muttered the words softly to himself.

"I'm going to get that damn horse."

†††

The Crusaders set up camp in sight of the docks. No one removed their chainmail that night, not wanting to become too comfortable. Richard took his horse, Comense, for a jog accompanied by Uther and the scribe.

"There she is."

A short distance from the shore, rising out of the horizon, was a small castle with at least a hundred Cypriot soldiers camped around it. Most of them were drunk, but they still dwarfed Richard's forces by three to one. The young scribe was visibly nervous.

Upon returning to camp, Richard and the knights spent the next few hours running stones along their swords. Arrow-firing arms were rubbed and stretched, and then shortly before dawn, with the element of surprise on their side, the king and his meager band stormed the Cypriots. By the time the emperor's hung-over soldiers were able to assemble a paltry line of resistance, the Crusaders had overrun the castle, but not before the emperor streaked off into the morning light with the yellow horse underneath him.

†††

When the Crusaders returned to camp in the morning, it was with a bevy of looted goods. Not far behind them was a cadre of Cypriot soldiers surrendering as slaves. Richard would not allow it. The men enthusiastically volunteered to join the king's army on the spot, and with that, the small group of sea-sick stragglers became a force of a hundred soldiers.

Not long after, a ship sailed into port, and Guy de Lusignan, the King of Jerusalem, stepped onto the Cyprus sand. Former king would be more precise, but the Crusaders wanted to delude themselves that the dethroned king would soon be restored and that the miserable state of affairs was only temporary. The only action that Richard's men were likely to take when they spoke his name was to spit on the ground afterwards. The Crusader kingdom in the Holy Land had stood eighty years, but it took the mighty King Guy one year to mess it all up. As much as anything else, Guy was the reason that they were all held up in Cyprus, fighting bastards and the elements in their way to win back Jerusalem.

Guy had paid for his mistakes with time in Saladin's dungeon. Eventually he was released, at which point he immediately mounted a horse and held the standard flag in the first attacks to retake Acre. Guy had not been back to Europe in almost fifteen years; he no longer walked like a noble and was threadbare and broken as he rowed into Cyprus. Having been denied any aid from King Philip, Guy was the perfect sad character for Richard to draw into his house for some useful purpose later.

"Guy, I've arranged for a camp for you, along with two thousand marks of silver and a chest of royal clothes. What news do you carry from the front?"

"Philip has arrived as I'm sure you've heard."

"Has he … achieved anything?"

Guy rolled his eyes. "It's not for lack of trying. His best catapult is focused on the accursed tower in the eastern corner of the city. He believes it's the key to bringing down Acre's walls, but thus far, heavy resistance on the ground has stifled him. Our spies tell us that the enemy believes that Philip only paves the way for you, and that if they can turn him back now, you may change your mind. The spirits of the remaining knights are waning. To them, it is becoming apparent that we cannot retake Acre and thus not the Holy Land either. I fear that they will falter without your arrival to the fight. Do we sail soon?"

Richard pushed out a fake smile and put his arm around the slumped, shorter Guy.

"Come, relax. You've earned it. Tomorrow you'll take command of the knights here as my first general. We'll cripple this son-of-a-bitch despot and then return to Acre together. To finish it."

Richard found Uther and quietly embarked on a fact-finding mission. Roaming town to town, they discovered a cowed, desperate people who stared with frightened awe as Richard spoke. Eventually, he met a girl who spoke French, and she helped translate and reveal the stories. One after another, Richard listened to the tales of the people's harsh lives in the emperor's twisted kingdom. Kidnappings, murder, children tortured in front of parents, all inflicted by the emperor and his soldiers. Later, after returning to the Crusader camp, Richard felt as though he had heard enough for a lifetime. Any doubts about whether they were justified in their actions were forgotten.

†††

Richard met his fiancé in bed for the first time that night.

"If you'd already married me this wouldn't be happening. A Spanish princess is not the same as the Queen of England."

"I highly doubt this fool would care about a difference in title …"

"He wouldn't have dared offend us in such a way, and we'd already be at Acre."

The next morning after a deep sleep, Richard looked out to behold one of the best sights he had ever seen. The entire balance of the Crusader fleet had caught up. Beaming, Richard turned to Berengaria.

"Heck with it all, let's get married today!"

With the grand English fleet overlooking, Richard Plantagenet married Princess Berengaria Navarre on the twelfth of May, 1191. The impromptu feast constituted the most vibrant event that Cyprus had seen in a long time, and there was a gathering sense among the people that Richard's presence alone could bring change.

†††

The next day the king split the Crusader forces. While Richard took the fleet southeast, King Guy took the knights and infantry overland. They would rendezvous in a few days in Famigusta, the eastern-most port of Cyprus, where Richard's sources believed that the emperor was hiding.

Richard arrived early, but the emperor had his own spies and had fled the city into the tall, shimmering meadows of the Mesaoria Plain that bled into the heart of central Cyprus like a great, strange, grass ocean. Its history was filled with tales of men becoming lost, confused, and dying of hallucination-plagued thirst. For these very reasons, Isaac hoped that his enemies would not follow.

While Richard relaxed and drank in Famigusta, the emperor made it a good distance into the maze. Though he was sure at first that it was a mirage, the emperor encountered a loyal remnant of his army, the strongest, most undisciplined brutes that had taken to the plains to plan their insurrection. The exposure and sun had likely taken hold of the emperor's brain when he decided that he could catch Richard before his army arrived and do what no one else had been able to do. With his militia by his side and a quiver full of poison arrows, the emperor doubled back and set out to kill the King of England.

†††

It took less than an hour for the small band of Crusader knights to slice through the emperor's troops in a grand display, but the emperor stayed calm, lined up the shot, and let the bowstring fly with Richard's throat in his sights.

Nicked. But not landed.

Richard whipped his head around and caught the emperor's eyes.

"That damned yellow horse!"

When Richard and his own horse closed the distance in half the time, the emperor must have dug his spurs into the yellow horse's side till it bled, and the panic-generated speed was the only reason he escaped.

†††

BUFFAVENTO CASTLE

Emperor Isaac Comnenus's trajectory was tracked in the direction of one of his castles, Buffavento, that was built hugging the side of the second highest peak in Cyprus's mountain range. It made perfect sense as a place of refuge. When the pursuing Crusaders arrived at the castle gates, they were greeted by wind so strong that they had to sheathe their swords to prevent the blades from blowing around and stabbing each other's guts.

Inside they found an empty structure that was lashed so hard by the high mountain winds that there was a persistent tremor about the place. It was almost uninhabitable, with a constant, horrid sound of the wind's wail. Looking out from the highest point, the knights saw nothing but clouds.

When Richard arrived, he loved the place, touring its spacious, high-roofed halls with joyous exuberance, yet there was little trace that the emperor had even been there.

DIEUDAMOUR CASTLE

The Crusaders regained their determination when an excellent tracking knight picked up the trail eastward, pointing to Dieudamour Castle, named for the Greek god of love. Set on a small peak in a secluded valley, it was known as the emperor's place to bring the virgin daughters that he would take as tax from his subjects. The girls would sleep for days afterward before rising, if they ever rose again at all.

When Isaac arrived there, he found his remaining soldiers useless. Any of their previous support for him had collapsed, and they all scoffed at his threats; they knew from what he ran and what his chances were.

The Cypriot soldiers removed their armor, broke into the wine casks, and relaxed on the hill outside the gate. When the sight appeared in the distance of the Crusader knights snaking their way up the mountain, the Cypriots could only exchange drunken laughter and mocking faces of the emperor and his predicament; he was running out of castles.

KANTARA CASTLE

The emperor rode as hard as he could for his most eastern fortress,

Kantara, known as the palace of a thousand chambers. Arriving there, Isaac lost himself deep within the labyrinthine, interconnected rooms. Surely Richard would not waste time having his knights search every last bit of space. Isaac could keep moving, keep changing rooms, keep them searching till he was able to slip out and escape.

Eventually, however, he lost his nerve; he could not just sit around and wait for them to come. He wanted to believe that they would not find him, but this was the only castle remaining, and they would be there soon. So he ran again, charging absurdly eastward onto the thinning land of the Karpas Peninsula. Ultimately, there was nowhere left to go.

The emperor arrived at the last, high, ocean-facing cliff at the end of Cyprus. His fear of what lay below was only slightly more frightening than the realization that there was no one there to talk him out of jumping. He begged God not to have to choose to either jump or face Richard. There was no answer, only the sounds of the waves crashing, and of galloping hooves rushing up towards him.

The king rode to the head of the army to meet his new prize. Although the emperor could scarcely look him in the eye, Richard could see the tears building. They eventually did stain the cheeks of a small man who wanted nothing more than to run and hide from all of the pain that he had caused in the world because of all the pain that he had felt.

Against his more powerful urges, Richard took pity. The king could have had horses split the emperor into four pieces if he wanted to; the locals certainly wouldn't have objected, but if Richard was going to win back for his people the holiest soil in existence, he had to remind himself why they cared about that piece of land in the first place. So he had the emperor taken away to rot in a Templar prison in Antioch.

Richard enjoyed a most refreshing ride back to Famigusta on the back of his new yellow horse. He had conquered Sicily and now Cyprus. Next up was Acre, then Jerusalem, and quite possibly the entire known world.

†††

The more that Uther learned about how Emperor Isaac had treated his people, the more he believed that King Richard had taken the right course of action. It was not so simple for the Cypriots though; they had been subjugated for too long. The initial jubilation and adoring crowds were quickly replaced by searching eyes that wondered what came next. Uther was not surprised, and he even sympathized with them somewhat. Blaming someone else was much easier than questioning how one had let such a bastard take control in the first place.

Maybe the emperor knew best, when, as he was being led away in the silver chains, not iron chains, he bowed his head before Richard's hand and whispered a few last words:

"It will happen to you. You'll see. One day they will chase you just the same."

†††

The order was dispatched for all the knights to prepare for an almost immediate departure to Acre, less than two days' sail. The king unleashed a small militia of local merchants, artisans, and blacksmiths fueled by the emperor's gold, to distribute daggers, patch burst water sacks, repair boots, re-shoe horses, and add extra armor to deficient knights.

When they all took sail, the richer, noble knights mingled less amongst the lower knights and archers, keeping to their own ships toward the back of the fleet. Though these high-born men had started out the trip playing cards and dice, as they drew closer to Acre, they ended the journey like the rest of the common fighters, praying and chanting hymns.

As Uther saw the glowing haze on the night's horizon from the fires, and heard the sounds of the battle, like giants smashing rocks together, the truth of the situation became unmistakable.

Richard was still tying up his affairs in Cyprus and would follow shortly. Uther prayed so; he was convinced that the King was the only one who could make sense of the inferno that they were about to step into.

Welcome to Acre; welcome to hell.

Part 6
Caught Between a Wall
and a Hole

With his entire fleet already sailing toward Acre, Richard made haste, kissed his new wife goodbye as she fought back tears, and boarded his ship the next morning. He had purposely sent everyone else ahead, including all of his guards and even his chaplain. Other than his ship's crew, he would go alone, as he was, with nothing but his cup and his sword. It was time for him to do this unaided—for himself, by himself—and arrive on the soil of the Holy Land in that moment that he had dreamt of so many times.

†††

Salah ad-Din sat inside a hidden cabin on a hill, close enough to the siege of Acre that he could hear it. He crossed his rigid knees and closed his eyes, and it was a good two hours before he opened them again. By then morning had closed in, and with it came a hush to the screams from the battlefield that had helped him concentrate on his prayers.

It was hot, even for June, even for a man who had spent his life exposed to it. At fifty-three, with hair now more white than driftwood brown, he was not the young lion of days past who could win a war without breaking a sweat. Now he broke a sweat without doing much of anything.

He rose and looked out over the besieged city thinking that maybe, if he stared at the tangle for just a few more minutes, the center would become clear. He had won enough battles to unite the Muslims from Egypt to Syria, the only man to ever do it, and he had recovered Jerusalem from the Christians and had been held aloft as one of the greatest leaders since the Prophet Muhammad himself. All those titles and accolades paled in comparison to the one for which it now seemed that he had been preparing his whole life. From the highest emir to the lowest grain farmer, they all looked to him to accomplish the impossible. He had to save their homes, and to do so, he had to become a giant killer.

Every day, more reinforcements arrived from all corners of the West, but no matter how many of them lumbered to the front, they were all ants compared to what followed in their wake: a newly crowned young king with a particularly acute bloodlust that had led him, in only a few months' time, to conquer his way through Sicily and Cyprus.

Doubt had crept in, and Salah ad-Din had begun to wonder if these stubborn enemies would ever hit a breaking point. He knew not to dwell on this foolish hope for too long. Maybe he had grown too comfortable? A lifetime of last-minute cleverness and dumb luck had balanced out every well-thought strategy or correct prediction. He would need to do it all again, or he would go down hard, and not just in defeat and death; if he lost this time, his name would be forever cursed as the ruler who let the Great Destroyer be unleashed on the entire Muslim world.

Salah ad-Din had begged every Muslim leader for more help, warning them that they would pay a price higher than any amount of treasure if this king were successful, and that the flags of the infidel would fly as far as Baghdad. They disagreed about the urgency, and it seemed to Salah ad-Din that his slow, overfed allies would simply rather wait for him to fail and then do their best with what was left.

It was time to admit that he didn't need them. It was just fear. And even worse, it was a loss of faith. Maybe events were not unfolding quite as Salah ad-Din had planned, but he would hone his focus, muster his courage, and remember his belief—no, his certainty in having God's favor. If that was the weapon on which he had the best grip, then he wouldn't need any others.

✝✝✝

Franco, a knight of the Hospitaler order, gave the report to Uther and the others on the boat, trying to sound calm despite himself.

"We've been locked in a stalemate for so long, it's hard to remember when it started. The King of France arrived and brought remarkable siege engines. It looked like the tide might turn, but then tragedy struck. The Count of Flanders is dead. He was one of the wealthiest nobles, yet he fought right next to his brothers. I personally watched him lay down his sword in the heat of battle to help injured men off of the field. He was a true knight. He ... succumbed to the sickness from the poison that their spies rub on our tents ... Satan's bastards! ..."

Franco trailed off, mumbling curses as another Hospitaler helped him to his seat. Uther sat nearby, clustered amongst a band of characters with whom he had become tight on the journey over. There was Sir Rotstark, an experienced German who wore chain mail so caked with dirt and blood that it was red; Jonas Chaucerwen, from the English infantry; the Frenchman, Coup; and Franco, who was the only one of them to have been to the siege already and the closest thing that they had to a leader till the king arrived.

Everyone knew that if the crusaders were ever going to have a chance of retaking Jerusalem they would have to win Acre first. With Richard not even there yet, it seemed an eternity of time away. Till then, they would do their best to fight and survive, girding themselves for the unknown without dwelling too long on the unspeakable.

Not so long ago, Acre had been the prized port city of the Crusader's empire in the Holy Land. Saladin had recaptured it, and now, two years into the Crusader's siege to re-retake the city, Acre emerged transformed into a pit of misery that grew deeper, daily—a dying beast, lurching through time, bleeding smoke and fire, and feebly trying to defend itself against each new assault. The Muslims held the city despite the constant attacks, but any hint of the once flourishing metropolis was covered in ash and blood.

As it became clear that they would be on the beach in a few minutes, Uther's heart raced, and although he took deep breaths, it was difficult to keep up. The skiff jerked as it hit the sand, and everyone moved. Uther raised his head to view his new reality.

From the beach, Uther could scarcely see over the city's high walls. A few stray arrows sliced through the nearby tide and reminded him that he needed to concentrate and move, though he wanted to run right back into the skiff and row far out to sea. In his mind, a competition began to drown out one phrase with another: I'm going to die here. I'm NOT going to die here. I'm going to die here.

He trudged forward, struggling to find focus through the screams of anguish and valor coming from every direction. A pot of Greek fire exploded on the ground nearby, and droplets singed Uther's tunic. Emerging from the recoil, Uther punched the side of his helmet twice, he spotted a row of siege engines, and charged for them with his shield up and head down. Just as he reached them, a catapult released with a sound so loud that it caused Uther to flinch and cover his ears over his helmet.

Uther quickly learned that arrows were the main concern at the front; silent killers coming from any direction, at any moment. The more Uther tried to stay aware and look out for them, the more nervous he became. No one could stay that alert all the time; it was too exhausting. The first time an arrow landed in Uther's chest, stopped barely from his heart by his pads, a minute passed before he accepted that he was not dead.

Uther and others were forced to defend the trench at the back line. One after another Saladin's fighters charged in crazed, futile assaults. Uther's size gave him advantage, and the other man always went down, but contrary to what he was told, it never got any easier.

Returning to camp one night, Uther found Coup using a dagger to whittle a tree branch into a crucifix. Coup had seen Uther fighting and offered advice.

"You must first and foremost respect the blade. It knows when you're misusing it, and the sharpness will … not … cut. Remember to let the blade, not your strength, do the work. If you strike confidently, you won't have to force it; it will slice clean every time."

"It's not the blade I'm concerned with; it's the hesitation," responded Uther.

"Forget faces. If you want to survive you must tear down everything that makes you think twice, because the only alternative is becoming food for the gulls. Become a killer to defeat a killer, your life or his—not many men, but one faceless man that you must kill, again and again, until the war is done. When it's over, you can remember faces again."

✝✝✝

The bonfires were lit and growing when King Richard sailed into Acre's harbor. As he placed that first boot through the thin surf and into the coastal sand of the territory that they called "the Holy Land," a shiver ran up his spine.

Richard ascended the tallest siege tower to survey the scene. The massive smoking ruin of a city sat on a southern-jutting peninsula, which was blockaded by Crusader ships to the south and surrounded by their fighters to the north. Behind the crusader lines was the menagerie of tents that made up their camp, along with a great trench farther on, dug two years before by men who were now dead. On the other side of the trench, pressed right to the edge, were Saladin's troops and their camp receding into the distance behind them.

The Crusaders surrounded the city, but they themselves were surrounded, thus the stalemate of the last two years. Richard rubbed his chin, still smooth from the morning shave, nodded to himself and headed for the French camp.

✝✝✝

Richard found Philip comfortably reclining in his tent. With a long absence between them since their arguments in Sicily, they embraced like reunited kin, and Richard spoke with earnest joy.

"It's so great to be here with you, brother, at long last, in the Holy Land! I am … feeling the spirit, brighter in me than ever before. God has brought us here, together, at the turn of the tide!"

"Yes, brother, it is … our time."

"What of Saladin? Has he shown his face yet?"

"Spies say that he is with the defenders in the city, and then they say that he is amongst the fighting men. Either way, his ability to anticipate our maneuvers has proven uncanny."

"I wasn't made to think that he would be an easy opponent. I'll set up at the north gate. I'll need timber for a ballista. I have an idea ..."

"Richard?"

"Yes, brother?"

"I'll expect my share of the Sicily and Cyprus conquests."

"What? Why now?"

"You haven't said anything about it, and on that point alone I will take offense, so do not cause further insult by pretending you don't know."

"Know what, Philip?"

"Our agreement, fifty-fifty, on all acquisitions. The language could not have been clearer. I want my share of the money, or we will have problems."

"Philip, I lost my entire fleet and have been shot at and pissed on by a parade of small fools blocking the way here. And now that I have finally arrived, this is what you trouble me with?"

"You agreed to it! Why must you put me in the position of calling you out on promises that you break?"

"There is a proper time and place, and we both know that it's not right now! You won't see one coin from me until I've conquered this city. And maybe not even then."

"You can't do it without me, Richard!"

Richard left in silence, finding Humphrey soon after.

"Humphrey, is everyone here going mad? Or is it, maybe, just me?"

"It's the Holy Land ... It does things to people. ..."

"Please tell me that at least you don't hate me?"

"You know that would never happen. Remember your words to me in Sicily. Stay focused. Stay in the moment."

"Humphrey, you understand this place like it's your bed. Please, old friend, tell me, what is the thing that is needed here most? What should I do?"

Humphrey swallowed and looked away. After meandering his hands through his hair aimlessly for a minute, he looked toward Richard with a clear-head.

"I know what you came here to do. I know you want to fight. Now is the time to unleash the dragon and finish this slaughter once and for all. Be the thing that is needed here now to end the suffering, and honor those who have died by killing enough of these bastards to break this miserable stalemate."

Nodding, Richard quietly thought to himself before arranging for a very specific proclamation to travel through the camp: Instead of earning the three gold pieces being paid by King Philip, if any man wishes to join the English army, he will be paid five gold pieces— up front.

✝✝✝

It had been days since Uther had eaten anything when his thoughts drifted to her. For the first time since he had left Sicily, he tried to sketch Gwen's face in his mind. The picture faded with harsh speed, as his memory only conjured indistinguishable features and a faint smile. When he thought about her name, it sounded alien in his head.

Uther had killed so many faceless men that he had finally become numb to it. Following Coup's advice, he cut them all down cleanly, one blank face after another.

When a true challenge finally arrived, the man walked calmly forward, holding his sword low, and cut a long slash along Uther's left leg. Uther prevailed and the cut healed, but when he was able to fight again, his drive was sapped. His blade did not slice well anymore, no matter how much he sharpened it, and his newer wounds were taking longer to heal. He imagined what it would be like when the next cut was not to his shoulder or knee, but to his ribs, or his wrists.

Eventually the enemy took advantage of Uther's lost focus. They swarmed him and dragged him down into the trench, but he vowed that he was going to see her face again, and that day was not going to be his last. When they were all dead except for Uther, he dug his blackened fingernails into the mud walls of the trench and heaved himself up onto higher ground again. He staggered back to camp and passed out at the entrance of his tent.

†††

Soon after his arrival, King Richard was touring the Crusader camp, trying to bring good cheer to the wounded, when he stumbled upon a gaunt but familiar face.

"Uther? Is that you?"

Uther rubbed his eyes and wiped his hand on his tunic to catch the one offered to him from the king to help Uther up.

"Sire… you are a good sight, as always."

"Jesus, Uther, where have you been?"

"Holding off the attacks at the rear … near the trench. …"

"Good god, man, why? You should be at the front—with me!"

Uther limped back with the king, who supported all of Uther's weight with ease. He put Uther down in a tent near his own, ensuring that Uther knew that he was expected to sleep till whenever he wished. It turned out to be just one very long night, for in the morning, feeling refreshed and vital again, Uther grabbed a new tunic of chain mail provided by the king and tossed his old one into the trench.

On order of the king, Uther was assigned to lead the newest

five-story siege tower, rolled into place near the main gate at night. The next morning, Uther and nineteen knights woke up and, with the element of surprise on their side, released a shocking offense of arrows at the unprepared defenders behind the wall. The defenders regrouped, but the distraction succeeded. It was the tower's real purpose to cover for the work of Crusader miners, digging under the wall with fire-starters in their pockets.

†††

When it came to warfare, the King of France was a tent-bound strategist, but Richard preferred the field. Uther had seen Richard fight, but it was soon clear that he had not seen his king at war. Energized and refreshed as he darted up and down the ranks, the king kept the momentum flowing at every station. Uther saw Richard truly in his element, and felt something for Richard that surprised him—pity. War was the only place Uther had seen the king so truly at ease. How could any man last so long with such an outlook? Then again, considering how many battles Richard had won, maybe that was the secret.

Occasionally Richard would have all of his siege engines loaded at the same time, and then have them all fire simultaneously. The effect was dramatic and humbling. One time he had them concentrate on a large building that, when hit, collapsed onto several structures next to it. As the death screams grew, it seemed to the Crusaders that maybe the awe-inspiring attack would be the catalyst that led to surrender. A tense anticipation spread amongst the knights just as the skies mysteriously darkened in the middle of the day.

†††

The abrupt darkness brought shock and panic to both sides. Previously valiant knights were reduced to babbling prayers on their knees, and in some cases even weeping, in the belief that God had finally, truly entered the battle.

Uther was on the fourth floor of the siege tower when he felt an impact. A rust-colored fluid dripped down the side, and Uther held his hand to it and then to his nose. It made the hairs in his nostrils tingle. And it was sticky.

Behind the city walls, the defenders took advantage of the darkness and confusion, and a horrific volley began, sending so much Greek fire at the Crusaders that it seemed as if the defenders had emptied their supplies. The purpose of the sticky substance was quickly made clear as flames from the barrage caught the tower, which became an instant inferno engulfing Uther along with it.

With instinct as his only guide, he jumped out of the window, twenty feet to the ground into a manure pile. He immediately doused himself with a jug of vinegar and writhed around long after the flames were out.

When he rose again, clammy and stinking, he tilted his eyes up toward the black, daytime sky that was now streaked by the flaming boulders raining down on the Crusaders. He stood frozen in awe and found it almost beautiful. When the mysterious darkness finally relented and regular daylight returned, the fires were extinguished, but the haze of smoke and stink made the front uninhabitable. Neither side had it in them for any more fighting that day.

†††

The next day the Crusaders resumed the attack without King Richard who had spent the night roaming by himself, killing enemy soldiers, before returning to his tent and collapsing. When he next awoke, it was with a scorching fever, boil-covered skin, and a piercing pain in his face. Those who heard the symptoms knew the name right away of the disease that had claimed so many in the camp before: trench mouth.

Richard's hair fell out, his nails splintered, and his gums were so swollen that he could not speak. To Richard, the sickness was surely punishment–for his overconfidence, his scattered-mindedness, or perhaps just his raw ambition to win. Or maybe just payback for every other sin he had committed before the Crusade.

He awoke during the second week of the sickness to find emissaries from Saladin. The men presented a basket of fruit along with a letter written by Saladin himself, containing only a few words in French, roughly translated as "Welcome to my home."

As his fever worsened, Richard was only rarely conscious and considered near mad. At one point, he demanded to see Uther. When Uther entered the king's tent, Richard's eyes were pinpoints and his jaw was clenched into a warped scowl. He threw shaking hands at Uther's tunic and pulled him in close.

"It … *cannot* end like this. … Saladin will not stop. … We must persevere … must defeat this man … or we will all perish … They will destroy our world … I swear it."

"Sire … what can I do?"

"A stretcher … bring me to the front. … I will stand when I die."

Uther agreed and left swiftly, if only for fear of catching the sickness. He marveled at whatever Holy Land-borne curse could have so quickly transformed a man of such unconquered strength into a frothing, crooked mushroom. Maybe God was punishing them all, or maybe just Uther, and his damned luck of ending up in such a fiasco.

†††

Richard was taken to a secret tent closer to the front. After more sleep, his fever broke, and he regained enough strength to rise and shuffle out. Though still spitting blood, he made straight for the nearest siege tower and took a seat at the top.

The king knew that his presence alone was no longer sufficient to inspire the men; it was time to turn to a more proven method. Crates of gold coins from Sicily and Cyprus were broken out along with a decree straight from Richard's pained mouth: *Two gold pieces given immediately to any man who kills an enemy soldier, and four pieces offered for removing a stone from the accursed tower and presenting it to the king.*

Almost instantly, the arrows poured out as the king's men competed with their newly acquired coins, placing bets on their shots. With this substantial cover, anyone with an ounce of strength dug their nails into every crack on the tower, piling a procession of bricks neatly at the king's feet. The tower's base disintegrated before their eyes, and when the final brick was pulled, the massive construct finally collapsed into a heap of dust and rubble.

The king picked up his sword and raised it over his head, doing his best not to shake it with sickly hands, as he stood out over his knights and basked in their cheers.

†††

As his strength returned, Richard felt that the time was right to look the enemy directly in the eye, so Humphrey rode to Saladin's camp to request a meeting between the two leaders. He returned faster than Richard had expected.

"Salah ad-Din says it would be improper for two leaders to meet before there's a resolution to the siege and terms have been decided."

Richard's smile shrank, and he looked away.

"You didn't do a very good job at the one thing you're supposed to be good at, Humphrey. It's in your favor that news of the miners has beaten you here. So now we'll burn them, as their dear, honorable leader burns me."

Richard was glad that he had placed his faith in knowledge

instead of negotiation this time, as the miners had indeed completed their work digging a tunnel that ran the diameter of the whole city, and was now filled with combustibles. Soon the fires were lit, and they spread up the walls, burning with divine intensity all through the night.

†††

In the morning, when the fires were mostly out, Richard stretched and tried to walk on his own but still leaned on his sword. He grimaced as he strapped on his armor, moving sluggishly and waving off others who tried to assist. He spat clean and looked out over the city. Seeing a single, scorched white flag waving, he summoned Uther.

Uther arrived to find the king's eyes looking whitish-yellow like boiled eggs. His hair was cut oddly short after most of it had fallen out, and his cracked lips moved awkwardly around each word that he spoke.

"The only way we accept Acre's surrender is if Saladin surrenders with it."

Not long after this decree was made to the Muslims, Saladin answered with his own, as his warriors crossed over the trenches in the largest numbers yet in a direct assault on the Crusader camp. With the Crusaders distracted by this chaos, another dramatic volley of Greek fire was launched from inside the city.

As the flames rose around him, King Richard sharpened his sword, with flinty sparks coming off of the pumice as it sailed across the blade's edge. After one last definitive swipe of the stone, he wiped the blade on the bottom of his tunic and sheathed the sword. Walking on crooked legs to a brand new, large ballista, he gave the order to have it loaded, cranked, and aimed at the gate. The load was one missile, made from a tree that was the width of a horse. Upon its release, Richard watched as it glided toward the walls and then exploded on target, reducing the gates to a pile of stone and splinters. Richard picked up his axe, smashed his teeth together, and waded in. He found Uther there, tired but lucid, with dust from the explosion blanketing his face. Nodding to Richard, he followed the king into the breach, and they cut till everyone was dead or on the run.

Later that afternoon a new round of white flags waved eagerly from inside the city. Richard ordered twice as many arrows fired at it and loaded up what was left of his siege engines. Amidst the bombardment, Uther presented new terms to the city defenders: Saladin, in defeat, must give up the entire Holy Land, including Jerusalem, or every last Muslim soul in Acre, down to the smallest child, would leave the city in chains.

Though the defenders took the terms and their white flags still dangled in the wind, their return arrows continued to prevent the Crusaders from fully breaching the swiftly patched gates. Richard knew that there was no way they could still have such potent supplies left. There had to be a way in, some kind of secret tunnel or breach that Saladin was using to bolster the defenses. Richard sent Uther to investigate the perimeter of the city as the fight continued, and then the king went to sleep.

That was when it happened: *the vision.*

Most Crusaders saw the divine face of the Virgin Mary, descending upon a column of heaven-born light with calming beauty and grace. The Muslims saw something too; to them it was the awesome sight of a million shining martyrs riding down on golden horses. Richard heard about it when he awoke, and his forehead was in his hands when Uther returned.

"Sire, I couldn't find any breach. There may be swimmers re-supplying them; we've heard stories from the Pisans in the blockading boats …"

"I don't care about the damned Pisans … What happened out there? What is this story of an apparition? Can I not have one minute of rest? Everyone has apparently gone mad, but you're not a God-fearing man, Uther, so you, if anyone, can give me a true picture, can't you?"

"I'm not crazy. Something did happen. It was like nothing I've ever seen. At first I thought it was some new weapon from the enemy … something of great engineering, an iron sphere, suspended in the sky. It … burned with white-light, so intensely that I shielded my eyes. I thought for sure that it would open and fire would shower down on us. Instead … the light flared to blinding brightness for a second, and then it was gone."

Richard searched Uther's face for any sign of folly.

"They must have dumped mushrooms and snake juice in our ale."

"No, Sire. The enemy saw it as well. They dropped to their knees quicker than we did. There's no good way to explain it without sounding like a fool, but I know what I saw, even if I don't speak of angels and holy light. Whatever it was, it was powerful enough to destroy us all, I think."

"What nonsense have you brought me, Uther? I thought, if anyone …"

"There is more. Word spreads through the camp that the Virgin Mary gave a message to stop fighting and that the city would fall in four days. Our knights still fend off Saladin's attacks at the rear, but they've put down their arms at the front."

The king stroked his unshaven chin, synthesizing what he could through his foggy outlook.

"All right. We'll wait."

†††

The torn bits of carrot and cabbage hit the butter in the cauldron with a hard sizzle. Richard released another handful of vegetables and inhaled the smoke.

"The trick is to let the butter foam a bit first. Then, just before it turns brown, the vegetables go in to cook."

Uther sat around the fire outside of Richard's tent, along with King Guy and Robert de Sable, an older knight who was recently dubbed the new Grand Master of the Templars to replace Reynard. Humphrey, who returned from negotiations at Saladin's camp, joined them shortly after. Next to the pot of vegetables was a stretch of chain mail that glowed red from the coals underneath. On it sat twelve, sizzling, misshapen sausages that spat and hissed. The men ate heartily, and the royal wine decanter was passed around. After a few swallowed mouthfuls, Richard nodded toward Humphrey to speak.

"Saladin has offered the return of three thousand Christian prisoners captured at Hattin in exchange for the entire Muslim population of Acre."

"He's in no position to bargain with us. My spies say that a eunuch and an old man lead the defenders in the city. All of their soldiers are dead or limbless, and they've sent word to Saladin that they intend to surrender any day."

Struck slightly lame by the experience of being amongst his noble betters, Uther had remained silent up till that point.

"I don't understand. How is it that Saladin will let this city fall if he has an army waiting to stop us from taking Jerusalem?"

"He doesn't have enough men to block us from Jerusalem, but he knows that once Acre falls, all of the sultans and caliphs and emirs will panic at our victory and send more soldiers. In many ways, he must let Acre fall, to save Jerusalem."

Richard took the last chunk of sausage off of the fire. Without even blowing on it, he bit it in half and washed it down with a large slug of wine before speaking again.

"Saladin will not roll over easily, but we must not be so concerned with the enemy's state of mind that we disregard our own. The path to victory lies in our right action at this moment, not in waiting for the enemy to make a false move. We must see this path clearly and then do everything that we can to create what we see."

Uther noticed that Richard was no longer looking anyone in the eye, but facing down, speaking in a tone that sounded as if he was trying to convince himself as he rambled on.

"Life itself is just a puzzle set forth to engage us while we search for an answer that doesn't exist. It seems like it's a choice, but choices do not matter. Down all paths lie the same paradoxes. How else is it that a married man will always wish to be free of his vows to enjoy carefree debauchery, yet the decadent bachelor will always long to escape his unanchored loneliness for the warmth of the right woman? …"

The group's attention to the King's words began to falter as a series of confused glances cascaded around the circle. Richard continued unaware.

"Saladin has gotten too comfortable in his home. When attacked, he will defend his realm violently, but each moment that passes, where he must fight off the attacker in his own home, is one more moment that it is now the attacker's home to defend as well."

Richard looked up. Despite the king's improved health, it occurred to Uther that there was still a sour look in the king's eyes that had not left him since he had been sick.

†††

Salah ad-Din sat in his palace in Damascus as if outside his own body, feeling like an empty sack on the ground. *I should have been there*, was all he could think to himself after a procession of grim messengers had visited him.

The first messenger brought a plea from the leaders inside Acre, begging to send more troops. Salah ad-Din had already begged the other Muslim leaders for help for the third week in a row without success. Maybe they were just running out of peasants and farmers to pour into the fight. The next messenger arrived an hour after the first, with shocking news that the Crusaders had broken through the inner walls and directly presented terms for surrender. The last messenger arrived and revealed that the defenders had accepted terms from King Richard and that the city was gone.

Salah ad-Din had thought they would be tougher, that they would have held out a little longer, even if it meant the possibility of becoming martyrs. The old sultan, however, was learning new things even in his later years. Apparently, sometimes people actually wanted to live rather than die for a cause.

He finally cried, like a mother who had lost a child. As the sobbing subsided and the cold shiver in his back turned warm again, he slept and in the morning felt like a new man, one who could accept defeat, move on, and hope that the feeling was temporary.

Part 7
Mission Rising

No one was surprised that Acre had been practically burned to the ground. Long before Salah ad-Din had captured it, people of all faiths believed that it was a city fated for ruin. It had been the most prosperous point of the sun-drunk Crusader kingdom in the Holy Land and had thus fallen prey to all of the same sins that Christ had died for in the first place.

During the siege, the Crusaders toppled the tower where it was said that Judas was given payment for betraying Jesus. Richard believed that this was a fitting symbol for the city to have a clean break from the past, but now, with the Crusader army and its many noble knights present, there was new money to be made. So cards were dealt, prostitutes removed clothing, and newly lit torches illuminated the night streets once again. Acre exhaled with new life, and as the Crusaders breathed it in, the appetite for pleasure overcame the spiritto fight. They left Richard no choice.

By royal decree, all Crusaders were ordered to exit the city by sundown and camp outside the gates. That night, the cursing of the king's name was audible throughout the camp. Uther struggled to find sleep in the unrelenting Mediterranean summer heat. Sweat soaked his bedroll as he listened to a group of nearby drunken knights discuss practical uses for hollowed-out Muslim skulls. Eventually he gave up and hiked to a hill overlooking the camp, where he finally found peace and sleep.

In the morning Uther squinted and yawned as a familiar figure sauntered up the hill toward him. Humphrey sat and spoke.

"Alone again, eh?"

"Couldn't sleep. There's a bad spirit in the camp."

"It's the sickness. They've been out here too long already. It makes them say things. They speak it with a smile, but don't mistake it for anything but despair."

"What would Christ think?"

"He would think we all should have stayed home and turned the other cheek, but what good has that ever done anyone trying to steal land?"

"Any word from Saladin's camp? Are the surrender terms set?"

"He's agreed to return five hundred of our captives along with ten cities' worth of coin in exchange for all the prisoners. A request has also been made for the return of the relic that he stole, the True Cross. When I asked about it, he moved his eyes away and tugged his beard. He's a wise man, but apparently he's unaware of the telling signs of a lie. My guess? The cross is ash in the wind, and who knows what else he's lying about?"

✝✝✝

King Richard slouched in his seat. Lifting his crown, he dragged his tunic sleeve across his sweaty brow. King Philip's envoy began to wonder if the king had forgotten that he was there. Richard slowly returned his gaze and spoke.

"*Too sick* to tell me himself? It's good to know some things haven't changed."

King Phillip's envoy clasped his hands tighter.

"Sire, he has had *several* relapses."

"Is this about Duke Leopold's flag? I told Leopold that I would never order something so heinous as having his flag crapped-on by my soldiers. It's not my fault that my knights didn't want to share glory with the late-arriving Germans. They're usually so punctual."

"Yes, Sire. Regardless, King Philip apologizes to be leaving so soon after the Germans, but he must attend to business in Paris."

"No. I'm not hearing it until he tells me himself—to my face like a true king, or at least a man."

"Sire, I beg your forgiveness, but the message is not a request."

Richard shook his head to himself and locked his teeth, trying to hold back the fire. His gums still ached when he bit too tightly. Finally he folded his arms and let it go with a swallow that he could not hide. He waved off Philip's envoy with a proud proclamation of "good riddance then," yet once the envoy left, Richard fell back in his chair, and murmured to himself:

"Damnit to hell."

✝✝✝

As Uther left the king's new headquarters, disappointed for the third time in two weeks, he wondered if this was the day that he would have to become a barefoot soldier. His boots had endured sand, sea water, and all manner of horrible human fluids, and had become so worn that they had split apart and were soaked through. Yet each time Uther had tried to speak with King Richard about obtaining money for a new pair, the guards had turned him away. The king had asked not to be disturbed. Despite Uther's frustration at another day of chapped soles, he took as much sausage and bread as he could stuff into his tunic as he left.

That night Uther met the other knights that he had befriended. It had become a daily ritual, with the price of admission being something for the stew pot. Coup brought hunted game, Franco brought oranges, Chaucerwen brought mushrooms. Rotstark brought rocks and grass, but they let him join anyway.

As Coup dipped stale bread into the resulting thin stew, a high, raspy voice begged for a taste. The boy, no older than eight, was rumored to be one of Coup's bastards that had followed him on Crusade. Coup called him "Peu Serpent," meaning "Little Snake." Franco had seen the boy actually fight in battles and said that he was scarily efficient, just like Coup.

The boy also had the mouth to match, annoying the men with inappropriate questions whenever he was around, except for Uther. When Uther turned to the boy, he looked away, not because Uther was the king's guard but because he was a Templar. The boy was right to distrust them, as Uther himself had learned when Grand Master Robert de Sable had visited him a few days earlier and revealed a curt, cryptic statement before disappearing back into the night:

"Recruit a team secretly. Draw them close, but do not reveal why. When the time comes, you will lead them on a quest."

Uther was horrified at this idea, but he did as he was told. He was just as leery of the Templars as everyone else and hated himself a little more each day for it. Coup could see the dark thoughts rolling through.

"Uther, when we have time in the days ahead, you should describe your Gwen to me, and I will sketch her for you, to help you remember."

The thought of this was a revelatory dagger to Uther. He had grown used to the hazy apathy that was the mixture of trying to remember a loved one's face that had been long unseen, and trying to forget them because you would probably never see them again.

"Thanks, Coup, that's a good idea. Is there anyone in France that you're trying not to forget?"

"I was married before all of this. No children. My wife caught the hay-plague before I joined the army. She was so sad in the end, and that's the last memory I have of her. I wish I'd sketched her when we were young and happy. You're still young, so I'll sketch Gwen for you, and you'll never have that problem."

†††

When he returned to the king for the fourth time, Uther was desperate. His feet were on fire with every step, and he *needed* those boots. He was prepared to push past the guards, but this time they let him right in.

The king sat low in his makeshift throne, while Guy and Robert de Sable played cards nearby. Richard rose briskly from his chair at Uther's arrival.

"Tell me, what news?"

"Sire ... I ... I need a new pair of boots."

Richard looked straight at Uther, whose words barely seemed to register.

"What word on the food? Has it arrived? Have the men eaten?"

"Uh ... food?"

"Humphrey said he would get word to you about food shipments from Cyprus?"

Uther was speechless while the king stared a spear through him.

"I have no idea what this is about, Sire. Humphrey didn't say anything to me."

Richard rubbed his temple and exhaled curses through his clenched teeth.

"Sire, is there anything that I can do?"

"Just … get out of here … See if you can find Humphrey."

Uther stood frozen for a moment as the king looked up.

"Are you deaf from plague? GO!"

The king sat back in his chair lower than before. He had run out of food and money. All he could do was wait, and hope that the remaining plunder on its way from Cyprus and Sicily was not sitting at the bottom of the sea.

Uther had stashed some extra bits of bread, so he was still lucid when the effects of the hunger took hold on the camp. Arguments broke out over the weakest animal to kill, and eventually the horse with the awkward gallop was still alive when the first chunks were torn away. A jostling frenzy followed as the starving men dove in for as much as they could scrape from the bones. For two days Uther kept to the edges of it all and waited for Humphrey, whose eventual response was a slow mix of muted surprise and head-shaking bewilderment.

"Food? I was near Tyre on personal business. I have no idea ..."

Humphrey stopped speaking as a vague memory landed.

"He mentioned something in passing. I nodded to humor him, but he's insane if he thinks that I took that as an order to actually go to Cyprus!"

Humphrey ran his hand through his hair and exhaled loudly.

"Christ save us, Uther, before this whole thing falls off the horse."

†††

Richard's eyelids were heavy when Uther and Humphrey

arrived, but he perked up at the sight and walked directly over to Humphrey, standing eye to eye.

"Well?"

"Richard ..."

"Just tell me, did you bring the food?"

"Richard, I never went to Cyprus. I had no idea—"

The king cursed loudly and threw his chalice of wine at the wall.

"Sire, if you want me to go to Cyprus I will, but it will be a week before we have anything, and even then it won't be much. I can put the sword to the people for what they have, but we might as well have left Emperor Comnenus in charge if that was the plan."

"It wasn't the plan, Humphrey, but our knights have carved up every last breathing dog, and on top of that I have two thousand Muslim hostages starving and rotting away, so what choice do I have? We can't march until I get the money that Saladin promised for them, and he knows that; so we're stuck."

"I'll return to Salah ad-Din immediately and see what I can do."

"Why do you do that?"

"Do what?"

"You pronounce his name the way *they* do, even around us."

"You question my loyalty?"

"You scold me like an untrained dog, but you kiss their feet to a fine shine."

"That's my job. I'm a negotiator, not a general. I bring your messages to Salah ad-Din and his to you. I do it politely, and that's all."

"Yes you do. You bring all his messages, but never the ones I want to hear."

"How is that my fault?"

"Humphrey, you've failed me. You're my only line to the man, and you haven't gotten anything. He's playing you. You've lost your touch."

"You can't be serious? Listen to me … the negotiations are working!"

"No Humphrey, not this time. He's *stalling*; can't you see that? We need food, and we need to get the hell out of Acre … a week ago."

Humphrey could sense the dragon rising and tempered his tone.

"Sire, be patient; the men will endure …"

Richard interrupted with a brisk swipe of his hand and a look of death.

"Get on the fastest damn horse you can find, and tell Saladin that if he doesn't pay all of the money in three days I'm going to take the hostages and make a pile of heads so high that he'll need a battering ram to break through."

"As your chief negotiator, I strongly protest that choice of wording …"

"Just do it, and get the hell out of my sight before I forget all the good times and remember all the bad."

Humphrey marched off as Richard turned to Uther with a subtle, unnerving smirk, staring through him.

"What the hell are you looking at?"

"I, uh …"

Richard cracked a smile.

"Uther, I'm just throwing jest. But please, get out of my sight as well. If anyone asks about the food, tell them to sharpen their swords, and remember that they're soldiers, not milk-starved infants."

"There has to be another way."

"Pardon?"

"Humphrey's right; it's not going to work. Saladin won't pay, and if you threaten to kill the prisoners, you'll look weak unless you follow through … and I know you won't risk looking weak."

Richard laughed to himself.

"Let me ask you something, Uther. What do you expect me to do with them? Sell them as slaves? Maybe ship them back to England? I could just leave them here and begin the march, with two thousand former enemy prisoners at my back as I try to take the most sought after city in human history. Is that what you're suggesting? If we aren't going to get paid for them, then they need to go away."

"We've won Acre; we have God's favor. If we kill all of those hostages … it will doom this Crusade."

Richard's eyebrows arched up in shock as he rushed Uther and spoke close.

"Not if you doom it first by even suggesting such a thing! Let me remind you of what's going on here. If the greatest king in all of Europe can't defeat the hordes of Saladin, then the Muslims will invade our homes as easy as the Vikings, only they'll be sober and organized. But I imagine, like most of the fools who shadow my feet, that you haven't thought it through that far. Trust me, *Saladin* most definitely has."

"I didn't mean to imply that I know …"

"Of course you did! You've got all of God's answers straight from His mouth to your ear the way it sounds, but there's really only one thing you *need* to know: I'm your lord. You *owe me* your allegiance, and you will kill and kill again to help me prevent these bastards from getting even a finger closer to our home-lands."

"Sire, for the sake of everything we've fought for, *think* before you do this, because once it's done, you can't go back. You asked me to be your conscience here."

Richard scrunched his mouth and eyes and blew air out through his nose before pushing Uther with a force that knocked him onto the floor.

"How dare you judge me from your perch. You think any of it is going to save you any more than the next man? The decision is made and stands. If Saladin doesn't give me the money, then *you* will cut off every last prisoner's head, and you can find out personally if that's what God wants."

Richard sat, and Uther left to the sound of the king's final words.

"And get some damned new boots. You're a royal guard, not a beggar!"

†††

A few days later, Humphrey returned with no money and ill news. Saladin had not minced his words; he believed that Richard was bluffing and would never actually kill the prisoners.

If only Saladin had not made that so unwaveringly clear. If only he had expressed even a nuance of concern for the threat. If only he had taken Richard's reputation seriously.

Uther was summoned as promised and given a freshly sharpened sword and a regimen of Templar knights. Their orders were to march the two thousand prisoners to a clearing, where Saladin's camping army could see, and cut off all their heads. The king stationed an additional group of knights to ensure that there would be no deserters from amongst the executioners, and the work began.

Eight excruciating hours later, Richard allowed the rest of the Crusaders to join in and have a taste of the vengeance that they craved. Previous to that, Uther and the small group of Templars had cut off the heads, one by one, of the crying, begging, sometimes silent, sometimes too weak from hunger to even notice, prisoners. As he did his share of the work, Uther slit throats first to spare the victims, risking his reputation, though eventually he stopped caring if the other Crusaders saw him do it.

Throughout this ghastly work, it was not the looks in the prisoners' eyes that Uther remembered; it was their expressions. It was the shapes of their mouths and the flare of their nostrils, even if they were already dead, as he sawed through blood-gushing muscle and bone. He remembered the sickly feeling of relief he experienced each time that the blade made it through the last bits of connecting skin, and the head hit the ground, and it was over.

These memories were grafted to him now, forever.

Afterward, his hands were crusted thick and dark. Though he washed for almost an hour, there was still residue: tiny brown flecks in his fingernails, and in his hair, and in the corners of his eyes. He dug his hands repeatedly into the ground, forcing dirt into the every pore of every finger to cover over the bits of the dead.

In the Muslim camp, a great collective cry of terror rose, followed by a re-invigoration of morale of which Salah ad-Din could only have dreamed. His soldiers foamed in sadness, frustration, and the overwhelming need for immediate revenge. The true fear had taken hold—not of Richard, but of the afterlife. Nothing less than the deepest pits of hell awaited them if they retreated in fear and did not try to stop him. They all believed it now: if Richard was left unchecked, he would tear their whole world to the ground, and God would weep and punish them for it, severely and forever. And thus, Salah ad-Din had a powerful new weapon in his arsenal: an enemy that his soldiers would willingly give their lives to help defeat.

Not far away, as King Richard made preparations to begin the march out of Acre, he had a nagging hunch that he may have just made the biggest mistake of his life.

Uther's voice echoed in Richard's ear:

"… You can't go back."

†††

Three days after the beheadings, Richard was able to secure enough supplies to feed his men and begin the march. The Crusader line pushed south along the old Roman coastal roads with the sea helping to cut off at least one side from attack. All Uther really wanted to do was board the first boat out, without a care for where it took him. He wanted that, but he was not a deserter, not yet. He was not ready to spend the rest of his life looking over his shoulder, so he pushed on.

As he rejoined the line, he immediately felt the stinging looks from the decent men who had not participated in the executions. They knew what he had done. He didn't care. He was tired of trying to please either the maniacs on his right side or the whiners on his left. Despite all of the reverent folklore that Richard inspired, he had turned out to be just another predictable disappointment. Uther remembered the words of the closest person that he had to a father in Beacan: "Eventually everyone will disappoint you. Even the best of them. Especially the best."

As the sun braised Uther's senses, he dwelled ceaselessly on his hatred. It had not been the first time Richard had acted as his friend before throwing him into the fire, and he had been stupid to expect anything different. The dark thoughts clung to him as he sweated a river in the thick midday air that scattered what was left of his attention. He was barely conscious when the attacks began.

The arrows came in waves from the surrounding woods, hour after hour, day after day, and everyone bled. Chaucerwen was one of the first to take a near fatal hit. Over the days the wound turned yellow, and he walked slower and slurred his words. Uther brought him to the back of the line, where Franco marched with his fellow Hospitalers, experts in the art of healing. Franco did what he could for Chaucerwen but did not look hopeful as he poured some water on his own hands to wash off the blood.

"We're assuming that the king will stop for camp at the Plain of Sharon. Chaucerwen can get some rest there, and we'll know then if he's going to make it. The Hospitalers are going to set up an infirmary to deal with all the wounds. We can use all the help we can get if you're interested."

Uther couldn't look Franco in the eye.

"Where are you right now, Uther?"

"Damn the king and this war. This isn't our land. We don't belong here."

"It's not *a choice*. We follow, or we prove ourselves the better man. If you think you can do it, challenge the king and become the lucky man in charge of all this ..."

Franco motioned to the enormous line of men extending in both directions.

"... If not, then may I suggest that you try to let it go. You and I, Uther, we're nothing. We're not moneyed and we're not noble, so we're pieces to be moved. Men like the king see greater things, greater actions, greater results, and all of the other effects down the line. It's a curse, not a blessing, and unless it's something you want to do yourself, we'll follow this man and muster what little faith we have that he will do the right thing."

"I can't just let it go. You don't know what I had to do ... what I've seen. It's not so easy just to pretend that it's just not there."

"You should probably think of it as a test. Nobody ever said forgiveness was easy. I know it was bad, but your choice lies straight ahead. You can hold onto the wrong that was done to you, or you can let it pass through like the air you breathe. Keep in mind; if you hold onto it, it won't rot *him* from the inside. The choice is still yours to make; he can't take that away from you."

†††

The grueling march, along with endless days of living on high alert, took their toll on the Crusaders, who grew increasingly frustrated with Richard's orders. The arrow attacks intensified, and the knights were anxious to take to the surrounding forests and root out the attackers. The king, however, forbid it on pain of death. Coup assured Uther that Richard was right and that he was preventing the knights from doing exactly what Saladin wanted—fracturing the line as each knight took his own path and became lost in the woods to be easily slaughtered, one by one.

"Besides," said Coup, "the more the king's decisions frustrate the common fighters, the bigger the release will be of their pent up anger when we reach Jerusalem's gates. Then the king will just have to stand back and watch."

The next day the march arrived at the Plain of Sharon. Many Crusaders had anticipated camping amongst the same sun-dappled limestone there that Jesus had walked over in exile. Instead they found a dense, creature-infested swamp. Swords became dulled from hacking through the growth, and foreign serpents sliced at heels. There was barely a dry square on which to place one tent, let alone thousands.

Deciding that he would not have much sleep that night anyway, Uther volunteered for guard duty, keeping watch as other guards screamed hymns in an attempt to scare away the creeping beasts in the night. Later, when most of the camp was asleep, Uther felt a tap on his shoulder. Spinning around, he found the Templar Grand Master Robert de Sable standing humbly in front of him. He had not heard as much as a ruffled leaf from the man's approach.

"Hello, Robert."

"Hello, Uther. I know you're not happy about what had to be

done at Acre. I want to assure you, though, that your mission is still incredibly important, maybe even more important than recapturing Jerusalem."

Uther hardly tried to conceal a sneer.

"So important that you won't even tell me what it is?"

"I'm still new to this job. It has ... changed my outlook on why we're here, all of us, as men with homes and families. *Your* mission, Uther, pertains to a weapon—something from the Far East that the Muslims have acquired—something so powerful that a wave of fear has possessed the Vatican and the Templars who know of it."

Uther listened, but it was only when Robert stopped talking that the weight of the words sunk in. For the first time since Uther had met him, the stone-faced Grand Master of the Knights Templar looked as tired as an old grandfather.

"Our spies report that, as we speak, the weapon is being brought to Saladin so he can test it against us. I await word on an opportunity to prevent that. *This* is your mission and our great need at this hour: to stop them and secure this weapon before they can deliver it to Saladin and ensure our plunge into darkness."

Uther tried as hard as he could to look past the massive wall of doubt and resentment and accept his role with loyalty and purpose, but everything that King Richard had done to him had cemented that wall firmly in place.

When Robert spoke again, Uther felt an unsettling sensation, as if the old Templar was looking right into his mind.

"Being forced to follow a man that you don't believe in can be as withering to the spirit as trying to climb a mountain with no peak. That's why no one shed a tear when my predecessor Reynard didn't make it out of Sicily. That's why it's important that you decide if you feel the same way now about your king."

And with that, the old knight disappeared again into the darkness.

†††

Word reached the Crusader camp that Saladin was sending a new negotiator that was no less than his brother, El-Adel. Richard wanted a fresh start, so he dismissed Humphrey and met the man himself.

"It's an honor, El-Adel. I've tried to convene with your brother directly, but apparently he views the importance of candid negotiations differently than I do. It is hard to accept his offers as honest when he refuses to look me in the eye and speak them himself. Since he's not here, I'll look you in the eye and tell you that we would be open to an end to the hostilities in exchange for the return of all territories seized in 1187, including Jerusalem."

El-Adel was momentarily stunned silent.

"Well … uh … that would be *all* lands occupied by Muslims in Palestine … where we outnumber you three to one. I would make a powerful guess that my brother will not agree to this. Perhaps, uh, we could begin by discussing the territory south of Acre, along the coast?"

Richard's reaction was a smile, a handshake, and opening the flap of his tent.

"Perhaps bring your brother the offer, and we'll let him decide for himself what he agrees to."

El-Adel left, and Richard turned to other matters. Before the meeting the king had learned from his spies that Saladin's forces were massing near Arsuf, two days ahead of the Crusaders. He found one of his guards.

"Send for Sir Uther."

†††

Entering the king's tent, Uther found Richard sitting with his face perched over a steaming cup.

"My advisor says these herbs will ensure solid sleep. I hope he's right; I feel as if I'm going to collapse. It would be a poor time for that to happen, to say the least."

The king looked weak, but Uther didn't care. He was weary of being lured in by the humbled king only to be burned by his rancorous second face. This time Uther was not going to hold back.

"The knights still worship you. The enemy mythologizes you. You could give orders from here without ever showing your face again, and it would only build your legend. They call you 'The Lionheart' without hesitation. Even the ones who hate you."

Richard smiled and laughed to himself.

"That name means nothing to me. It's a nickname from when I was a young duke in Aquitaine, when I made war against all sorts of men for one ridiculous reason or another. I always had something to blame them for. I was a young fool who'd been given power without understanding what that really meant, so I attacked those who I saw as ogres, when the real bastard sitting under the bridge was me."

Richard motioned for Uther to sit.

"I'm going to try to make this brief. I want to apologize for my words to you at Acre. As I believe yours were rash, so were mine. I put you in an advisory position and made you feel at ease to speak, so it shouldn't have surprised me when you did. There are times when a king must be open to all that's coming toward him and times where he must be strong enough in his own decisions to trust nothing else. That was a challenging moment for me, and the truth is that you would've had to carry out the executions whether you had angered me or not. You're a Templar, and that's what Templars do—the dirty work. So I hope you can forgive me. I won't hold it against you if you can't."

Uther had no answer. Richard apparently was not seeking one as he continued.

"I also hope that you have recovered from whatever trauma you experienced, because unfortunately there's a good chance you'll have to slaughter twice the number in the coming days. I only wish for you to go toward that task untroubled, and not hold scorn for me, as I will be fighting beside you. None of us knows what we face ahead, but I hope that you and I enter the fight as brothers instead of separate and alone."

Uther took his time in responding.

"It won't be easy for me to just let it go, even if I wish to."

"Life is short, Uther, and mostly pointless. We're about to enter an ambush. Though I've gained knowledge of it through our spies, it won't lessen the blow. Saladin's army outnumbers us four to one. The skirmishes on the march have only been a taste. *Acre* was only a taste. The true test of our resolve lies straight ahead. There's no going around it, no other path to choose. Even if we retreat, they will double back. The stark truth is that we are surrounded; he's everywhere now, around us like a glove and he apparently chooses this moment to attack and blunt our advance. We knew this was the price to pay for the journey south, and we will win this struggle, but it won't be an easy next few days."

Richard saw the change come over Uther as his shoulders lightened and his eyes unclasped their scorn.

"Maybe I'll attend mass tonight," said Uther.

"Maybe we both should. I have supplanted my own faith with the words of gypsies and card readers at times. One told me that I would never have children; certainly no male heir, but no girl either. Nothing. Another one told me that I would die young. He didn't say when."

Richard half smirked and shrugged, before adding, "Maybe I

will see less fortune tellers in the future."

†††

EARLY MORNING

The next morning, the Crusaders extinguished their campfires and formed up the line. The cavalry hugged the shore to the right, with the infantry and bowmen marching together to protect the exposed left flank. There was one goal for the day: secure shelter behind the Arsuf ruins, five miles down the road, before Saladin attacked.

As they reached the end of the second mile, not one arrow had come their way, when suddenly a roar erupted from the surrounding woods, and a collective Crusader flinch gave way to wide-eyed shock. The first wave of Saladin's horde, dark-skinned Moorish scouts swarmed into the open. They were designed to unsettle, and the effect was a success. When the first volley of spears rained down on the Crusaders, their jaws were still gaping. As the survivors recovered, the charging scouts parted, and Saladin's mounted archers rode through and rained down more razor sharp speeding points on the Crusaders. Richard yelled a defiant command.

"Do not break formation! Keep the sea to your right, and get to the ruins!"

Within minutes, the Muslim assault doubled, and they were everywhere. Under the determined Saracen blades, the unified Crusader line disintegrated into a panicked mob as the blood sloshed up around their ankles. Amidst the chaos, Richard focused his eyes on the back of the enemy ranks where a decorated soldier with a graying beard rode a large horse. *Could it be him?* It seemed to Richard as though the man could almost see him too, and was smiling.

AFTERNOON

The screams of the accursed dying and maimed competed

with the constant beat of the Muslim war drums to drown out all sensible thought. The Crusader line was shattered, and the knights on horse were backed against the shoreline with the rear guard all but decimated. All indicators pointed to defeat.

At the head of the line, Richard pulled an arrow out of his chest armor and swung his blade, separating an enemy's ear and then a vocal cord. Out of the corner of his sweat-soaked eye, he spotted the familiar maroon cloth of Sir Garnier de Naplouse, the Grand Master of the Hospitalers, riding toward him.

"Our horses are being cut out from under us. We must charge now, or there will be nothing left to charge with!"

"No, not yet; not till I give the order! Keep moving toward the ruins, and hold the line as best as you can! I'll man the center, but you must defend the rear."

"Eternal infamy is upon us! All will be lost if we don't charge now!"

"I have given my orders!"

As Richard watched the knight gallop away bitterly, he knew that the man was close to the breaking point, and Richard hoped that the rest of the knights were feeling exactly the same way. Uther had spotted the exchange and rode over to the King.

"Sire, we're close to falling apart. Why don't we charge?"

"We have to hold back just a little longer. Saladin's men have spent their rage and are near fatigue. You have to trust me. Ride to the rear guard, and help there."

Uther joined the stifled, enraged cavalry at the rear where Franco spotted him.

"What does the king say?"

"Hold the charge and keep fighting."

"Damn him! What's he thinking? His scheming ways will be the end of us!"

"No, Franco, we have to follow the king's orders!"

Franco saw Uther's eyes under the shadow of his helm and, remembering their talk from a few days before, nodded hesitantly. Another Hospitaler nearby had overheard Uther and exploded.

"Damn his oily English hide!"

The Hospitaler signaled to a nearby French knight, and they threw their helmets to the ground, raised their swords, and galloped in a hard charge toward the enemy lines. Other Crusaders followed in a cascade, and soon the cavalry was in full charge.

Over his shoulder, Richard spotted this, and his adrenaline fired. He smiled giddily, held his royal blade as high as he could, and yelled: "GOD BE WITH US! KILL THEM ALL! CHARGE!!!"

The Crusader line had been whittled down and hammered into one unified body that now unleashed a torrent of pent-up energy. The closest Muslim infantrymen stood frozen in shock at what approached—a mass of down-pointed lances, flaring horse nostrils, and the kicking legs of both man and beast. There was nowhere to run as the gleaming wall of steel, iron, and muscle sped over them like a rushing tide. As the Crusaders regrouped for a second and third charge, the decimated Muslim lines scattered in every direction.

Salah ad-Din lost his composure, cursing and threatening deserters. Right before he accepted defeat and signaled his horse to gallop, he spotted a warrior on horseback at the front of the Crusader lines wearing a crown and a maniacal smile while hacking gleefully and scattering Muslim body parts all around him. King Richard's teeth clenched, and the corners of his mouth turned up even higher, providing Salah ad-Din a glimpse of something that sent a shiver down his spine. The stories that Salah ad-Din had heard were true; this was the man who would end him.

EVENING

The Crusaders had won the day but at a steep price. They limped into Arsuf, and a marathon began of the removal of arrowheads from wounds and the cauterizing of stumps that used to be limbs.

The bloody rage that had propelled the Crusaders through so much had finally given way to the inevitable hangover. After taking Acre there had been relief, even joy, but now apathy was all that the un-maimed survivors had left. Richard sensed that if he gave even one more order that the army did not like, they would conjure up just enough strength to hang him from his standard flag. This was an inconvenient reality that he was going to ignore in his determination to push them down the road again to the city of Jaffa, a day's hike away, where they would be significantly better protected and could recover in peace. It would be worth it, even if they would curse him every step of the way. Once there, in the accommodating port oasis, they would all get the much-needed rest that they craved and quickly forget their wrath toward the king.

He hoped.

†††

When the Crusaders made it to Jaffa, they took off their armor, let their swords sit dull, and drank. Uther was the exception. Robert de Sable found him shortly after they arrived, and Uther immediately began training with the Templars for his mission. His crew was gone; Chaucerwen, Franco and Rotstark had all died in the battle of Arsuf. The only one who remained was Coup, who was anxious to help and was officially knighted despite his lack of title or property. Everything was coming together, but something still did not add up, so Uther paid a visit to the Templar Grand Master's humble tent.

"Hello, Robert."

"Hello, Uther. What troubles you?"

"I'm confused. Why send a few untrained men on such a crucial mission? Why not send the whole army if it is as dire as you say?"

"Because outside of the Vatican, no one knows about this, and it has to stay that way. King Richard doesn't know about the weapon, and even Saladin himself doesn't know what he is about to receive. It is that sensitive."

"Then why put all this trust in me? I'm just a farmer."

"Maybe that's what you once were, but we both know that you are different now. You can pretend otherwise, but you're a knight, a Templar, and a respected guard of the King of England. Surely he has told you that you are destined for great things."

"Your definition of great things is ... a suicide mission."

"Maybe. Maybe those who have chosen you for it have a little more faith in you. I know that I've been vague at times, but I want you to enter this mission with complete confidence, so I've decided that you should know the full truth and understand the weight of the task. The weapon that you're going to steal is a book..."

✝✝✝

Despite another crushing defeat, Salah ad-Din wedged righteous indignation into his mind to squeeze out the doubts and fears. He was not going to let this boy-king best him so quickly. There was no question that Richard was a skilled general, but he was still an interloper in these lands. For fifty-three years Salah ad-Din had lived there, eaten there, starved there, taken life there, and learned how to defeat an army there. It was time to slow down the pace and really put Richard to the test.

Salah ad-Din doubled his cache of light-skinned spies and dispersed them throughout the Crusader ranks where they mixed in and disappeared. As their reports returned, Salah ad-Din learned that even while Richard's men ate grapes at Jaffa, the king remained vital and ambitious, repairing the town and assembling a proper forward base. Obviously Richard would use Jaffa as his stage to attack Jerusalem, but what Salah ad-Din really worried about was the place to which anyone with the guts to take Jerusalem would eventually turn: Ascalon.

If Richard could occupy the more strategic southern port city of Ascalon, he could use it as a base to conquer much more than Jerusalem and keep Westerners in those lands for generations. He would start with bringing nearby Egypt and its riches into his war chest. With that to fuel his fire, he would topple Baghdad, solidifying the Near East. After that, he would be unstoppable. Ascalon would be the key to it all.

Salah ad-Din knew what God was telling him. It made his stomach hurt, but he had to face it and do what needed to be done. Trading temporary pain for long-term security, he would burn out the disease and thus let a part of his soul go with it.

Ascalon had to be destroyed.

†††

News had reached Richard that Saladin was burning Ascalon, the largest southern fortress in the Holy Land. This meant that Saladin did not believe he could defend it and would rather destroy it than risk it falling into Richard's hands. If Richard did not counteract this, it would obliterate what was left of the Crusaders' respect for him, let alone any motivation that they had to follow him to the gates of Jerusalem. The relentless heat of the Holy Land summer was waning, and once the rainy winter season began, the muddied sand would be as constant as the sky, and an attack on Jerusalem would be impossible. Richard knew what he had to do.

Ascalon had to be saved.

✝✝✝

When Uther woke on the morning of his mission a feeling of calm lingered on him and all of his questions were gone. The moment had arrived, and though he had dreaded it every day till then, he was surprised to find that he was no longer afraid. It was all so clear. He knew what he had to do. In service to the most powerful men in the land, to prevent great suffering and evil from being unleashed on the world, his mission was stark and simple. He did not need to worry about the *whys* or the *hows*, only the *when*.

After the mission was complete, with his debt paid to the Templars and his innocence back home in England guaranteed by the king, he would be free to walk away. First though, he had to face it.

Everything was executed perfectly. The enemy arrived when they were supposed to and were effectively surprised. And they had the book, as big as a shield, and too large for the enemy to hide effectively. Uther held it in his hands, for a moment at least.

It had deceivingly been too easy. Uther had seen victory in his mind, and it had almost happened, but things changed, up became down, and suddenly there was nowhere to run. The enemy reinforcements sprang from the trees as if by a magic spell and showered Uther and his team with a point-blank barrage of arrows.

In panic, Uther ducked behind the closest tree that was too thin. He was pierced in both calves, and his right palm was pinned to the tree. The rest of Uther's team was either dead or had run off, and now the bastards had him too. He had failed. Two Muslim soldiers approached with drawn swords and satisfied grins, until someone dropped down from the trees between them. It was Coup, bloodied but swift. One enemy soldier fell quickly after two strategic cuts, but with a stab through the sternum, the other bested Coup. Though defeated, Coup surprised the man who had just killed him with a head-butt, a slice across the eyes, and one last strategic stab. Coup slumped to the ground with a look of relief spreading across his face.

Uther tried to pull the arrow out of his hand, but it would not move, and he was not brave enough to pull free of it. He watched helplessly as his friend and savior exhaled his final breaths in rare silence.

"Coup! Are you all right? Say something!"

"Uther … good Uther … do you remember the places I told you to strike a man to defeat him without killing him?"

"Coup? Are you? …"

"Recite it for me if you remember …"

"The gut, the groin … the knees."

"If you remember any of the lessons, remember that one."

"It won't be the last lesson…for either of us."

"Don't mourn me, Sir Uther … great things await you in life, and greater things await me in death … I go willingly to the gates, to serve the One … who will save us all, eventually …"

There was no sound after that, and Uther did not disrespect the dead by calling his name. The next few minutes of sadness, anguish, and fear felt like an eternity before a familiar face peered out from the brush. Coup's little friend Peu stood solemnly over Coup's corpse, looking more childlike than ever before. Uther called to him.

"Boy … come here!"

Peu, whose true name Uther had never learned, approached sheepishly.

"I've never seen men fight like that, Sir Uther. What were they protecting?"

Uther should have just given Peu the book, but with pain and panic setting in, Uther worried that the boy might give it to the wrong person, so he simply sent him for help, and then waited.

Alone with his thoughts, nailed to the wood, and with certain doom bearing down on him as he waited, Uther truly discovered his faith. Not in God, or in religion, but in his friends. The king, no matter what had happened before, was Uther's friend. If Peu could reach him in time and Richard still cared enough about Uther to make haste, there was a chance that Uther could still be saved.

Part 8

Descending the Other Side of the Hill

Richard paced his chamber like a caged beast. While everyone else was relaxing in Jaffa, the king had not stopped moving. His mind swirled with possibilities. Saladin was occupied with burning out Ascalon port, which meant that he had taken his eye off of Jerusalem, and Richard was anxious to snatch the unguarded prize.

And yet, he was utterly conflicted. Philip was back in Europe now, along with the Germans, and they both hated him and would take advantage of the situation as much as possible. He had no proof, so rather than tempt paranoia, he dispatched envoys to assess the situation. No matter what they discovered, he still needed to walk out of the Holy Land high if his reputation was going to survive. He might have been crazy, but he was not insane; he needed a backup plan. Saladin's brother El-Adel had proved to be a virtuous negotiator, and as trust grew between them, so had options. A deal that would allow Richard to detach from the Holy Land honorably had become a legitimate option. Still, what incentive did Saladin's own brother have in helping Richard?

Perhaps El Adel wanted something too, not just as a negotiator for Saladin, but for himself. Richard had his suspicions as to what that might be and thus a strategy was born. He promptly located a squire.

"Tell the servants to gather. We're going to plan a party."

Richard would send for El-Adel, along with Richard's wife and sister in Acre. To ensure their safe passage, he would have his most valiant knights leave immediately, but before Richard could seek them out, the guards found him. By their side was a boy dressed in oversized knight's garb as if at play.

"He seeks you specifically, Sire. He says he was sent by Sir Uther."

"Speak, boy, what of Uther?"

"He was on a mission for the Templars, but he's pinned down."

"What mission? Where's de Sable?"

Richard sent for Robert de Sable who made the decision, as Grand Master, to reveal the true nature of the mission to the king.

"There is a book of arcane knowledge from the Far East. The Vatican calls it the 'Liber Ignium.' In its pages are instructions for how to create a type of fire, in powder form, that can propel an arrow one hundred times faster than a crossbow. This could decimate an army before a single sword was raised. It's the recipe for conquering the entire world, and with this book, one man could do it. This is what they are bringing to Saladin."

Richard put his hand on the boy's shoulder and spoke calmly to his guards.

"Prepare my fastest horse, round up a hunting party of the toughest Templars, and meet me at the gates in fifteen minutes."

†††

As the fifth nail tore away, the tears streaked Uther's grimy jaw. He wondered if Peu had even made it to Richard. Perhaps the king could not come, or simply did not want to. It did not matter which now; Uther had seen his captors put the swords on the fire and remove the glowing blades a moment ago. As he said goodbye to Gwen, he wasn't sure if it was inside his head or spoken out loud.

In those last moments he clung to a shameful wish: he hoped that Gwen was already dead, that he had been wrong about Heaven—that it really did exist, that he had not sinned too much to get in, and that he would see her there soon.

As Richard rode out of Jaffa, he kicked his horse so hard that he drew blood. Feeling his hair lift in the wind, he prayed, promising to restart the march to Jerusalem immediately, regardless of his plans, as long as he was not too late to save Uther. Simultaneously he damned God and every angel in heaven if he was too late and pledged to fulfill what he was told by the Pope was God's true wish, and murder every last man in Saladin's camp.

Six men were in the process of torturing Uther when the Crusaders arrived. With ferocious speed, Richard rode down one of them and swung so hard that he cut clean through the neckbone. He jumped off his moving horse and bludgeoned another man's face to pulp with his crossbow. After a minute there was not a trace of life left in it, but he unleashed an arrow into what was left anyway.

When the last man attacked, Richard threw his crossbow away and faced the man defenseless, blocking the enemy's sword with his arm gauntlets before annihilating the man's nose and eye socket with a strong left hook. He pulled the man up by his collar and whispered.

"You're going to die soon, so I encourage you, while I finish speaking, to offer any last prayers that you wish your God to hear before he delivers judgment. Though I can't say that I'm one to enjoy torture, it's important to send the proper message in these types of situations. However, I will show you true chivalry and spare you from enduring it. It's what Christ would have wanted."

Richard cut the man's throat, right before another enemy soldier dashed out of the woods, jumped onto a horse, and practically trampled Richard as he sped away.

The pursuing Templars approached the king.

"He's got the book!"

Reaching into his belt, Richard retrieved two tiny pouches and emptied the contents onto the ground in a uniform pile. Within seconds a small flame erupted. He dipped the crossbow arrowhead into the fire just as the man rode out of range.

Richard leveled his arm, squinted, and calmly pulled the trigger. In the distance, the arrow made contact with the rider's back, and the man erupted in flames. Richard stared, transfixed, before looking down in anger as the Templar spoke.

"Should've aimed for a headshot without the fire; could have saved the book."

"Better to let it burn."

The king sighed before helping to dislodge Uther from the tree.

Before they rode back to Jaffa, Richard took time to leave his message for the enemy reinforcements, who, when they arrived, found all of their men burned to ash except for one, who was fanned out on the ground in six pieces—limbs, head, and torso—with King Richard's royal monogrammed sword protruding from the chest.

†††

Richard felt liberated. The rescue had revived his spirit, and more importantly, he had saved Uther's life. The lost book was forgotten, and even Jerusalem was distant. There was a party to assemble, and there would be no humility about it; the king aimed to make an impression.

Ale was laid out in barrels throughout the streets in Jaffa like water, and every cook in the city was hired to prepare enough food for a week-long banquet. Richard was flush with loot that had finally arrived from his conquering adventures on the way to the Holy Land, and he took utter joy in knowing that it would have been hard to find a party in the known world that night that compared.

El-Adel was the first to arrive, laden with gifts, along with trays of roast lambs and casks of brandy. He came with full arms, almost as if he wished to receive his own gift.

"You've really spared no expense, Richard; your generosity shines."

"It feels good to make people happy. Hopefully you can find some fun in what passes for merrymaking in our world. Excuse me for a moment..."

As the night progressed, Richard ducked away to check on the wine levels for a very specific group: the Crusader infantry and lower knights, who were given a lavish feast of their own, separate from the king's party for El-Adel. There would be no drunken masses breaking out into hymns in front of his guest, not tonight. Tonight was for El-Adel.

The king's sister Joanna arrived next, making the most dramatic entrance yet. Richard knew that she had been clawing at the walls of her dwelling in Acre, hoping to find a new husband, or at least something to occupy her time till she did. Richard practically had to rip her away from the city, where a traveling minstrel had been writing songs for her. She came as requested and brought a motley band of drunken musicians, sweaty jesters, sharp-eyed jugglers, and swarthy cooks armed with all manner of fish mousses, cheeses, livers, and vinegars to entice the noble tongues.

As the band played loud, joyous songs with unhinged abandon, Joanna danced, flirted, and darted back and forth in a manner not that different from Richard manning the siege lines. Her perfumed, strawberry-blonde hair left trails of her scent that the war-worn men eagerly inhaled. The party shone brightly in the dark desert sky, but the spark that kept it lit was Joanna, or at least El-Adel's eyes would testify as much. Richard wasted no time grabbing Adel and walking toward his sister, who immediately noticed the dashing stranger with the kind, dark eyes.

"Adel, this is my sister Joanna, Queen of Sicily. Joanna, this is El-Adel, the great general and brother to Saladin."

Joanna's eyes widened. El-Adel reached for Joanna's hand to kiss it, but she pulled it away before his lips could touch. Instead, she ran her fingers briefly through his hair.

"Yes, Saladin; the man we're here to crush. I didn't know he had a brother."

Just then, to the king's great joy, Uther sauntered into the party and presented the perfect opportunity for Richard to leave El-Adel and Joanna alone.

"Please excuse me. One of my men-at-arms was injured in battle, and I should give him a proper toast."

Richard threw an arm around Uther and raised a cup for him with the other knights. With Richard gone, El-Adel made his move with Joanna.

"The king tells me that you're a fan of poetry?"

"I am, though your Muslim variety is vulgar, even for my filthy tastes. Your poets are quite obsessed with the roses down below as opposed to the roses up here."

She pointed to her face. El-Adel moved closer and spoke with focused sincerity.

"It is my deepest belief that the roses with the sweetest nectar are the lips that adorn a woman's face, especially a pair as perfect as yours."

Joanna smirked and blushed.

"Well, it must be a rare treat for you to view a woman's face. I'm told that you keep your women's faces covered."

"We prefer our women to be … unattainable … until we attain them. We … enjoy a sense of mystery and longing; it's tradition, if you will, the build-up and the *dance*—for the road traveled should be as pleasurable as the destination. Some of us are more permissive … or should I say, adventurous than others. And, if you will allow me to say so, your beautiful eyes suggest great depths to be … explored, by an equally adventurous soul."

She chuckled and gulped back the remaining contents of her wine goblet.

"If your wish is to dishonor yourself, please continue," she said.

"My poetry only reflects a society whose God does not forbid them from enjoying the pleasures of the world that He has created for them, as opposed to your own people's views, which seem to indicate a very distinct fear of … pleasure."

"On that note you have found something that we can both agree on, completely. In fact, it's my most cherished goal to help my people overcome this fear and embrace romance, in any way possible. Tonight, perhaps?"

She smiled at him, holding her eyes on his for what seemed to El-Adel like an eternity before drawing them gradually downward to pour more wine.

El-Adel's lips turned puffy, and his heart raced. He savored her lingering scent before releasing a profound exhale and turning to one of his emirs with a conquering smile.

To Richard, who watched from the corner like a game hawk, it was clear that Adel was smitten and Joanna was desperate; and perhaps the king had just won the whole damn war in time to be home for Christmas.

As Uther drained the last of his cup, the king abandoned his goblet in favor of the wine pitcher itself before speaking.

"Just so we're clear, I didn't race to that scene because of a book. You deserve a better death than that, Uther—an honorable death, not in Jerusalem, not even in England, but in the new worlds yet to be explored. It's my sincere hope that you'll have the chance to use the skills that you've learned on this quest to save lives instead of taking them."

"Sometimes, I think I'm OK with ending my part in the fight, one way or another."

"I doubt they'll be taking you down just yet, old man. You were right though, about many things, and I won't forget it. And now, with what's coming, I'll need your help more than ever."

Richard looked at Uther with a glint in his eye that Uther had seen before—when they'd left Sicily, when they'd pursued the emperor in Cyprus, when they'd won Acre, and right before they'd left it. It was a look that had frightened Uther to the core, and that was when he knew that he was not leaving. Richard still had plans, and Uther could not just abandon his king, not after Uther had been saved by him. Just as the original Templars had remained in Jerusalem when others returned home after the first Crusade was won, out of loyalty to an idea, Uther was in it till the end now out of loyalty to his friend;

no matter how much of a bastard he could be at times. Somehow, reaching that place of surrender brought Uther more peace than he had felt at any time since leaving England. *This* was his true mission.

✝✝✝

A few days later, when El-Adel told his brother what Richard had proposed after the party, Salah ad-Din almost laughed out loud.

"Adel … what are you thinking? This is, without a doubt, the most ridiculous, scheming …"

"He is serious, brother. So am I … if she'll have me."

"A Christian woman and a Muslim man getting married and sharing the kingdom…as if everyone is just going to lay down their weapons while you're on honeymoon?"

"If Joanna and I marry, all of these lands, including Jerusalem, would be jointly owned, but technically contained under my name, *our name*. This could be the secret to the peace that has eluded us for over a hundred years!"

"Mischief is all I sense. You've become too close to this king."

"That's because he is a good man. I swear that you two have more in common than you know. If you would just meet him … you'd see it. He wants to leave, and he's trying to find a way for us all to get what we want."

"They will never leave. Look into my eyes, and tell me that you are not blinded by love … or one night of love."

"Have you given up on hope completely?"

"Don't say that word. We are at war. I don't know why you're suddenly forgetting that. … What am I saying? Of course I know why."

Salah ad-Din knew exactly the right gaze combined with a certain tone of voice that would make his younger brother feel six years old again. But Adel was not yielding so easily this time. He addressed his older brother by his first name.

"Yousif, you once told me that letting go of fear is the key to understanding life. I know you remember this …"

"I was young then. Things are more complex now."

"Only because you choose to see them that way."

"You can't possibly appreciate the burden that I carry, and it is truly unfair for you to put me in this position. Besides, while you have been feasting with our enemy, there have been recent developments that may flip the board in our favor without any of these stunts. Conrad of Montferrat, the Lord of Tyre, has just proposed his own plan for peace. He despises Richard, and with my assistance, he intends to ambush Acre and kick Richard, along with all of his high ambitions, out of our lands. This is a very appealing offer, Adel, even if Conrad is a Crusader. You must understand that Richard is the most dangerous of them all. He wants Egypt and more; I'm sure of it."

"No, he doesn't. You have to trust me; he wants to fight for Jerusalem, yes, but he knows that he needs to save face and return home as well. He is ready to deal, and he understands the power of compromise. There is trust between us, and once we have an agreement, he will leave; then we'll have peace, pure and simple. No more death, a time to rebuild—isn't that what we have wanted?"

"You have seen this man fight, yet you can honestly speak these words to me that he wishes peace? I think you've forgotten yourself, and forgive me for saying it, you've done a disservice to God by putting your trust in this devil. But … for you, my beloved El-Adel, I will pray on it and hold off on Conrad's offer—for now. But I implore you to do the same, and ask yourself, ask God, if she is really worth it."

†††

By the time Richard received Saladin's answer to his proposal, it didn't even matter; Joanna had flatly refused on principle, even though she would have sat on the throne of Jerusalem in the apex of luxury. If there was one thing Richard could count on, it was someone in his family stubbornly messing up his plans. Regardless, it was clear to him now that he had been delusional and that the scheme had been faulted from the start. Even if everyone agreed to it, Richard still would have had to convince the Pope, and wait weeks, if not months, for an answer. Also, Richard's dogmatic Christian army was so collectively shocked by the idea of a Muslim marrying a Christian woman that all of the goodwill built up by the party dissipated instantaneously. They had come to the Holy Land to charge Jerusalem's walls, flay its occupiers, and walk the streets as bloody winners, so why was the king trying to cut a deal on the side with the enemy?

Richard knew that he had messed up. He had held out for the high stakes when he could have cut an easy deal and made a clean break. Now there would be no deals, just an army that was increasingly hesitant to follow him, yet furious that he was not leading them to glory. He decided that, if nothing else, he would call their bluff. He had spent too many nights bent over his plans by candlelight anyway; he needed to get out and start doing something.

The squires were given the royal decree to spread.

"In three days, Jaffa shall be empty of anyone who has pledged the oath and can fight. We leave to take Jerusalem."

✝✝✝

As Richard prepared to leave Jaffa, his mind dwelled on the past, and he could feel his father's claws digging in. He realized how much scorn he had heaped on the old man for the same indecisiveness, rash thinking, and hastily planned schemes that he himself now committed. He wondered if it was simply inevitable that he would descend along the same disappointing path without any chance to break free.

In truth, he missed his dad and tried to remember a time when they had still gotten along, hoping to recall some advice that his father had given him to use as a beacon. Neither good memories nor words of advice could help him now though; he was on his own, and he would need to forget his father's mistakes and figure out how to deal with his own if he ever wanted to find the path to Jerusalem.

✝✝✝

The Crusader march started up again and wound slowly southward from Jaffa toward Jerusalem. Richard left behind as much baggage as he could, but he wished that he could have left his army. They were a sack of hammers around his neck—pacified, slow minded, and fat on fruits and nuts. Even the tougher knights, fresh from their new mistresses' homes, had naïve smirks and unfocused eyes. These men were not ready for the next twenty-two days of punishing hail, freezing wind, torn-up tents, rotten bread, rusted armor, drowned horses, and endless mud everywhere. The strongest man, who only a few weeks ago was walking tall in the gardens of Jaffa, was now stooped, shivering, and cursing Richard's name.

Trying to imagine attacking Jerusalem with this hung-over procession was so horrifying a notion that Richard refused to face it. He pushed on relentlessly, dragging them as far as they could go, until eventually, despite all awful odds, they made it to camp in a clearing near Beit Nubar, a day's march from Jerusalem.

Richard was once again exalted in the minds of his army, and a celebratory joy washed over the camp. They were suddenly within reach of everything for which they had worked, and Richard was closer to his goal than ever before. As he settled in that night, an envoy visited him with eagerly awaited news from England.

Just when the situation had been looking up, Richard's worst fears were confirmed; his resentful younger brother Prince John was openly working with King Philip to carve up all of Richard's territories in England and France. The longer it took Richard to win back Jerusalem, the more likely it would be that when he returned to Europe he would no longer have a kingdom of which to be king.

In the moments of reflection that followed, Richard held tight to an unfortunate but impossible-to-deny revelation; he had to dedicate his energies less toward conquering the Holy Land and more toward pulling free of it, or it might permanently soil his reputation and ruin his entire life. This drove him to put his energies rashly behind a new plan; he would take the focus off of himself by initiating the process of choosing a new "King" of Jerusalem to sit on the throne once Richard had presumably won it back and left. This would imply to the common soldiers that, despite what Richard knew in his heart, victory in Jerusalem was all but certain.

Against his better judgment, Richard turned to the old guard Franks for advice on whom to nominate for king. These were Humphrey's and Guy's people, the Europeans who had grown up in the Holy Land since their great-grandfathers had conquered it in the First Crusade a hundred years before. They were the ones who had governed the place before Guy had lost Jerusalem to Saladin.

They had no new ideas, mostly because they were too busy being terrified. They had grown too comfortable in the Holy Land and had forgotten that they were thieves squatting in someone else's house. As Richard grimly showed them to their horses, they pledged allegiance to anything he could come up with to win.

After the meeting, Richard stayed behind to dine with King Guy, Henry of Champagne, and Robert de Sable. After his third cup of wine, Guy brought up what no one in the room wanted to think about.

"I hear news of the King of Jerusalem to be crowned once again.

Though we may not possess the holy city, I will hold my crown high and gladly rule in exile in Acre."

The next thing that Guy felt was the edge of Richard's fist crushing his nose. He did not even fight back as Richard locked his fingers around Guy's throat.

"It's your fault ... We're only here because you lost it ... I should have been ruling England ... I would have brought Europe out of the dark and built a land of glory. ...Instead I'm stuck here with you, branded by your spreading legacy of trash."

The only sound Richard heard as the others tried to pry him off was Guy's heaving gasps and the clanging bell in his mind. Guy's tongue dangled over the edge of his lips, and the only noise he heard was Richard's roaring whisper in his ear.

"... You will never be king...I will put my worst enemy on the throne before I give it to you..."

Finally, after Guy had accepted his fate, with his face almost purple, Henry and Robert succeeded in pulling Richard away.

†††

At first light, without warning, Richard packed up and led the Crusaders out of Beit Nubar. The abrupt departure did not sit well with anyone, but when they arrived at the still glowing embers of what was once Ascalon, the anger became livid confusion; why in hell were they turning away from Jerusalem to occupy a port that the enemy had just burned down? Once again, Richard had lost the fickle mob.

Richard knew exactly why he had returned to Ascalon, and he did not care what anyone thought. His legacy would forever be linked to the status of Jerusalem, and if he could not conquer it himself, then whoever had the guts to try after him would use the nearby, rebuilt port of Ascalon to launch their attack. If they were successful, they would owe their victory to Richard, and his name would live well down the line, no matter how many sins he had committed.

There was an initial wave of deserters, but for those who stayed, something extraordinary happened. Amidst the fog of failure that blanketed the smoldering port, they lost themselves in the work at hand. The rebuilding gave them something to do with eager muscles, and it was not long before they stood tall and cursed Richard less. With clear eyes and reborn strength, they seemed like an army that could do great and terrible things again.

Uther had finally healed enough to return to guard duty, where he expected to find the king's morale soaring. Instead, while walking to the king's tent, he encountered Richard in disguise as a poor pilgrim. He caught the king's gaze, and Richard smirked, pulling his hood in tighter and ambling over.

The king had stopped shaving and now had a regular beard, along with a weary, distant look in his eyes. He pulled two sacks of wine from his belt, handed one to Uther, and eagerly polished off the other with gulping mouthfuls that dribbled down his chin as he spoke.

"When I started this quest, I thought I was the luckiest man in the world. Anything seemed possible. Now look at me."

Richard and Uther spent the day together rebuilding a burned-out sea wall. Working in silence, Richard stayed until he was the last one there. That night he had vivid dreams in which he constructed a magnificent tower made of cubes of light solidified like stone. It soared into the sky and spread across the land until it was everywhere and everything. It was so blindingly bright that it overwhelmed Richard, and with his bare hands, he smashed it all until there was nothing but dust.

✝✝✝

Since the day Richard had joined the Crusade, one name had stalked his mind around every moment of confident joy and unhinged optimism: Conrad of Montferrat. It was the name of every person who second-guessed Richard, was not afraid of him, or would not follow his orders just because he was king. On top of the fact that Conrad had stolen the wife of Humphrey, Richard's ally, he had also denied Richard a safe port in Tyre when the king had first arrived in the Holy Land. Worst of all, Richard's spies had recently confirmed that Conrad was actually working with Saladin against Richard. As such, it was with the utmost shame and regret that Richard arrived for the meeting that morning to make Conrad the new King of Jerusalem.

Richard's scheming had truly, definitively backfired. His plan for establishing a new king had been all but decided without him by the scheming Crusader nobles, and now the man who was Richard's last possible choice to succeed him in the Holy Land sat expectantly in front of him. Richard was in too deep to change course, so he would eat his shoes and make an ally of an enemy to help pick up the pieces of the mess he had made.

"Conrad, thank you for making the journey south. How's Tyre?"

"Expanding. My engineers are irrigating a patch of land that we kicked some heathen farmers off of. They'd barely been able to scratch out a few olive trees. I'm going to turn it into an oasis."

"That's … wonderful news. Our great Christian cities of Tyre and Acre shall remain pillars standing strong as testaments of our achievements in God's land."

"Ah, but wouldn't it be something to add the only city that matters to that list. Saladin has disbanded his army. Any half-practiced band of marauders could pick Jerusalem as easy as spring carrots," said Conrad.

"I hear similar things. Our intent is to go there and do just that, but

I'll confess that several concurrent issues distract me. One day when you…perhaps, attain a similar title, you will find a great difference in the responsibilities of a township administrator and those of a king."

"A great man once told me that a lord is a lord. His name was King Philip," responded Conrad.

"He is someone that I, too, think of lately."

"I'd imagine you would."

Seeing Conrad grin after these words tested Richard to remain civil.

"I don't want to drag this out, Conrad, so I'll confess that my desire is to depart soon, regardless of what happens in Jerusalem. The time has come for me to admit my accomplishments and let the True King attend to the affairs of the Holy Land. Our territories here— what remains of them, will need strong leadership."

Richard rose and stood in front of Conrad, looking down at the short, unkempt man insipidly wearing double layers of chain mail for protection. Richard could not help but sneer as he continued.

"I've brought you here to make you King of Jerusalem. Whether I am able to retake the city or not in this Crusade, if you wish it, you will be the one who is in charge of all that I have won, after I leave."

Conrad had expected this, but actually hearing it made him giddily unsteady.

"I shall … accept … but, I must … think it over, to decide if … ah, I mean, to…"

Richard backed away slowly, never breaking eye contact as Conrad continued.

"What I mean is … I just need some time to think about this … I mean to uh, I'd like some time to prepare for accepting this."

"You shall have none. Do not misunderstand me, Conrad; I need someone to do this, and if it's not you, then I'll find another. You are detestable enough maybe to be able to do what is necessary to hold our interests together here."

"Then I will. I deserve it."

"Yes, of course you do. GOOD, it's done then. My envoys will facilitate the proper transfer of power. I will march on Jerusalem and eventually back to England, and if I don't make it to either place, then all of these bets that we've placed on the table together disappear, and you can sit in your oasis in Tyre and call yourself whatever title you wish. Now, please, get out of my sight."

✝✝✝

Richard rubbed his scratchy chin and pushed a burgeoning smile onto his face as he marveled at the rebuilding efforts that were slowly pulling Ascalon up and into something that resembled a city again. A weight had come off of his shoulders since making peace with Conrad. Despite any misgivings, it was perfect timing as it coincided with a grim letter arriving from Richard's mother Eleanor in England.

In a dire tone, she begged Richard to disembark immediately for the two month journey home. Richard's brother John had brought in mercenaries, propped up by King Philip's money, who roamed freely and harassed anyone who did not swear loyalty and pay tribute. People were truly suffering, and there was no one to help.

Reading the letter put Richard's heart in a vise. He could not ignore it any longer; his deluded dreams could only carry him so far. Now that he had a solution, and someone to take over the problems, he owed it to his father's ghost to go home and save the land of his ancestors. Still, for a moment he contemplated letting it go. If his brother John wanted it all so much, let him have it. Richard was so close to his dream now; maybe it was time for him to think more about his own future and less about things from his past.

He was roused from his gloomy trance by the bark of an envoy from Tyre.

"I'm sorry, Sire, King Conrad is dead, stabbed by Muslim killers called Hashishans as revenge for looting a ship of theirs that had wandered into Tyre."

Richard felt as if his whole body had been stuffed into a small hole. The words that he muttered to himself pinpointed the only man who hated Conrad more than Richard, a man whose grudge had apparently driven him to seek an alliance with the best killers in the land; a man who had grown up there and who had the contacts, and who could afford to pay the right people to enable the Hashishan ship to gain access to Tyre, thus creating an easy alibi; a man who had long since let the part of himself die that cared about anything other than revenge.

"Damn you, Humphrey."

✝✝✝

Word spread quickly of Conrad's death and with it came the assumption that Richard would abandon the quest for Jerusalem. It did not take long for a consensus to build amongst the Crusaders to disregard the king either way and go it alone; they had had enough of Richard's fickle moods. Upon hearing this, Richard barked a rage-filled laugh and, with a malicious glint in his eye, wrote a note to Robert De Sable in Jaffa to gather every able-bodied Templar, along with the siege engines and any knights that he could find, meet in Ascalon in a few days, form up the attack, and begin the liberation of Jerusalem. Till then, Richard wanted to ride, and he did not care where.

When the scouts brought word of Muslims raiding the supply lines, it seemed like a gift from heaven. Richard rode out with a detachment of guards, including Uther, and it was not long before they encountered a band of Saladin's soldiers.

The enemy swords were sharp and well wielded, but they could not compare to the king's crossbows. Soon there was a pile of dead Muslims, and Richard rode-on in mad triumph, kicking his horse faster up the hill and praying for more enemies to cut down. When he arrived at the summit, he glimpsed something that caused him to stop his horse abruptly. In the distance, a vision came into focus of an austere walled city, standing just far enough away that Richard could cup his hand around it.

Jerusalem.

It felt like his heart would shatter in his chest. Less than three miles away was everything that he had fought, bled, and probably lost his entire kingdom for, and he knew in that moment that he would never have it. Now that it was finally in front of him, he was ready to admit it; with his army limping and half-mad, he couldn't take the city, and even if by some miracle he did, he wouldn't be able to hold it. He would be overrun in a few months, and then he would forever be known as the man that let Jerusalem burn. As brave as he was, he didn't want to die for a lost cause. There was no way, no sensible chance, and in that moment he reached the end of his rope. He dropped to his knees, put his head to the ground, and finally erupted.

"WHY?! WHAT MUST I DO?! HOW MANY MORE MUST I KILL?! WHAT MORE MUST I PROVE!? JUST TELL ME THE ANSWER! TELL ME!!!"

He wished he could cry, but he had nothing left. Dry frustration transmuted into hollow acceptance, and he rode as fast as he could in the other direction.

†††

Salah ad-Din had arranged a meeting with his most trusted counselors to discuss an alarming development. One of his envoys had returned as the only survivor of an unprovoked ambush by King Richard on a ridge near Nabi Samwil, less than three miles from Jerusalem. The king was clearly restless and eager to fight, and this combined with increased activity on the Crusader supply lines meant that it was only a matter of time before the siege on Jerusalem would begin. Despite this, Salah ad-Din comforted himself with the thought that even if Richard did attack, between the deteriorating Crusader spirit and the king's indecisiveness, the Muslims could outlast it. He realized, however, that he had thought the exact same thing almost a year ago to the day, before Acre had fallen.

To assuage his nagging paranoia, he sent another detachment of riders to spy on Richard, just as the last guest arrived: Baha, Salah ad-Din's childhood friend. Once inside, Baha was clearly happy to be away from the clamoring soldiers departing for certain death. Salah ad-Din was quick to change the subject.

"I need to eat; I've been starving myself with grief and stress, so I'm having a banquet brought. We'll indulge like men who have made God proud."

Along with Salah-ad Din's best generals, they sat in a circle and ate quietly as if a sandstorm was passing outside. Baha cut through the silence.

"There is a reality beyond the King of England. He is just one man, and this is just one war. God doesn't force our hands to fight him, He lets us make our own decisions, and He'll judge us for them just the same."

Salah-ad Din was taken aback and responded hastily.

"Baha, remember why we're fighting. Remember what happened after Jerusalem fell. You can still see the bloodstains on the walls; Muslim, Jew, gypsy, man, woman, child, anyone who didn't pay allegiance to the cross, all cut down…"

Becoming flushed and gesturing excitedly with his hands, Salah ad-Din continued, "… Because, let me tell you what happens next. If Jerusalem becomes a Christian city again, they'll flock to it and multiply and spread out, until they completely surround us. We'll be refugees in our own homes. Everything rests on Jerusalem, and we must do everything we can to defend it."

Salah druh-Mehtria, whom Salah ad-Din considered his wisest general, interjected.

"I believe, as you do, that this man can end our way of life, but as difficult as it is to say, we must not make a final stand at Jerusalem. Ascalon is what's important now. Our spies say that the king has rebuilt it. Whether it's him or another, they'll use it to light a fire under us worse than anything we've seen. We must let Jerusalem go in order to focus our efforts on Ascalon. If not, we risk losing everything."

Salah ad-Din's lower lip fell, but no words followed. Salah druh-Mehtria was his most objective, honest strategist, and if he said it, it was scripture. There was little to talk about afterwards as everyone hastily finished eating and retired to their tents. Salah ad-Din never left; sitting alone, he sipped tea late into the night and quietly prayed for a way to hold it all together.

✝✝✝

Uther's eyes creaked open. As he shakily raised an arm to rub away the crusted blood in his eyes, his whole body rippled with pain. Slowly he remembered attacking the Muslims with Richard—the fight, the swift enemy rider that chased Uther onto a narrow ridge, and soon the path that ran out in front of him. With quick thinking, Uther had stopped his horse suddenly and surprised the enemy who rode right into a dagger in the sternum, killing him instantly. The knife, however, had not pulled free of the thick leather armor, and as the body fell, it tangled Uther in the straps, and the combined weight caused one of the horses to pitch a foot near the side of the ridge. The last thing Uther could recall was both sets of man and beast tumbling over the edge and Uther's disbelief that it could all end that simply.

But it had not; a Templar who sat nearby had apparently found him.

"When you did not return, the king sent me to scout. With your horse dead and mine exhausted, I made camp for the night."

The Templar handed him a bowl of broth, and Uther knocked back a mouthful.

"Not bad. Where did you get the meat?"

"I hope you weren't too attached to your horse."

Uther's hunger and the deliciousness of the soup overrode any shock he might have felt at what was considered a high crime amongst knights.

"I'm Uther Pendraig. From England."

"I know who you are, Sir Uther. We all do."

"I'm sorry, have we met? I'm a Templar, but I work directly for the king."

"I'm Sir Paul Amblefet, from France. We haven't met, but you're well known to the Templar ranks. I'm glad I found you; you made it far from where the king last saw you. I was almost ready to give up."

"What happened? Is the king all right?"

"The king… has taken the army back to Jaffa and soon to Acre. I believe the Crusade is over."

Uther responded with a slight, confirming nod.

"I wish I could say I'm surprised, Sir Paul."

"I always assumed that Richard and Saladin would be locked in it till the bloody end. If I was a betting man, I'd have wagered good coin that their spirits would battle between the Christian and Muslim heavens after they died."

"You really think Richard is going to heaven?

"Of course. That was decided from the moment he took the oath of Crusade. No matter what else he may have done, it guaranteed the ultimate reward.

"Doesn't that strike you as a bit too easy? Killing and stealing land are sins. Sins send you to hell, don't they?"

"That's for God to decide."

✝✝✝

The next morning, Uther felt well enough to travel, yet after he and Sir Paul arrived back at the camp, they spent the rest of the day vomiting. Saladin had poisoned the wells within a three-mile radius of Jerusalem not long before Paul had made the soup. Uther, who had eaten only one bowl, had passed out vomiting and awoke feeling weak but stable. Paul wasn't so lucky. Uther buried him just as the last Crusaders were starting their march out of Jaffa.

Richard was already in Acre, having left secretly a few nights earlier. As hard as it was for him, he was decisive this time in ending his quest. Once settled in Acre, disguised in monk's robes, he found a comfortable chair at the tavern and began the process of drowning his days in a bottle. All of his previous accomplishments seemed like a great ascent to enable a harder fall. He did not deserve the prize; that was clear now, but what frustrated him most, was that there had been a part of him that had always known it. If he had only been brave enough to admit it to himself, he knew that he could have saved them all a lot of trouble.

He remembered something that his father had told him when he had reached manhood: "Don't expect too much, and you won't be disappointed; life has a way of luring you into the hunt, thinking the fox is soon to be trapped, only to leave you lost in a strange shire, wondering how you ended up there, with the fox long gone."

At night, when Richard stumbled back to his quarters where his wife slept warmly, instead of slipping in behind her and wrapping his arms around, he laid a blanket on the floor and curled up on it like a dog. There he spoke the words that had become his regular refrain before sleep, whether said softly aloud or repeated in his head, aimed at no particular person, deity, or himself, but just to say them.

"I'm sorry."

†††

When Uther finally returned to Acre, he found Richard weeks drunk, with hired musicians playing loudly nearby while he sat alone with his head in his hands. He was not ready for Uther's urgent news.

As Uther was leaving in one of the last caravans out of Jaffa, Saladin's soldiers commenced a surprise attack, swiftly overrunning the skeleton crew of mostly one-limbed knights who had been left to defend the city. The crescent flag now flew over Jaffa's walls. Uther had escaped by the skin of his teeth to tell the king.

Richard immediately dunked his head in water, had one more glass of wine, and began planning.

†††

The next morning in Jaffa, Salah ad-Din smiled as he felt the early sun shine on his face. He had outwitted Richard, who was now far up the coast in Acre, and with the wind at his back, Salah ad-Din would use Jaffa as a stage to retake Ascalon. As his men set up checkpoints around Jaffa, Salah ad-Din was permitted barely a few days of accomplished pride before receiving the news that Richard was on his way.

†††

At the head of a cluster of ships, sailing as swiftly as hunted fish toward Jaffa, stood the sober, focused Lionheart. During the trip, the king took the opportunity to speak privately with each of his confidantes, including Uther.

"Sire, will it be a long fight?"

"I'm trying to make fewer predictions about combat strategy these days. We'll leave the Holy Land soon, but first we'll rescue our brothers. Tell me though, have you thought about what you'll do after all of this?"

"I guess I'll go to my village and try to find my family—my parents, my brother. Gwen. By now it's hard to imagine that she ever existed at all, or any of it, really. I'm not so sure that I can just go back to turning soil. It will take some adjustment not to expect an arrow through the neck."

"Rest assured old man, your hands won't touch a speck of dirt again. Your accumulated royal back-pay alone will be enough for three manors."

It took a moment to sink in, but Uther felt a little less naïve this time as he quickly remembered all the false promises of the past. He played along anyway.

"Thank you, Sire … I don't know what to say. Thank you."

"I know that you might be considering my… changeable manner, but you've earned every coin and more. You'll get everything I say; I swear it to God and on my ancestors' souls in heaven. After all of this is over, promise me that you find me, and it shall be made so."

"I promise … I won't forget."

"Good, because there's one last thing that I need to request of you when you return."

†††

Six days into the occupation of Jaffa, the Crusader fleet arrived. When they emerged onshore, Richard promptly began the carnage on foot. With each life-robbing stab and slice of his blade, Richard imagined what the attack on Jerusalem might have been like. He could only have hoped that he would have seen his flag flying over its walls as quickly as it was over Jaffa's again.

That night, fully expecting a counter-attack in the morning, Richard took the bold move of setting up his camp outside the city walls. He had had the monks salt-cure the best parts of cattle rounded up in Jaffa, and now they turned them on spits and washed them down with freshly cracked barrels of ale.

"To our last merry adventures in the Holy Land. To Saladin for giving us a sporting chance, and to the maidens for greeting us when we return home."

The cups were clanked, and the men ate heartily while chanting drunken hymns and celebrating what could be their last night alive. The king drained his cup and retired to bed earlier than usual. When he woke in the morning, he immediately rode into the hills to scout the area. Nothing.

The king looked up at the day's young sun and decided that he would call Saladin's bluff and make first contact. It was time for a final face-to-face, even if Saladin still would not meet with him.

✝✝✝

Salah ad-Din himself was there to meet Uther as he was led into camp. To Uther's surprise, the Muslim leader was bright and jovial, with kind eyes and an easy smile. He did not walk with the chest-out stride of a noble but rather with a relaxed, humble gait that would have made it easy to mistake him for a merchant who had never picked up a sword in his life. He looked Uther over as if weighing something.

"It's fascinating to meet you, Sir Uther. You are not a stranger to my soldiers; you've survived many battles with luck that seems gifted by God. I myself have watched you just barely avoid death before splitting my soldiers' skulls. They call you 'Rabah-Iblis,' 'The Conqueror Devil.'"

Upon hearing this, Uther's stomach dropped. The Muslims must hate him to the core. Perhaps Richard made a mistake in sending him. As it rolled over in Uther's mind, Saladin must have seen it clearly.

"Please relax; I'm only trying to be light. Trust that you're welcomed here as a respected envoy and are in no danger. I swear it to God and on the souls of my family."

"Thank you for your kindness, Great Sultan."

"No need for formalities. Saladin is fine; I know that it's what your people call me, and I wear it proudly. I'm just a man who has a knack for strategy, no more, no less. Did you know that when I first recaptured Jerusalem, your people said that I was the spawn of dogs and that I had a forked tongue?"

He smiled again, squinting his eyes and pushing out his tongue like a child.

"See, even if I am a son of a bitch, at least my tongue is normal."

As Uther relaxed inside Saladin's palace, bountiful plates of food were served. Saladin boldly grabbed a pile of lamb and onions and chewed with a messy, beaming grin, motioning for Uther to do the same. They ate together heartily like adrift sailors who had just found land.

"I can't begrudge any man who honors my table with such a solid appetite. I can only hope, Sir Uther, that your time in these lands has been inspiring in some way."

"It's beautiful here. It really is like Eden."

"You know, my scholars believe that they know where the real Eden was! Southeast of Baghdad there's an inlet near the sea where they believe that there was once a great, lush forest that was washed away by a massive flood, just like our myths of Gilgamesh and yours of Noah. So we aren't so different after all, right? Can I be honest with you? I love Western culture. Your Arthur stories are some of my favorites. Tell me, do you miss your home?"

"I miss my life before the war. Bad leaders have overrun the land there, which is why my king wishes to end his present condition here and return. He believes, as I hope you do too, that there's no advantage for either of us to keep doing this."

"Good then, I accept the offer."

Salah ad-Din smiled and nodded.

"… Additionally, I propose that you can have the country from Tyre to Caesarea and that the place where Christ was sacrificed in Jerusalem, the Church of the Holy Sepulcher, valued so highly by Christians, shall be open to pilgrims without question. This is in accordance with your agreement that my flag will fly over the uncontested city of Jerusalem. Also, Ascalon must be destroyed."

"My king will not look favorably upon that last item, for he holds Ascalon close to his heart, having rebuilt it after you burned it down. He's prepared to share it with you and even offer you the services of his troops stationed there."

Saladin laughed loudly in a mocking manner.

"How does he expect to hold onto all that land after he's gone? Even if he stays, we'll take it back—God willing. My men will keep coming, and they'll whittle away your king's holdings, and you personally, Sir Uther, may not survive as you have in the past. You're still in the prime of your youth, and what a sad thing to dash away your life in these old men's wars. That's why I'm so glad that you're here."

Saladin's words were followed, again, by that beaming, boyish smile that was starting to make Uther uncomfortable. Saladin continued.

"You've accomplished so much here, but now it's time to leave. I want peace as much as you do, but the terms are in my favor. If your king truly wants the same, then he must do what he knows is right, and go without quarrel. I know that he wishes to secure something for his legacy before he leaves. I respect that, but he no longer has the army to carry that out."

Saladin did not look angry, but the change in tone reminded Uther again where he was. Every Muslim grunt that Uther had slain haunted him where he sat. No matter what Saladin had said earlier, the enemy surrounded him now and could swarm him like locusts at any moment, especially if the wrong words fell from his mouth. That was when he decided to drop any pretenses.

"Saladin, the king has a name to protect. He needs to leave with something."

"Yes, he has Acre. He has Jaffa … for now. I want you to understand something, Sir Uther, and help your king to understand as well: I freely acknowledge that I'm not young anymore. I have no more use for the pleasures of the world; I've had my share and have long since forsaken them. With age comes focus, and I can wait here as long as it takes, in the lands of my forefathers, surrounded by my family, to sweep the dust off the bones of any man who your king leaves to hold onto his winnings. He's more than fought his way to a name that will live through the ages, but if he truly wishes to put his legacy down in chiseled stone then let him stay and take his chances. I'd be happy to give him the chance to write a proper end to his story."

Saladin smiled one more time before having Uther escorted to his horse. Uther suspected that the message meant for Richard hinted at other messages of which Uther could only peek at from a distance. It almost felt as if the old sultan was goading them on, wanting to see what kind of show Richard could give him, and knowing that Richard had one more good show left to give.

†††

On the morning of the attack, the scouts identified Richard's tent at almost the exact moment that he awoke. Hope for a surprise attack was gone; Richard rode out immediately and saw the formations. Deep in his bones, he knew that it was time for his last battle in the Holy Land.

The flaccid Crusaders were woozy and vastly outnumbered, but they were ready to fight as much as their king was. They hastily formed up the lines; a throng of archers backed the infantry, and behind that stood eighty of the toughest remaining knights who, with only twelve horses remaining, would mostly charge on foot. The king strapped on his armor with disregard as he rode down the back line and saw vital men made of steel who deserved an honest victory.

"This will be the end of your pain. When you arrive in heaven, you'll be forgiven for everything. Go with a smile on your face, but first, let's avenge our deaths."

Richard held his lance aloft, the Crusaders mirroring him, and then it began.

They stampeded as hard as any of the charges from their previous battles, but the enemy's clustered shields repelled them, and the Muslims seeped in around the edges in endless numbers. Richard kicked his horse, broke from the Crusader column, and screaming in Latin, charged at full tilt straight into the two-thousand-strong Muslim line. He drove his sword into one neck, then another, then two more to his left, and onward in every direction as a radius of dropped bodies expanded out from his point of existence. He had been looking forward to this for a very long time.

Salah ad-Din watched nearby, just close enough to make out

faces. Though his line had been set up strong, Richard had crushed it, and ten minutes in, the dead were piling up as Richard worked methodically to even the odds. A large Muslim sergeant ran up and finally gave Richard pause by cutting out the legs from under his horse. For this pointless temporary triumph, the man paid for it with eternal sleep. Salah ad-Din called for his brother.

Now fighting on foot, out of the corner of his eye Richard saw an enemy galloping fast straight for him. He cocked back his sword and fixed his weight to stab through the man's face—until he saw that face and stopped.

El-Adel calmly dismounted and handed Richard the reins to the horse.

"My brother said that no matter what happens, he'll always want to fight you fairly, on your horse, as a true knight should be."

Richard flung himself coldly onto the saddle, nodded to El-Adel, and rode off.

†††

Hours later, more than three hundred of Saladin's men had fallen under the king's sword, and Richard just kept fighting. His face was the last thing that fathers, sons, brothers, and husbands saw that day; a ghoulish image that was burned into them as they left the world for whatever lies beyond.

Later, as the sun fell, seven hundred dead Muslim bodies hid the grass, and Richard had not stopped yet. Salah ad-Din was older than Richard by twenty years. He had fought in many wars and had killed countless people, but he had never seen anything like this. For the first time in his life, as a general, he knew that he would throw every man that he had at Richard before he would have to face the king himself. He was not ready to die and thought of his daughters and their children, before giving an order that he both regretted and hoped would bring an end to it all. Requesting that one of his top generals attack the king, Salah ad-Din was pleased as Nam-Sadeem immediately volunteered. He was a master rider, and he truly believed that he could surprise Richard and end the horror.

Fueled by frustration and pride, while tempering fear with focus, Nam-Sadeem rode up quick and light, just as he had promised. The general squared up for the perfect surprise kill, but at the last moment Richard flipped around and swung his sword downward in an arc so hard that it cut off the general's head, shoulder, and right arm in one chunk, all flopping to the ground in a spreading pool of red.

Richard dashed his hand in the blood and wiped a long streak slowly across his face. Knocking the decapitated body off of the horse, he jumped on and rode down the front of the Muslim line, holding his sword over his head. Hundreds of enemy soldiers stood frozen as Richard rode once more in the other direction for good measure, and then rode off into a nearby field and collapsed.

†††

The aroma from the gore-soaked grass floated up into Richard's nostrils. Every inhalation was embedded so deeply with the stench of extracted life that he would phantom-smell the odor for weeks. It was a massacre and an atrocity, accomplished by his own hands, and now he was paying for it as a fever descended upon him like none in the past. Over the first week, he wavered in and out of consciousness with no sign of improvement. By the second week, he was so mad with sickness that he ordered his men to carry him out to meet Saladin's envoys. It dispelled rumors that he was already dead, though he might as well have been to their eyes. He spat blood through chattering teeth and insisted that his army was staying. Salah ad-Din did not believe this story, so he sent El-Adel to confirm it.

"It's true. He's fevered, almost near death, but aware enough to request peace. We mustn't let this opportunity pass. If we make a decisive treaty now, they will break up and leave; I'm sure of it."

"There will never be peace! Why do you all refuse to accept this? The men from the West will haunt our doorway for a million generations down past our children!"

"What then? What are your terms?"

"Ascalon. We must have Ascalon. That or no deal."

†††

Richard was dying. He knew it. He had been sick many times before, but he had never felt this ill. He imagined that it was the unique sensation of one's body shutting down because it believed that it no longer deserved to live. For a third week, he drifted in and out of sleep, barely existing, as blood was drained regularly, and a woman was stationed to put his head in her lap and dab it with a damp cloth, which was customary for men near the end. After three more days, the fever finally broke, and with it, Richard's silence ended as he wrote to Saladin.

"This must end. If you agree to a truce now, I will leave, but if you deny me, I will stake my tents and push my will to the absolute brink to destroy you. I have renounced my quest for Jerusalem, and as you wish it, I renounce Ascalon. Save it or destroy it, I no longer care which. Accept this difficult concession, along with my respect; you beat me. I wanted so very much to see the view from the throne of Jerusalem, but it was not meant to be. If I could, I'd stay and joust with you as long as needed to find your weakness and win, but you've bested me for now. Fulfill my wish: make a pact with me, and let me go."

Salah ad-Din had the terms written up, brought back, and read to Richard who was still dazed from lingering intermittent fevers.

"Five year peace treaty, all pilgrims permitted freely in the

Church of the Holy Sepulcher, Crusaders keep the secured coastline from Acre to Jaffa and lose everything eastward, and the fortification at Ascalon to be destroyed."

"No, no, no! I said that I must be paid for Ascalon. I rebuilt that city with my bare hands! That has to count for something!"

Uther reassured the sickly, confused Richard that he had agreed to the terms as they were written. Richard turned back, extended his hand out from under the blanket to the surprised envoy, and spoke something in a mumble.

"All right. I will make peace."

†††

As summer slipped to autumn, Richard healed slowly in Acre. At night he slept before all others, and in the morning he was the last to rise. During the day he was coherent but depleted. As his condition improved slightly, he prepared to depart. A final correspondence from Saladin indicated flatteringly that he would rather lose the Holy Land to Richard than have any of his own sons take it over. The king crumpled the parchment and threw it off the dock.

Most of the knights had already departed for Europe. One in twelve that had arrived with Richard would rest their bones in the dirt of the Holy Land. Richard personally saw his friends Henry of Champagne and Robert de Sable off, and they each promised to return and finish the march to Jerusalem soon, or as soon as they could— or someday. The king equipped Uther and Robert of Locksley, his top Yeoman archer, for their journey back to England ahead of him, where Uther would fulfill the king's last request of him, made back on the boat trip to rescue Jaffa.

"After this is over, I do not expect to return home soon ... or really ever at all. I'll be hunted throughout Europe where Philip, John, and the Germans have poisoned my name with well-spread and repeated lies. I wish you could accompany me, but I need you in England. You'll find, I'm told, pockets of resistance in the deep woods and especially in the Sherwood forest near John's stronghold in Nottinghamshire. Go there and train the people's armies to take back their homes."

The king set them up with enough money to start, telling them to rob from John and his men "vigorously" and to spread it around to the commoners in the name of the true King Richard.

Before Uther left, potentially never to see Richard again, he offered words that he believed the king needed to hear.

"This was just one quest, one dream. It may be over, but it's not the only dream to be had, and it's not always our fault when they don't work out."

Richard nodded and then handed Uther a book. It was a Bible.

"I'm done with this for a while; the answers I'll need will be found elsewhere. I'm not giving it to you because I think you'll find God with it; I want you to hold it as a reminder of something besides this failed quest. The people who wave this around like a weapon are right about one thing: the world is crooked. It will beat you into the ground until you're up to your knees, so you must protect your heart, because that's what will keep you going, even when it's been torn to shreds. You must protect it, but not by closing it; keep it open, never hide it, show it to them, and walk with heavy steps that make the ground shift to hold you."

Uther took the Bible, and then he and Locksley, along with their band of insurgent knights, boarded the ship for home. Locksley took the everyman moniker 'Robin Hood' to hide his noble origins, and Uther was laughingly given Richard's favorite nickname for his traitorous little brother.

"Uther, have them call you 'Little John.' They will remember you from your size, and the name will remind them that the cruel man that has brought them so much pain is just another small person."

After boarding the ship, Uther opened the Bible that Richard had given him and found the inside cover signed, stamped with the king's royal seal, and containing a list of all of the possessions that he had promised to Uther on the way to Jaffa.

Then, at last, Uther was sailing to see his England again on October 9, 1192.

Three years later.

Part 9
Wolf's-Heads

Uther woke suddenly to a flash of ambient screeching sound. He closed his eyes again and tried to ignore it—probably just a wolf with a broken leg. It might have worried the other men in the brush—a cook, a boot smith, three farmers—but Uther had experienced enough real horror not to let the noises in the night keep him from a few more moments of rest. It was late and still dark, but the light would emerge soon, along with three horse-drawn carriages full of noble coin. The roadside traps had all been set, and Uther's band was ready to fight. The men with him were not Crusaders, just victims of Prince John and his thugs. Bullied and taxed, those oppressed by John felt that they had no choice but to fight back. Whether this was helpful or not, Uther was not sure; he had dealt with desperate men long enough to know that their thinking was not always the clearest.

Richard had predicted his own fate well and had disappeared on his way home. In the year since he and Uther had left the Holy Land, the only word of him had been rumors of his bloody royal tunic being found in a German tavern. Without their king, it had not been easy for Uther's band of rebels to stay dedicated to the cause. Locksley had been harder to work with than Uther had expected, losing his composure easily, doubting Uther's plans often, and worrying more about the views of the church than Uther cared for. Despite this, they had held it together and built something resembling an organized resistance.

The carts coming down the road included pay-offs meant for John's most loyal man in Nottinghamshire, a noble letch who had taken to designating himself "Sheriff" and who had been funded by John to put the whip to his neighbors. Uther's spies had indicated a large haul, so there would be substantial guards that Uther would do his best not to kill; he had seen enough blood, and these were still his countrymen. With his last words, Richard had instructed Uther in how to fight John but not in how to heal a broken kingdom. When Richard returned, England could be fully healed, but till that day arrived, even if it took many dusty decades, Uther would keep himself occupied with the basics: resist, rob, and run like hell into the night.

With the procession in sight, Uther readied himself for another successful heist, or the last one. As the first horse's hooves clicked the trip line and its skull launched into the ground, Uther's merry mob were on the road with swords drawn before the carts had even turned over. Uther had insisted that no harm come to any women under the guise of chivalry, though in reality he hoped that one of the women he would encounter would be Gwen. As he helped a lady out of one of the carts, she told him that her name was Marion and that she had fantasized about meeting the leader of the rebels. Marion's beautiful gaze abruptly transformed into blood-splattered, twitching shock as an arrow pierced her throat. Uther's crew had barely sifted through the wreckage before the ambush rushed in, and they were outnumbered; it was a trap.

Uther bolted for the woods with the sheriff's men in tight pursuit. He was surprised at their substantial numbers, which meant that the Sheriff was beginning to take the rebels seriously. The slight trees of the shallow woods would not provide cover, so the race was on to escape into the deeper forest.

It seemed as though they never stopped running, and these were the times when Uther understood Locksley's frustration. Uther was tired of running too, but he was not ready to die, so he pushed himself as fast as he could go. His chest burned while his feet smashed through the dirt, but he was not pulling away. He could hear the mail around the pursuers' wrists clicking against their sword handles and their breath snorting through their helmets. In his mind he imagined the sound of his own death soon to come from a blade in his back. He could hear their boots moving closer, and he could hear the leaves swaying above it all. And then one more sound: the thump of arrows piercing arms, chests, and throats. Uther had reached the escape line, where Locksley and his archers were waiting in the trees.

Locksley may have been a spoiled noble snob, but he could shoot a carrot through a keyhole from three fields away, and he had taught his disciples well. As the arrows rained down on his pursuers, Uther reached the edge of Sherwood's deep forest and collapsed in exhaustion. His opponents fertilized the ground with their blood as they limped back to their sheriff, and Uther was home and lucky, one more time.

†††

At Salah ad-Din's palace, Hubert Waller was escorted in. Today the halls were made up more elaborately than usual; Bishop Waller was from England.

After the war ended, Salah ad-Din had made a point to invite European intellectuals passing through to discuss their beliefs and share ideas. Bishop Waller had asked him specifically for an interview. People in England followed the Crusades like spectators at a joust, and the bishop delighted in peppering his sermons with stories that he collected.

"How is King Richard?" asked Salah ad-Din almost immediately after shaking the bishop's hand.

"You are mistaken; our king is now John, Richard's brother. Richard never returned from his journey home. A page bearing the royal seal was discovered near Vienna with his throat cut and with no sign of the king. I pray for Richard's soul, wherever it may be."

The interview began with the two men discussing additional rumors that surrounded the king's disappearance. Bishop Waller, a respectful, eager man with kind eyes and a clean smile, softened the old sultan by clarifying details on his many famous battles and victories, before seeking the information that the bishop truly desired.

"If you'll oblige me, Sultan, there's something that people in England wish to know from you more than anything else: How were you able to defeat Richard the Lionheart?"

"It's a fitting name. I witnessed something more than a man in those few years that he was here, but I didn't defeat him; he was a victim of his own shortcomings, which, to be fair, is the predicament of many great men. He was tougher than anyone I'd ever fought, but his strength was his flaw. A lack of confidence prevents most people from achieving what they truly wish, but he had the opposite problem; he forgot that he had to do more than just fight, and it exhausted him. If he had put his mind to it and followed through, he would have decimated my weakened defenses, and you would be asking him this question about me, in Jerusalem."

This passage turned out to be one of only a few provocative moments in an otherwise boring interview, with the other coming toward the end when Saladin promised to fulfill any wish that the Bishop had, without question, as a show of respect to England and Richard. Bishop Waller requested to have English priests replace the ones that the Muslims had installed at the Church of the Holy Sepulcher, and as promised, it was enacted immediately.

A few months later, in the spring of 1193, Salah ad-Din finally succumbed to illness. He had lived out his last months in declining health amongst a full, loving house that was tempering sadness with joy in celebrating his life. Banquets were held, and his grandchildren crowded around their old Papa's bed. When he died in his sleep, a subtle smile reached across his lips. Before he passed, he had willed an ample inheritance to his family and donated whatever remained to charity, dying with nothing in his vaults and not a yard of land in his name.

✝✝✝

On the day that Richard let go of the Holy Land, he packed lightly and left the rest behind. He hit the sea in the late morning with a small group of guards and low expectations, imagining that the journey ahead would be like trying to step across a thin sheet of parchment without breaking through.

As the inevitable storms blossomed, the ship's crew doggedly pushed forward, hugging the coast to avoid the deeper, choppy waters. The wind took control and tore at the ship until it wrecked, forcing them to continue over land.

The goal was north, where refuge could hopefully be found with Richard's brother-in-law Henry in Bavaria, who might still feel forced to turn him away. There, held up in Germany, the King of England was just another outlaw. Every petty lord, poor bounty hunter, and wandering thug knew that Richard had departed the Holy Land, and their eyes would be extra sharp for him. Richard was not sure he could blame them, considering the massive bounty that had been offered by the German emperor.

All traces of noble royalty were stripped from Richard's small band. He disguised himself at various times as a monk, a Templar, and a merchant, switching clothes as routinely as the hours passed. They hid by day and traveled at night, broken into two sections to avoid arousing suspicion. Although they moved quietly in the dark, they were eventually discovered. Luckily for Richard, the leader of the gang of hoods turned out to be a former soldier who had fought with Richard at Acre. Instead of turning Richard in, the leader warned Richard of another ambush and gave him their fastest horses. The king's group scattered, leaving Richard with only one Templar guard and a page.

Uncertain of where they were even going, the king's fellowship of three rode far and fast. Three days passed as they journeyed through the freezing Alps without food, driven by starved perseverance. In a cruel coincidence, they were unknowingly riding directly toward the man who hated Richard the most: Duke Leopold.

The duke had arrived late after the capture of Acre and had tried to share the glory. In response, Richard had had his men pull down the German flag and deface it. Leopold left Acre in disgrace; it was not Richard's finest hour. Now he would be paying for it—possibly with his head.

Richard and his cohorts eventually made it to town and found a modest inn. The king gave the page money to buy food at the market. Though exhausted and desperate, Richard still should have known better, for the merchant selling stew meat was impressed and asked the page where he had obtained such funds. Upon the boy mentioning his rich master, the wrong ears were listening. When the German magistrates raided the inn the next day, Richard had nowhere to run. After searching every room at the inn, the magistrates found a tall man hunched over some pots in the kitchen with a soiled cloth draped over his shoulder that barely concealed his face. Richard made a solemn request for his travel mates to be spared, but their throats were cut, and the king was blindfolded and spirited directly to Duke Leopold's castle.

The duke had his entire court waiting there when Richard was brought before him. The king was forced to endure Leopold's satisfied, seething tirade where he spat on and kicked Richard, as he told the whole story of the king's inevitably failed quest to capture Jerusalem.

Richard had gone from hero to vagabond in a few years. His hair was short, his beard was long, and he was at the mercy of his worst enemies, but inside, his heart was still vital. Throughout the seemingly endless rant from Duke Leopold, retelling the tale of the king's high adventures, Richard's smile grew until he was practically laughing at each new sound that fell from the Duke's mouth. He was forced to endure three nights in the lowest dungeon sleeping with the rats, before being sent to the castle of the Holy Roman Emperor and ruler of Germany, Henry the Sixth, who had coins bursting from his eyes at the thought of the ransom that English royalty would fetch.

✝✝✝

Uther still had the picture, sketched by a dead man's hand, of Gwen. On the trip home he had made sure to keep it well covered and dry. It may not have been an exact match, but it was all that he had left. As far as he was concerned, he was staring right at her.

The trip was uneventful, and Uther soon found himself once

again soaking his boots in the English shore, not far from where he had left it. He wondered how that impetuous fool could be the same person he was now. The realization dawned on him that it had been a long three years away and everything would be different. That's when the arrow landed in the sand, inches from his foot.

At first he just stared, transfixed, wanting to believe that it had simply blown there on a strong wind, but when one of his shipmates went down with another arrow in his chest, the grim reality sunk in. Uther, Locksley, and the others darted into the woods in the direction of the shooter, but no more arrows came. Whoever it was, they were gone now, along with Uther's hopes of a calm, discreet return.

The attack proved to be a sad omen, as the land was crawling with Prince John's henchmen. Uther did not want this; he was done fighting and wished only a peaceful life, but he had made his promise to the King of England, his friend, who had saved his life many times, so he did as he was asked and went underground. Though Uther, Locksley, and their gang of veterans had spent the previous two years fighting for their country, they were now outlaws in their own home. Rebels. Fugitives. Outlaws. Wolf's-heads.

The weeks and months that followed were not easy. Uther's men stashed their supplies, but the hiding spot was looted, and for a while they lived in the dirt and robbed to survive. All the while, Uther wondered about Gwen. He was so close now, but he was still an outlaw with a pardon from a king in exile. Some nights he would rub dirt on his cheeks, shroud himself in a hooded cloak, and travel the taverns to see what he could find. He would talk to whomever looked trustworthy, subtly trying to find a connection—a cousin who lived near her village or an old neighbor's son's wife out for the night—anything that would lead to some information about Gwen's fate. He felt as if he had covered half of the towns in England when he finally found a relative by marriage of Gwen's aunt who revealed the unfortunate truth: Gwen had married a rich merchant, who had worked with her father, and now lived far north, near Scotland. Gone.

Maybe it was better this way. She had moved on and had probably forgotten about him. Maybe. Probably. It didn't matter; she was gone. There was nothing he could do about it, so he got back to work.

Along with his trifling band of outlaws, Uther robbed anything with John's royal seal on it. It was enough to seize the attention of John himself, who needed every coin he could muster to keep his men armed and well paid just in case Richard returned. John increased the amount of men that the sheriff had at his disposal. Though hammered and squeezed by the hunting parties, Uther and Locksley stayed light and moved often, maintaining their edge because of their low numbers. If the plan was to progress as intended, though, the numbers would not stay that way for long.

Change came quickly. The initial acts of thievery by Uther and his band accomplished their intended function and word spread of a band of veterans from the Crusades who were fighting back against John's tyranny. Locksley made inroads with nobles that he knew before he had left England, and many, even if they had paid-off John, were still loyal to Richard. Anyone who could be trusted was told to look for King Richard's seal carved into trees, leading a path to the constantly changing rebel base. Scouts were stationed at easy distances to prevent an ambush, and anyone new was watched very closely. Uther and his men had to be extraordinarily careful in the beginning or their plans could snuffed-out before they had even sparked. John had spies everywhere, and for most people, the fear of what John would do to those who crossed him outweighed the will to fight back. Even so, before Uther and Locksley even knew what they were doing, they had a number of recruits—ordinary, tough-willed men who were sick of what John had done to their country and were ready to do something about it.

Uther tried to keep a low profile, but his image was hard to forget. "Robin Hood" Locksley was the proclaimed leader, but his right hand man, the taller one that they called 'Little John,' was suspected to be the real leader. He had the Bible with the king's seal as well as the king's sword, and some even whispered that he guarded the Holy Grail, captured in Jerusalem. A few times Uther even impersonated Richard to fool some of John's men and help keep rumors about the king alive, but the longer they waited for true word of Richard's fate, the more frustrating the silence became.

✝✝✝

Richard was kept blindfolded for the entire three day travel to the palace of the German emperor where he was brought to his quarters that would be his cell for God-knows how long. The accommodations were bigger than he had expected and well furnished by royal standards. Though the guards insultingly lorded over him with swords brandished, Richard was just glad to lie down, spending many hours simply resting silently and still, contemplating all that had transpired from his long youth at battle with his family to his last few years playing bloody chess with Saladin. Jugs of locally pressed white wine were brought to keep him docile, and Richard took advantage of this to assist in marathon poetry writing sessions at night, while his days were filled with greetings from sympathetic visitors. He lost track of the hours and lost care of when he could leave. Eventually the guards became his friends, and he would greet them each morning and play cards to pass the time.

1192 wound down and passed into 1193, which dripped-by slowly like tree sap. Richard wiled away his days writing, reading, and sometimes just breathing the air with closed eyes—detained but carefree. Finally, as 1193 dried up and 1194 arrived, the massive ransom that Richard's steadfast mother Eleanor had raised, more than all of the money in the English economy, was placed in the German emperor's royal exchequer. Despite a tempting last minute offer from King Philip to pay more to keep him shackled, Richard was released in early spring, almost a year and half after they had cuffed him.

††††

When John received the parchment note about Richard's release, he tore it to shreds with his teeth. Little Prince John, the "soft sword" as they called him behind his back, had had a good run, but his brother was coming home, and all that John had done to prevent this confrontation was going to be tested.

John's bands of soldiers grew larger, moved faster, and tracked better. It had become a regular occurrence for Uther's scouts to run into the camp in the middle of the night with alarms to move quickly, and they took losses every time. Though they had grown used to staying in one place only briefly, they decided to make a permanent base deep in Sherwood, a forest whose narrow ridges, steep hills, and heavy growth made it difficult to travel. Around this time, however, one of their closest men was discovered to be a spy. Knowing their location and having the route in, the sheriff would unleash the full force of John's well-equipped henchmen to crush Uther's band for good. There would be no more robbing and no more running; they would be surrounded soon and outnumbered. It was time to take a stand.

They prepared for the impending attack by sharpening their swords and planting traps. Uther had forbade revenge killing, always insisting that the king would return soon and the rebels would need to call their traitorous countrymen neighbors again, but there would be no rules against carnage in the coming battle; they were fighting for their survival, and for many of them, it would be their last fight.

Uther and Locksley laid out plans for a layered defense with the archers sending an initial volley and then retreating to function as snipers, while Uther and the others battled back the intruders on foot. It was around this time, with final preparations made, that a scout returned with news. King Richard was alive, recently freed from a German prison, and on his way to England!

That night, Uther, Locksley, and their band merrily toasted the bittersweet news with what little they had. Though buoyed by the rumors, even if they were true, it would take Richard a few weeks to return, which meant that he would be back just in time to sort through the rebels' burnt bones. The news had also certainly reached John, which meant that, backed against the wall, he would be even more ruthless. All these thoughts made for an uneasy sleep that night for Uther, which was only slightly offset by the ale. He woke the next day and steeled himself for what was to come. It turned out to be more news, and a specifically corrected message: King Richard had not just been freed from Germany in the last few days, he had been freed weeks ago and was *here*, now, back in England.

 Poets and minstrels worked overtime spreading the news, and those who had hidden tight from John's tyranny opened their shutters, let in the light, and took to the streets, ready to do what they could to honor the return of the king.

The next morning, a tall figure with reddish-gray stubble covering his face stepped out of the mists with no signage and no sword, riding a slow horse toward the gate to John's castle in Nottinghamshire. When he presented himself, the defenders did not even believe it was him. How could it be, when he had died a thousand times according to the stories that they had heard? They spat in his face and laughed.

"Get out of here old man, before we arrest you."

The Richard of two years ago would have head-butted the man through his helmet, but now he just smiled, turned his horse, and returned to his tent. The next day Richard arrived again at John's castle, only this time he was not alone. A loud procession stretched behind him including siege engines, all his loyal knights, the entire resistance from the woods, and a gallows. The guards that Richard had met the day before greeted him again, and shortly afterward, they were in shackles. John, who had fled the castle the day before, was charged with high treason and ordered to return to stand trial in forty days or face the forfeiture of all of his royal inheritance. The word reached John a week later across the channel in Normandy, where he had no intention of leaving.

As the king strolled through Sherwood Forest barefoot in the warm spring morning, he found a few familiar faces amongst the cheering loyalists. He spoke to Uther directly.

"In prison, I prayed that if I ever made it home alive, I'd never have to view that distorted mug again. Yet as I gaze upon you now, old man, it seems that God has yet to forgive me for my sins."

Richard hugged Uther, practically picking him up off of the ground. The king looked much thinner and somehow shorter but still with bright light in his eyes.

"It's good to see you again amongst the living, Sire. We've done our best to keep things together for you here while you've been gone."

"You have done your jobs well; I wouldn't have expected less. I hope you'll forgive me for not lingering amongst you too long here today. I think if I'm forced to remain, I might have nightmares about our little trip eastward a few years ago. I could use a decent night's sleep, preferably in anything besides a tent."

Richard visited his mother and his sister who badgered him

immediately with plans for his homecoming.

"I've been thinking about ways to revitalize the economy with fairs and merchant festivals. Richard, you could tour with them for the summer—relax, eat, drink, greet the people; it'll be just the thing to raise spirits and reignite prosperity. What do you think?"

Joanna tried to sound reasonable, even stern, but her begging eyes betrayed her. She had a strong hunch that she knew exactly what Richard was going to do, and her hopes of dissuading him with a well thought out plan were all that she had.

"It's not a bad idea, dear sister, but I won't be involved. I'll be leaving soon for France. I have interests to look after and a scheming French king to harass.

"But you just arrived home?"

"I apologize for saying this, because you're my sister and I love you, and I know that these will be hurtful words for you to hear, but this isn't my home. The road has changed me, and I can't stay here."

"You've barely spent time here to know that ..."

"There's no use in protesting it. Your idea has merit; consider me a full sponsor, but I won't be around to see it."

After a second coronation in Winchester on Easter followed by a sparse celebration, for which Richard barely had enough coin to pay, he was gone a week later to Normandy to begin to reclaim his stolen lands from Philip. As promised, before the king left, he installed Uther as a baron with land in the South along with materials and workers to build a castle. He requested Uther's company for one last gift.

"I'll be boarding a ship next week. I wanted to make sure I had time to fulfill this."

"Fulfill what?"

"Any request you have. Anything. Ask it and it will be yours, as true payment for your time in the English army during our quest and as proper thanks for your service here afterwards."

"Sire—the land, the titles, they're truly enough!"

The king's face turned severe.

"Don't play up your modesty now, Uther; it's not the time for it, and you'll just insult me. When I leave soon, it will be toward battle at some point, and I may not return this time. Don't rob me of my intention to repay a friend as I see fit. What is it you wish?"

Uther did not need to think about the "what," only whether or not it was right to request it and whether the king truly meant "anything." Since Richard had so far been good on his promises, Uther decided that this was his chance to receive what he wished for most, no matter the consequences. He asked the king about a certain lord married to a woman who was an old friend of his, and if a dissolution of that marriage was possible.

"I did say 'anything.' So is that it? Are you sure you want me to remove him?"

Uther was surprised by Richard's blunt response, until he realized that the king was probably giving Uther one last chance to think over the consequences of what he was asking for. He used those precious few minutes as wisely as he could.

"If your men determine that she's happy there, then don't disturb her. If she is any less than pleased with her situation and desires at all to leave, then please make it so."

"And so it shall be."

†††

A few weeks later in France, a humbly dressed friar visited Richard. The man explained that John wished to gauge Richard's thoughts to see if there was any desire to settle their grudge. Richard was matter-of-fact in his response.

"Tell him to come home. He's still my brother, and I still love him. He was probably led astray by unwise counsel from nobles who had their own interests in mind. Probably. I have forgiveness in my heart for him, so inform him of this in any way you please."

John, who was penniless and starving, had nothing to lose when he returned to Richard, groveling on his knees as a scruff of a man. His predicament was made all the more shameful by the great compassion and mercy that Richard showed by seating him at the royal table for dinner that night, where they toasted and let old grudges die in the wine.

✝✝✝

Back in England, Sir Uther Pendraig, Baron of Cambershire, dismounted his horse. He was inside the gates of the manor house of Lord Bradford, who had been recently sent on assignment to the English royal cavalry in France to pay his feudal burden to his lord, King Richard. The king had made a personal request for Lord Bradford's "great courage and unique fighting prowess," even though they had never met.

In the absence of her husband, Lady Bradford was there to greet the Baron, but when she saw his face she almost fainted. Their equally watery eyes met, and she grabbed his face with both hands and kissed him on the mouth before staring in disbelief.

"How is it possible? Is it possible? Tell me you're not a ghost or a dream?"

"Hello, Gwen."

"You came back to me ... you ... know the king?"

"I have a lifetime of stories to tell you. For now, I hope you don't think that I'm an awful person for using royal privilege to see you again. Or if you do feel that way, can you ignore it just for tonight?"

"Lord Bradford was an old, goat-legged bastard. He treated me well enough at first, but when I didn't produce a child for him, he turned sour. I'm so happy to be free of him, but that means nothing. To see you means everything. There are some important things I need to show you."

After a long embrace, they walked hand in hand out amongst the woods, into the night, and repeated a late meeting that they had first had all those years ago, and fell asleep together under the dark shining sky.

†††

Five years later, in a needless fight stemming from an insignificant dispute with a rogue vassal in France that he had never even met, King Richard took a stray arrow through his unprotected neck.

As he lay in his quarters, though he had stopped spitting blood, death was pronounced certain and imminent. Richard demanded that the attacker be brought before him, and soon found himself staring into the eyes of a child. With a look of shock, Richard had only one word: "Why?"

"Sire, you killed my father and two brothers in the siege. Before he broke the arrow off, my father made me swear to take a clean shot at you if I could to avenge my family."

King Richard's men punched the child in the face.

"What shall we do with him, Sire? Shall we rack him? Can we rack him?"

The king tried to speak, but his words were swallowed by his bulging-eyed coughs. He waved his hand and croaked out for the men to leave him alone with the boy. After catching his breath, he was able to speak.

"I forgive you for killing me. You don't deserve to be brought down for it; I would have done the same thing. I may die here, but you will live and, by my grace, behold the light of another day."

He called his men back in, instructing them to release the boy with fifty pieces of gold and defend his exit from the castle territory.

Richard proclaimed his brother John his successor and asked to be buried at the feet of his father. When Richard finally gave up his last breath, he left life with a smile on his face.

ACKNOWLEDGEMENTS

As I worked on this book, most of the people in my life were very supportive, and I want to thank them all, but some specifically. My writing mentor Ben who was always a source of gruff, driving encouragement. My design mentor Bob who always listened. Alysha, who read what I sent her and then demanded the next chapter as soon as possible. My parents, who, once they realized I was serious, encouraged me and helped me to keep things in perspective. Also, I want to thank the people of San Francisco and New York City who inspired me and added depth and color to my world as I worked on this. They helped me to remember that there is more to life than just my own experiences and desires, and that if I really wanted to be a good writer, I had to write for them as much as for myself. Finally I'd like to thank Eleanor Gagnon who was a staunch advocate and made contributions, including considerable encouragement, to the final edit that you are reading. She prompted me to clean up the original edit so that her students could read it to learn a bit about the time period referenced in the story. In a way, that's the highest compliment that an author can receive.

ABOUT THE AUTHOR

Seth I Friedman is a third generation artist and designer living in New York City. *The Pilgrim* is his first novel. He began research in 2007 for a story that was intended to be a series of scripts for a TV drama about the Western Medieval world and the Crusades. After a year of research, he came to believe that the idea deserved a format that could allow for a more vivid and intimate picture of such a lush, elaborate, mythic time in human history. Instead of a script, he began work on a prose story that eventually evolved into *The Pilgrim.* His remaining research and story development from the initial phase will be utilized directly in the creation of a sequel to *The Pilgrim.*

www.ingramcontent.com/pod-product-compliance
Lightning Source LLC
Chambersburg PA
CBHW050339030726
47503CB00008B/2526